"So...this is awk...

"We have a child toge... ...ow anything about you," Alex said.

Kaylie was the reason for all of this.

Paige wanted a family, so much that on her twenty-fourth birthday she'd decided to take life by the horns and create the family she dreamed of. The sweet, smart, silly girl was everything Paige needed. No men needed to apply and since Kaylie had been born, not even a handful had stuck around through dinner.

And here was one more.

A man so gorgeous the rebellious part of Paige, the part of her she couldn't get rid of, was glad her daughter wasn't here.

Because she wanted to flirt. She wanted to flirt and touch and see if the attraction she felt for him was mutual.

Alex offered her a half smile, making his eyes crinkle at the corners and accentuating a little scar at the corner of his full lips. The tension she felt when he brushed past her ratcheted up a notch and she admitted to herself it wasn't fear at all. It was flat-out excitement. Want. She couldn't remember the last time she'd felt such an instant attraction to a man.

Dear Reader,

I've been trying to think of the right words to tell you about *The Daughter He Wanted*. I thought about telling you about the small town where I grew up— which was right across the state from Bonne Terre. I thought about telling you the crazy adventures I had as a child—some of which inspired Kaylie's adventures in this book. I thought about telling you about my own daughter, who is a Kaylie in every sense. At the heart of this book, though, isn't the small town or a single childhood. At the heart of this book is choice.

We all choose who we will be—the athlete or the wallflower, the rebel or the rule follower, the corporate success or the small-business owner. Alex and Paige made their own choices leading up to Chapter One: Paige to start the family she craved in the only way open to her and Alex to distance himself from family because of the pain in his past. Writing their journey not only to love but to personal fulfillment was amazing, and the fact that I was able to write this book for Harlequin Superromance is a joy that has blown me away.

I've been reading Superromance books for more than half my life, having stolen my very first one from my mom's bookshelf when I was about eleven. I hope you have as much fun reading about Alex and Paige and Kaylie as I had in writing their story. I love hearing from readers—you can find me on Twitter (@AuthorKristina) or Facebook (facebook.com/kristinaknightromanceauthor), or shoot me an email the old-fashioned way.

Happy reading!

Kristina Knight

KRISTINA KNIGHT

—

The Daughter He Wanted

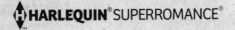
HARLEQUIN® SUPERROMANCE®

Recycling programs
for this product may
not exist in your area.

ISBN-13: 978-0-373-60895-9

The Daughter He Wanted

Copyright © 2015 by Kristina Knight

Printed in U.S.A.

www.Harlequin.com

Once upon a time, **Kristina Knight** spent her days running from car crash to fire to meetings with local police. No, she wasn't a troublemaker—she was a journalist. Her career took her all over the United States, and along the way she found her very own Knight in Shining Cowboy Boots. Just like the characters from her favorite books, Kristina is living her own happily-ever-after with her Knight and their Princess.

Books by Kristina Knight

HARLEQUIN E

Rockers

Light My Fire
Start Me Up
Call Me

Visit the Author Profile page
at Harlequin.com for more titles

For Janell and Roxanne, my sister-moms who have the patience and encouragement that inspires me.

For my mom, who read the books and told the stories. And who busts all of us with her amazing ability to recall every life event.

For Shelby, the daughter we chose, who is everything.

CHAPTER ONE

HE DIDN'T HAVE to know.

Alex Ryan sat outside the pretty white house on the quiet street in Bonne Terre, Missouri. It was an older home with a wide front porch and ivy growing up the two posts on either side of the three steps leading to the front door. It had a peaked roof with gingerbread trim. It wasn't a true Victorian but someone along the way had added a few Victorian touches to the two-story home. He could see the tops of a wicker couch and rocker on the porch. Pots overflowing with red snapdragons and bleeding hearts hung from the ceiling and wound their way over the steps. In a few more days those plants would begin to die off, but for now they were pretty in the October afternoon sunlight.

There was a hopscotch course painted in sunny yellow on the front walk.

It looked like a happy house. A peaceful house. The kind of place he'd have liked to have grown up.

He didn't have to knock on the pink front door. Didn't need to introduce himself. He could turn the key, put the gearshift in first, make a right at the corner and be back at his own house within twenty minutes.

He could forget about the phone call that led him here. Go on with his life. A gauzy curtain in the front window flicked but he couldn't make out more than a shadow inside. There was a late-model Honda parked in the drive, and the woman who lived here would probably like him to start up the truck and leave.

Alex looked down at his knuckles, white from gripping the steering wheel. He'd been fine before that damned phone call. His job as a park ranger at St. Francois State Park and St. Joe State Park was demanding and required all his focus. When he went home to his big, rambling house in Park Hills he was so tired that all he needed was a TV dinner, a sitcom laugh track and his bed. But the phone call came and now all he could think about was the tricycle he hadn't been able to resist buying four years ago. The trike that was gathering dust in his attic, and was an almost exact replica of the pretty pink model that sat in this front yard now.

The trike he bought had been green, a compromise because Deanna insisted that, when they finally became pregnant, she wanted to be surprised at the birth.

But Deanna had gotten sick, so there hadn't been a baby at all.

What could he gain from pushing himself into the lives of a strange woman and her daughter?

A four-year-old you didn't know about until a week ago, he reminded himself. *A four-year-old who lives in a pretty house on a quiet street in a town with an almost invisible crime rate.*

She and her mother had been doing fine for four years.

You have a daughter. The soothing voice of the lawyer tasked with telling him about the mix-up at the fertility clinic echoed around the truck cab as if she sat beside him on the leather seat.

He had done the love thing. Married his college sweetheart and had a good life, but all that changed when Dee died. What could he give a four-year-old kid? He didn't know how to act around adults anymore, much less children. It was one of the reasons he turned down every promotion in favor of hiking the park trails alone as a ranger.

Late-afternoon sun peeked from behind a cloud, caught on the chrome handlebar of the pink trike and winked at him.

He had to know.

The front door opened slowly and a slim woman stepped out onto the porch. Watched the truck for a moment as if she needed to think about something. Like whether or not to call the cops because a strange man was loitering on her curb. She started down the steps toward his truck and Alex swallowed hard. Too late. No chance for a clean getaway now. Sweat rolled down his neck, and he switched the air conditioning on. It didn't work. The air conditioner pumped out enough cold air to make an elephant hypothermic but the nervous sweats continued. The woman shot a glance back into the house.

She was pretty, in a girl-next-door sort of way. Faded denim outlined her slim hips and red flip-flops protected her feet from the warm concrete. The old tee she wore with "Navy" emblazoned on the chest was splattered with paint. She tucked a long strand of honey-colored hair behind her ear as she opened the front gate and let it slide closed behind her.

Then she stepped onto the pavement and tapped on his window.

Alex hit the button to lower the glass and inhaled a slow breath filled with the smell of fall leaves and something tropical. Like mangos and bananas. Her. Sea-green eyes met his gaze. A splash of freckles played over her pert nose. He'd always been a sucker for freckles. Freckles and laughs. Deanna had both, along with white-blonde hair, short legs and an infuriating habit of finishing his sentences. Physically the women couldn't be more different. Where Dee was short, this woman was tall. Willowy. Alex shifted in his seat.

He would not be attracted to her. Not, not, not. *You're not here to be attracted to the mother.*

Definitely not. He had nothing to offer her, but the little girl, maybe he could give her…something.

Still, he was mesmerized by the light tan dots over the woman's nose and those long, long legs covered in tattered denim.

"I've had four neighbors call to let me know a strange man is casing my house. And Mrs. Purcell—" she pointed toward a green-shuttered home with a cracked sidewalk and an old Chevy Impala in the drive "—has probably also called 9-1-1. So, unless you just like being interrogated for sitting in your truck you might want to come in." She offered him a kind smile but her hands trembled against the door. Her voice had a light twang to it that a lot of Southern Missouri residents had. Not so twangy that single-syllable words became multisyllabic, more of a slow, I'm-not-in-a-hurry twang. "Unless you've decided against it?" The words were semihopeful and Alex couldn't blame the woman for that.

He tapped his booted foot against the floorboard and flipped the key. "I haven't really decided anything but maybe we could talk?"

She blew out a breath, nodded, and the strand of hair she'd tucked behind her ear slipped forward, hiding her face for a moment. "They told me you'd like to meet. I kind of hoped we could talk over the phone first."

Alex shrugged and his shoulder pushed against

his seat belt. He pulled the key from the ignition and then released the belt. "It's easier to hang up a phone than not answer a doorbell." He got out of the truck and shut the door. Paige, the lawyer told him her name was Paige, watched him, arms folded over her chest and an annoyed slant to her full lips. "I didn't— Not that you wouldn't answer." This was going wrong. So wrong. This situation was completely out of his grasp. "I'm not sure where to begin."

Her voice was quiet, resigned. Like she knew she couldn't stop what was coming, but wanted to all the same. "I'd rather not have this conversation on the street." She stepped away from him. "I'm Paige Kenner, by the way. And you're Alex Ryan."

"I know." She raised her eyebrows at him. Alex ran a hand over his face as if that might wipe away the discomfort he felt now that he was face-to-face with Paige. It didn't. Paige seemed…normal. Nice. She hadn't run screaming for the cops when a strange man sat outside her home, anyway. And he'd just swung from arrogant to meek and back to arrogant in about two seconds. He held out his hand and waited a long moment before Paige reached out. Her skin was soft against his and he told himself the little shock he felt was from his smooth-soled boots rubbing against the carpet on the floor of his truck and not because he was attracted to her.

"Sorry, yeah, I'm Alex. I'm your daughter's father."

PAIGE WANTED TO do anything except lead Alex Ryan into her home. But there were at least four pairs of eyes on them right now and one of those pairs—Mrs. Purcell—would be right back on the phone with the Bonne Terre police department if Paige ran screaming down the street.

Maybe that wouldn't be the worst thing.

The police would come, and crazy teenage reputation or not, the officers would take her seriously. She was a teacher now, a single mom. Valued member of the community. He might look perfectly adorable in the black tee with the park ranger logo over the chest, faded jeans and boots, but there were only a few reasons a stranger would sit outside a home for hours. None of them good. The cops would take Alex Ryan into custody and delay this meeting. Maybe even make him reconsider stepping into her life.

God, let him reconsider. Her life worked now. She liked who she was, liked being Kaylie's mom, giving her daughter all the love and attention Paige was denied in her own childhood. When she was a child, her parents either ignored her completely or interfered to the point that Paige couldn't take it and lashed out. Those actions had sent her down the road of rebellion until she realized the one person she hurt with her antics was herself. It was a shock and had sent her down a new path. A path that led to the stupidest fertility clinic in the tristate area, apparently, but as crazy as it was that they'd used Alex's semen instead of the donor she'd chosen, she still had Kaylie. The most amazing four-year-old on the planet.

For a moment she wondered about the strange man in the truck outside, and then she caught a glimpse of tawny hair and saw the way his head cocked to the side as he studied her home.

Both characteristics were exactly the same as her daughter's.

Paige opened the front door and waited for Alex to pass by. His broad shoulder brushed against her and tension bubbled up in her belly. She took a moment to steady her hands against the doorknob at her back and mentally shook herself. There was nothing to be afraid of. Those four pairs of eyes would keep watch over her house until the blue truck sitting on the street had driven away. It was one of the reasons she chose this neighborhood. The house was the perfect size for her and Kaylie, and it was one of those places where neighbors watched out for one another.

Paige's mom side appreciated the sentiment, even if the Mrs. Purcells of the world sometimes paid a little too much attention to her.

Alex stood in her entryway looking around as if he was lost. Her paint supplies took up most of the space in the living room to the left and Kaylie's latest infatuation—Lalaloopsy dolls—took up the rest. She led the way through to the open-plan kitchen and family room.

"Would you like some iced tea?" Prim and proper and not at all what she wanted to ask. She wanted to be direct, tell him he had no business here. That he needed to leave. Something held her back.

Alex shook his head and Paige motioned him to sit at the island counter while she refreshed her glass. She wasn't thirsty but it was something to do with her hands so she fussed with slices of lemon and added more ice before putting the pitcher back into the fridge.

Finally there was nothing left to do so she turned back to the man at the counter, trying to ignore the assessing way he watched her. Despite the casual clothes, Alex Ryan was the mirror image of everything she had left behind in her parents' home, from the set of his shoulders to the judgment she saw in the thin line of his mouth. Rigid standards and rules she could never live up to. Expectations that had left her heartbroken and wounded. She didn't need his approval, she reminded herself. It wasn't like she'd asked him to come into her home and disrupt her life.

It wasn't as if she'd had his permission to use his semen, either.

The clinic sent a file with his pertinent information, but Paige couldn't force herself to read it. A small piece of her had hoped that if she ignored the report the man would ignore her. Now she wished she had read it cover to cover instead of putting it in her bottom desk drawer.

Her gaze caught on the picture of Kaylie at her fourth birthday party, cake frosting up to her eyebrows, princess crown askew, charging after the boys with her blue lightsaber.

Kaylie was the reason for all of this. Paige had wanted a family, so much so that on her twenty-fourth birthday she'd decided to take life by the horns and create the family she dreamed of. The sweet, smart, silly girl was everything Paige needed. No men needed to apply and since Kaylie had been born, not even a handful had stuck around through dinner.

And here was one more. A man so afraid of commitment he hadn't known whether to get out of his car or run screaming into the warm Missouri afternoon.

No, that was unfair. She didn't know anything about Alex Ryan.

A man so gorgeous the rebellious part of Paige, the part of her she couldn't get rid of no matter how much she tried to pretend it didn't exist, was glad her daughter wasn't here. Wanted to flirt. Wished

they'd met at a bar or under any other circumstances so that she could flirt and touch and see if
the attraction she felt for him, he felt for her, too.

She glanced at her watch. Just over an hour until
her best friend, Alison, would bring Kaylie back
from her swim lesson at the rec center. The prin-
cipal at her school required impromptu meetings
now and then; today Alison was able to step in and
help Paige. She was grateful. Alison was her biggest supporter and cheerleader. Paige hated missing the lesson, but Alison liked playing auntie for
Kaylie from time to time. This introduction needed
to get moving and get over with because, until she
knew exactly what Alex Ryan's intentions were,
he was not getting anywhere near her daughter.

"So, this is awkward." She blurted the words
out, not sure where else to start. "We have a child
together but I don't know anything about you."

He offered her a half smile, making his eyes
crinkle at the corners and accentuating a little scar
at the corner of his full lips. The tension she'd felt
when he'd brushed past her ratcheted up a notch
and she admitted to herself it wasn't fear at all. It
was flat-out excitement. Want. She couldn't remember the last time she'd felt such an instant attraction to a man. Attraction was bad. Very, very
bad. Attraction meant throwing all her rules about
relationships out the window. Attraction led to
mistakes and mistakes could hurt Kaylie.

Hurt Paige.

She gulped some tea, hoping it would put out the sizzle of heat that seemed to grow with every second Alex was in her kitchen.

He shrugged, the motion defining his upper arms—as if they needed more definition—and her heart seemed to skip a beat. "I always figured if I were to have a conversation like this it would be because of a drunken night in Cabo, not because a fertility clinic marked my, uh, sample, as 'anonymous donor' rather than 'IVF candidate.'" He gave a chuckle, and the deep sound sent another hot zing across her nerve endings, as if her ears were now an erogenous zone.

She was going to need a lot more than tea. *Focus on the tea,* she ordered herself. But the way his muscular arms filled out his short sleeves was an even bigger distraction. She focused on a picture of Kaylie on the back wall, her daughter smiling at the camera with Mickey Mouse ears atop her head.

That did it. Seeing her baby's smiling face did more for Paige's focus than the past fifteen minutes of ordering herself around had. Kaylie was important—not Paige's hormones.

"So, you weren't a donor?" Once more she cursed herself for not reading the clinic file on Alex. The lawyer merely told her that the man whose donation she'd used would like to contact her. Over the next ten minutes, which seemed to take ten hours, Paige had worried he was contacting her to tell her he had cancer or AIDS or some congenital disease that might affect her precious girl.

Learning he only wanted to meet her was almost a relief until the implications hit her. He only wanted to meet her so that he could be part of Kaylie's life.

"No, my wife and I were IVF candidates. It was after the first embryos were implanted that we learned she had cancer." Sadness flickered in his eyes. "The embryos didn't result in pregnancy and we decided everything, even the precautionary donations I made, should be destroyed."

Thank God, he had a wife. Thank God she hadn't made a move on him. Wait, a wife. And cancer. She sucked in a deep breath, ignoring the instinct pushing her to reach out to him.

"I didn't realize you were married." There, her voice sounded normal.

He smiled, but instead of crinkling his eyes, it left them bleak. "She died. Just over three years ago," he said. Paige reached across the counter, brushing her hand across his and mentally castigating herself for the little snap of attraction at the contact. He was a widower, for crying out loud, and this was her kitchen, not the Low Bar. They were discussing the possibility of him creating a relationship with her daughter—not with her.

And, damn it, why couldn't she keep her hands to herself? This man was a stranger who would mess up the pretty, uncomplicated life she'd cre-

ated. He didn't need her pity and she certainly
didn't need to feel this overwhelming need to comfort him.

She squeezed his hand. "I'm so sorry." It was no
wonder he'd come looking for her. No, for Kaylie.
His wife died, then he learned his sperm was used
and a child came of it. He was probably trying to
recapture some of the joy he'd expected when he
and his wife began IVF treatments.

And she still didn't want him to mess with her
kid, but this wasn't some frat guy who suddenly
decided to see if he had any progeny. This was
a man willing to go through IVF and who knew
what else with his late wife so they could have a
child.

That was commitment.

This time the clench in her belly was less attraction and more fear. How could she share her
daughter with a virtual stranger? A stranger who
was the antithesis of everything she had decided
she wanted when she left home.

"It was a long time ago," he said, his deep brown
eyes focused on her, as if he could see through the
paint-splattered tee to the heart beating erratically
beneath. Paige shifted, suddenly uncomfortable in
her favorite tee.

"What is it that you want from me? Us?"

"Honestly, I don't know. I couldn't not try to
find you, not after the clinic called."

Not what she wanted to hear. Or was it? If he

didn't know what he wanted, maybe this one meeting would be enough. Maybe her world didn't have to change.

"You work in the parks?"

"Ranger, so most of my days are spent hiking. Making sure the streams aren't overfished. That kind of thing."

"That explains the tan, then." Paige's eyes widened. "Not that I thought you were lazy or anything. I mean, you're here in the middle of the afternoon but—" There was no way to recover. Alex laughed.

"Not even my closest friends call my job a 'job.' And the best part of it is that I'm not stuck behind a desk and I rarely have to wear a suit."

"Both definite pluses, I suppose." Paige laughed with him. Laughing got her through a lot of days, especially those when Kaylie was whiny or needed every second of attention Paige had. "I'm a teacher, so no suits, either. Although I regularly come home with paint or chalk all over me."

"What grade?"

"Elementary school, art, actually. So I get to hang with the kids for an hour, do fun stuff and then send them back to homeroom."

"You don't look old enough to be a teacher." Was that appreciation in his gaze? He watched her for a moment and Paige forgot to breathe. Then, the look was gone and he was just a guy sitting in her kitchen. A gorgeous guy, but just a guy. He cocked his head to the side and a half smile spread across his face, stretching that tiny scar near his mouth until it almost disappeared. "From what I remember all my teachers, kindergarten on, wore orthopedic shoes, had gray hair and liked to smack at my hands with a ruler."

Nope, not just a guy. Alex Ryan was dangerous from the tips of his tawny hair to the soles of his booted feet. And all the muscled, tanned areas in between.

"I assure you twenty-nine is old enough to be a teacher. For the record, you don't look like those grumpy old guys in the Smokey the Bear hats, either." He scrunched his eyes together, as if searching for something. Some kind of common ground, maybe. She would certainly like to find some.

"I'm thirty-two. Born and raised in Park Hills." He mentioned a town only a few miles from Bonne Terre. Paige had driven through it many times in her life. "I'm surprised we've never run into one another."

Paige wasn't. Her parents had sent her to a private school near St. Louis when she was ten, telling her she deserved a better education than she would find in a small town. Then, at sixteen, they'd tired of her antics altogether and sent her to a Swiss boarding school known for discipline and year-round school. During the rare summer or winter breaks when she was allowed to come home, she made sure her parents knew she was there. Dating the wrong guys, ignoring curfews, whatever it took to make them notice her. But that wasn't the conversation that would get them on more even footing.

"My parents sent me to boarding school. I was rarely here as a teenager." It wasn't a lie, just an omission of all the facts that might leave Alex with a bad impression of her. Paige reached for another glass. "Are you sure you don't want tea? A soda?"

"Water?"

Paige nodded and filled the glass with ice and water, adding a slice of lemon at the last moment. Alex plucked the lemon from the glass and sucked it between his full lips, drawing out the juice. Her belly clenched at the action and Paige swallowed hard.

He sat up a little straighter and dropped the wedge back into his glass. "Sorry. Habit. I like lemons."

So did Kaylie. She waved the apology away and hoped she hadn't been looking at him like a missing hiker desperate for water.

"You're a park ranger. I'm a teacher. How did we wind up here?"

Alex shook his head. "I've been asking myself that very question since the lawyer called." He took her hand in his, held it for a long moment, and the world seemed to stop moving. The ticking of the kitchen clock faded into the distance. The breeze that had been blowing through her windows stopped billowing through the curtains. She forgot to breathe for a long moment. "When the lawyer called I didn't want to know her. I didn't want to know that she's four years old. But now all I can think about is when is her birthday and what cereal does she like for breakfast and can she spell her name yet? Do kids even know how to spell at four?"

One meeting would not be enough, not with those kinds of questions, Paige realized.

The kitchen timer beeped, usually a reminder to put her paints away and start dinner for Kaylie. And just like that Paige's world started spinning again, this time reminding her to finish this meeting and get Alex out of her house. He had so many questions, and none were what she had expected when the lawyer had called or when she'd looked out her window and seen the unfamiliar truck parked on her curb.

That didn't mean she had all the answers; not yet, anyway.

"Not all kids can spell at four, but she can." She withdrew her hand from his grasp because, while he seemed to be the opposite of every commitment-phobic man she'd ever known, that didn't make him good date material. Getting a handle on this weird attraction she felt had to be her first priority. She tucked her hair behind her ear and busied herself with the empty paper-towel container. "Well, a few words. *Bat, cat,* that kind of thing. And she can count to thirty without mixing up too many of the numbers."

Paige blew out a breath and then bit the corner of her lip. She took the picture of Kaylie off the windowsill and held it out. "This is her, last May on her birthday. She is kind and smart and the way she sees the world is…so funny." Alex took the frame, holding it so tight the tips of his fingers turned white. "I know I'm biased because I'm her mom but she's just…the best." Paige bit her lower lip again. The impulse to ask him to stay, to get that first meeting over with was nearly too much to bear. He looked so lost and confused sitting at her counter and gazing at the picture of her—and his—daughter.

But her impulses had gotten her into plenty of trouble in her life and she'd learned to push them away.

Paige was Kaylie's mom and not this man's girl-friend or confidante. She would not fix his problems by endangering Kaylie's stable world.

"What does she know about her father?"

"She's never really asked so I haven't told her anything. All the pictures in her baby book are of me and her. I thought I would cross Daddy Bridge when she started to ask questions."

He traced his index finger along the image of Kaylie chasing the boys and smiled, a softer smile this time. No self-deprecation. No sadness.

A sweet smile that she'd felt on her own face when Kaylie said her first word and took her first step.

"She likes *Star Wars*."

Paige nodded. "Jar Jar Binks is her favorite. And she thinks Amidala should have been a Jedi rather than a senator or queen. Although she usually calls her a princess."

"Smart girl. Amidala would have made a great Jedi fighter." He handed the picture back to Paige. "How did you know I'd come by today?"

"What?" Paige replaced the picture on the sill and turned back to the quiet man at the counter.

"I'm guessing she isn't here because no four-year-old could be quiet and out of sight this long, right? How did you know today was the day you should get her out of the house?"

"I'm not trying to—"

He held up his hands. "No accusations. I'm not sure today is the day to drop all this on her, either."

Paige took a moment to breathe before answering. "Good. I didn't send her away. It's her swim-lesson afternoon. She swims at the rec center during the winter months and at the public pool during the summer. My best friend, Alison, took her because I had a meeting after school." She pointed to the partially finished canvas in the family room. "Then I decided to work on a project I'm painting for her. She'll be home—" Paige swallowed the lump in her throat but still didn't invite him to meet Kaylie. She couldn't. "She'll be home later."

Alex blew out a breath. "Would it be okay if I met her?"

"Okay," she said after a moment. "But not today. Not yet." Paige finished her tea and started to pace. She waved her hands at him like she was spreading oil over a canvas with her hands. "You seem completely normal, have a legitimate job. There's not a neck tattoo under your collar. But she is still very young. I can't just tell her you're her dad over Cheerios—that's her favorite cereal, by the way—tomorrow morning and send you two on a play-date after lunch."

She watched him intently for a moment and finally Alex nodded. "So how do we approach this? I could give you references that note my stellar work reputation, the fact that I play in the rec leagues during the summer and that I haven't had more than a speeding ticket in my adult life."

"No references. I want a promise from you."

"I could quote you the oath I took when I joined the rangers."

"Don't do that. Don't be flippant. This isn't wanting a lobster dinner and then changing your order to steak. She's a person and she deserves your best. If you aren't willing to give her that then you can turn around, get in your truck and go back to Park Hills."

Alex was quiet for a long moment. His eyes

were fixed on her but it was as if he wasn't seeing her so much as... Paige wasn't sure. Something else.

"I swear to you I'll do my best not to hurt our daughter. I just need to see her." There was a sincere edge to his voice that Paige couldn't ignore. She nodded.

"Okay." She took a breath. "Could we meet for coffee? I have a meeting at the clinic tomorrow, so Friday? Before you meet Kaylie, you and I need to get to know one another better."

"Kaylie." He breathed the word like a prayer and Paige realized he hadn't known his daughter's name. "My daughter's name is Kaylie." Her heart melted a little at the breathy way he said Kaylie's name, the mistiness in his eyes.

Paige swallowed. "Kaylie Ann Kenner."

Alex stood quickly, the high chair squealing across her tiled floor and making them both wince. He whipped a card from his wallet and handed it across the counter. "Coffee would be great. My numbers are there, and my email. Just text me when and where and I'll be there."

He hurried from her kitchen and the screen door slammed behind him. Paige watched from the little hallway as the man she never thought she would meet got into his big truck and pulled away from her house.

He was coming back and she had no idea if she should be happy or sad about that.

CHAPTER TWO

As soon as the truck turned the corner from Paige's house, Alex pulled to the side of the road. Took a couple of deep breaths and tried to make sense of the jittery feeling in his stomach. He'd been fine talking to Paige about the clinic, been fine seeing his daughter's face for the first time covered in cake icing. Sure, when she brought up Dee his hands got sweaty, but that was normal. No one liked talking about dead spouses, did they?

Everything was fine until Paige said Kaylie's name.

Then he couldn't get out of the little white house with the pink door and wicker porch furniture fast enough. He hit his head lightly against the steering wheel. It was just a name. An innocuous name.

A name that changed everything one more time.

The call from the lawyer had him taking a day off work just to make sure the little girl's life was ordered. He never took off work. Not since the funeral. Work was real and the reality was that his world imploded when Dee got sick. He'd made sense of what was left and built a decent life again.

Sure, he avoided places like the Low Bar and no, he didn't really like the summer and winter rec leagues, but it kept his friends off his back and distracted him from the big, empty house in Park Hills.

Maybe he should have moved. He got as far as donating most of Dee's things, but moving out of the house she loved had felt…wrong on some level. So he stayed.

Kaylie Ann Kenner. Paige's voice echoed in his ear. The plan had been to knock on the door, make sure everything was in place and go back to work. Put the little girl in a box in his mind, but leave her and the mother alone. He had needed to know and now he knew.

And the plan was out the window. He couldn't see her picture and know her name and not know her, too. Alex swallowed.

Kaylie was real. Paige was totally and completely real from her paint-dribbled feet to the freckles over her nose. Why did he have to take her hand? That little jolt of electricity he'd felt in the truck was nothing compared to the full-on sizzle that'd raced through his fingertips at her kitchen counter.

For the first time in three years he wanted real. Tangible. Not the memories that floated around the big house. Not the too-loud laughter that sometimes escaped him when everyone watched to make sure he got the joke, that he was really there with them, in the moment. Paige hadn't looked at him like that, not once. And not once had he mentally escaped the pretty white kitchen with the hardwood floors and black granite countertops. He couldn't remember a single time in the past few years when he'd been as present as he'd been from the moment he parked the truck at Paige's curb.

A low-slung convertible swerved around his truck, honking, and Alex shook himself. He pulled back onto the highway and started for Park Hills, and as usual took a right at the light rather than the left that would take him home. The wrought-iron gates were still open, the tree-lined lane shaded from the afternoon sun. Alex pulled through the gates and drove past the statue of the floating angel, turned at the mausoleum that always looked haunted. Stopped the truck before a gray headstone with Dee's name and dates.

And didn't open the door. He sat there for a long time with his hand on the door handle, unable to move. What was he going to say to her? *Hey, honey, you know how I didn't want to do IVF? Well, thanks to your insistence now I have a daughter.* He could imagine the back-of-the-head slap Dee would give him with that one.

Don't be so flip, she'd say and demand all the details. Not that he had that many. He had a meeting scheduled tomorrow with the head of the clinic, but for now he only knew what the lawyer had told him on the phone: his sample was mislabeled and used as donor sperm instead of being destroyed. She'd turned four in the spring, according to the picture on Paige's windowsill, so Kaylie would have been conceived sometime in the three-month window between when they learned about the cancer and when they learned it was terminal. Before he sent in the paperwork to have his samples destroyed. And he definitely couldn't tell Dee that for the first time in three years he felt alive and it was because of another woman.

No, he couldn't tell her that, not any of it. Because he had a daughter, thanks to her, and he had a life, such as it was. All she had was nothing. No babies to hold. No more laughter when he burned the steaks on the grill. No more life to grab on to.

Alex restarted the truck and pulled past her marker, down the shaded lane and back onto the main road. He grabbed dinner at a drive-through window and continued to his big, empty house. The forest-green shutters needed to be repainted, he realized when he pulled into the drive, and this weekend he should probably do a final mowing of the grass. In the kitchen he opened the cupboard door but instead of picking up one of Dee's fancy plates he dumped his food on a paper plate and grabbed a beer from the fridge.

The canned laugh track from the sitcom annoyed him so he flipped over to a sports channel rerunning a Cardinals game from several years back. He ate his dinner sitting on the sofa Dee had bought, surrounded by the plants she liked and with her picture still on the mantel.

He wished like hell she was sitting on the sofa with him—and kicked the coffee table when he realized the woman he was imagining was Paige.

"WHAT I REALLY want to know is how this happened at all." It was just before noon on Thursday, the day after meeting Alex, and Paige was expected back at school in just over an hour. She should have taken the entire day off work rather than just this morning.

While they were in the waiting area, Alex asked why she kept checking her watch. One thing led to another and they waived their confidentiality rights to face the lab supervisor together. They both wanted the same answers: how and why did this happen?

Alex sat in the chair next to her, arms folded over his chest. The supervisor looked uncomfortable. The longer this meeting went on, the nicer it felt to have someone on her side. Not that he was on her side, not really.

Paige glanced at the watch on her wrist. The drive from the fertility clinic to Bonne Terre would take at least forty-five minutes. She did the math. If the paper-pusher across the heavy oak desk didn't give them some answers in about ten minutes she would have to leave and come back.

Not going to happen. And she wasn't going to be

pushed into another phone conversation with the lawyer, either. During the first phone call, she'd been too numb to ask questions about what happened four years ago. The donor she'd picked was a college graduate, Caucasian, of average height and weight. All of which fit Alex, except Alex wasn't a donor. He'd been an IVF candidate along with his wife.

Now he was in Paige's life and she needed to know why. Why, when she had been so careful in her choices, when she had made so many changes in her life, did this have to happen now?

The lab supervisor seemed honestly upset on their behalf, but he was still a company employee.

"My wife and I were assured that samples were checked and double-checked. That there was no need to worry about—"

"Human error," the man across the desk interrupted and pushed at the lock of hair he was trying to use to cover his bald spot. His blue eyes were faded and the crow's-feet at their corners seemed to be growing new legs the longer he was in the room. His nameplate read Merle Nelson. "We vet our employees very well. They are all smart, efficient and well paid, but mistakes do happen. We do know it wasn't a case of an employee intentionally replacing samples."

"Intentional or not this is a little more than a 'mistake,' though, don't you think?" Paige couldn't believe the man was talking as if this happened every day.

Mr. Nelson folded his hands over the desk blotter, pressing his thumbs together so hard Paige thought they might snap right off his hands. "Yes, I do. I can assure you this kind of mistake has never happened in our facility before."

"Well, that's comforting," Alex said sarcastically.

"What we can tell you is that there will be restitution made to your families and, with DNA testing of the remaining samples, we can tell you with authority if there were any other, uh, mislabelings."

"Remaining samples?" Paige's voice was a squeak.

"I might have— Son of a bitch." Anger laced Alex's voice and he stood to pace.

"We don't believe there were. We have run initial tests on the other samples and all indications are they belong to the original donor and not to you."

Paige felt sick. For the past half hour Nelson had danced around how sperm samples were stored and why vials were labeled with numbers rather than names and how those numbers referred to the names attached. He skipped over the part where Alex's sample should have been in a different section of the storage facility than the donor sperm. Now there was the possibility that this could have happened to other families. It wasn't right.

"What is it that we can do for you, Mr. Ryan?" His words snapped Paige out of her thoughts.

"You can tell me there aren't more children out there with my DNA inside them, for starters." Alex gripped the back of his chair and his knuckles turned white. Paige wanted to comfort him somehow, but what could she say?

"We sent the samples to a DNA lab for complete analysis. A mouth swab from you and from the child… It won't tell us why this happened, but you will know definitively how to move forward." He turned his focus from Alex to Paige. "Ms. Kenner?"

What could they *do* for her? They could go back in time and give her the sperm she'd chosen, that's what they could do. Only…

Would Kaylie be the girl she was with different DNA inside her? Paige's attention and mothering would be the same, but could she truly complain about the DNA that gave Kaylie her silly laugh or the curl in her hair? Or that made her so curious about the world around her? So eager to learn everything about it? She couldn't.

He didn't wait for her answer. "I've been authorized to offer a settlement to each of you. While our facility is focused on helping men and women create the families of their dreams, we do realize that our error may have caused you some mental anguish—"

Anguish? He thought reading Kaylie Dr. Seuss

at night caused anguish? Sure, Paige could do without the nightly arguments over veggie consumption or the ten-minute monologues that helped Kaylie decide which princess movie they'd watch on a Friday night. But those things weren't exactly anguish-inducing.

"—and we applaud your decision to begin the process of blending your families." He pushed an envelope across the desk as he named a figure that made Paige's ears burn.

Her hands fisted in her lap.

Alex's fingers were nearly white under his fingernails until he reached for the envelope and tore it in half. He tossed the pieces on the desk, turned on his heel and slammed the door.

Paige was in shock. Nelson thought a check for five times her yearly salary would make her forget the sleepless nights she'd had since the lawyer first called? The worry over how she could let a stranger into their lives? The insecurities that this crazy situation brought back to the surface? Paige knew she was a good mother, but was this some kind of sign she really couldn't pull off single-parenting without messing up her kid?

She swallowed and reached out, pushing the envelope back across the desk with her fingernail. How many times had money been used to keep her in line? There was the cruise for her sixteenth birthday, the extravagant car her parents offered on her high school graduation, an upgraded model when she graduated college. They always said the boarding schools were for her benefit but Paige knew the truth: boarding schools were a way to keep her under control and give them a way to forget about her.

She wasn't taking another penny. Not from her parents. Certainly not from a fertility clinic.

"I didn't come here for your money, Mr. Nelson. I came here for answers. The fact that you don't have the answers I need—" she shook her head "—it's typical. But I still won't take your money because when I came here five years ago I had one thought in mind, making a family. My daughter is amazing and this situation leaves a lot to be desired, but it doesn't change the fact that without your colossal mistake, I wouldn't have her." Paige picked up her bag and slung it over her shoulder. "I hope you continue to reevaluate the humans working in this office so no more of these 'errors' occur."

FRIDAY MORNING ALEX'S cell phone chirped and he pulled it from his pocket. It was Paige, texting the address of a coffee shop in nearby Farmington. Probably didn't want rumors to spread in her small town about them. A sigh of relief escaped his chest. He couldn't blame her. Meeting in Farmington meant he had more time before telling his in-laws about the change from widower to father. He had no idea how they would react to the news but figured it couldn't be good. Alex added Paige's number to his contacts list and then replied that he would be there.

He put the phone back in his pocket and blew out a breath. He shouldn't be attracted to her. It wasn't like they were dating or even should date. She was the mother of his daughter, a little girl he'd never met. He'd done the love thing and it was great, but there were enough complications between him and Paige without adding attraction to the mix.

The promise he made her, not to hurt Kaylie, felt like a promise about Paige, too. How could he hurt a woman he barely knew? Another of the million unanswerable questions plaguing him lately.

He didn't want to hurt her or the little girl, and making sure everyone came out on the other side of this without a few bumps or bruises would take all his focus. Only he couldn't forget about those adorable freckles, the way her upper half filled out the navy tee, the tight behind she showed off so well in jeans and the pretty, paint-splattered toes.

How many women still blushed, much less admitted to blushing when they could just as easily pretend nothing happened? He liked her. Didn't want to, but there it was.

Paige Kenner tripped all his buttons in the attraction department.

Not that that had anything to do with anything. Alex turned up Mooner's Hollow Trail to check in on the hiker's kiosks. So far it was a quiet afternoon at St. Francois State Park. He swiped a bandanna over the back of his neck. Hot but quiet. October was almost over, but so far Mother Nature seemed to be ignoring the fact that fall was here. He knelt beside Coonville Creek, dipped the bandanna into the water and then squeezed it over his head before replacing his black ball cap and continuing down the trail. Any day now the leaves would begin turning. First brilliant reds and then more subtle oranges and yellows would peek through before the first frost.

His walkie crackled and Tucker Blevins's deep voice echoed around the quiet trail.

"Any campers in the past day ask about setting up camp off-trail and away from the usual sites?"

Alex hadn't seen many campers, period, for the past week. The park was open to them from March through November but once school was back in session traffic died down significantly.

"Other than the RV that checked in two nights ago, I haven't seen anyone."

Tuck was quiet for a moment. "I've got an off-grid camp, maybe a day or two abandoned, just off Pike's Run. You close enough to get over here so we can look around for any lost hikers?"

Tuck described his location and Alex left the trail to start in that direction. Off-grid hiking wasn't unusual but it might have occurred be-cause someone had gotten hurt or more experienced hikers wanted to rough it for a night or two. Either way, they needed to check for anyone lost and make sure the campsite was cleared.

Two hours later what was left of the site was packed into a couple of sacks, but there were no campers to be found. No real trail, either. Which led Alex to believe it was kids on a dare. Most experienced hikers would have marked some kind of trail so they could easily get their bearings and return to camp.

Of course, most experienced hikers would also not leave most of their campsite behind.

Alex hefted one of the sacks over his shoulder while Tuck grabbed the other one and they started the cross-country hike back to the park office. They hit the creek within a few minutes and then rejoined Mooner's Trail. Alex pushed his black ball cap off, wiped his forehead with the bandanna and replaced the cap. Tuck followed in silence and it ate at Alex.

"What?"

"What, what?" Tuck feigned surprise.

"You never hike in silence." Alex rolled his eyes. "Since we were kids it was what girl let you get to third base, how hot the girl at the honky-tonk was or how women seem to go from fun to clingy in a heartbeat. You haven't said a word in more than a half hour. I repeat, what?"

Tuck kicked an acorn off the trail as they curved around a creek bend. "I wondered how it went with the baby mama. And then I remembered how mostly I do the talking because you don't like to talk about anything important anymore and decided to keep my big mouth shut." He elbowed Alex. "But since you brought it up, how'd the big meeting go?"

"How did you know I went to see her?" He shifted the pack on his back but that didn't ease the tension in his neck. Tension that had nothing to do with carrying an extra fifteen pounds of gear and everything to do with how Paige looked standing in her kitchen. Then again in the clinic office. A little scared, a lot focused. Sexy and ruffled and damn it, why did he have to keep thinking of her at all?

"Dude, since Deanna died you haven't talked about much of anything except the weather, baseball and tourist traffic. A month ago you tell me about the fertility clinic screwup and two days ago you call in for a personal day. Same thing yesterday. It's an easy jump from Alex-Never-Takes-Vacation to Alex-Met-The-Mom."

"We talk about more than baseball and tourists. And the weather is important." Alex scowled as the office came into view.

"Wrong. I talk. You mostly listen. I'm not gonna go all girl on you and say I've missed our friendship, but when you told me what happened, it was nice to see a little of the old Alex coming through again."

Alex unlocked the park office and dumped the excess gear on the tiled floor so they could catalogue it and then box it away. "The old Alex?" he asked.

"You remember him, don't you? Got excited about things, got mad about things."

"I'm not mad or excited about this mix-up. It's messing with my life."

"What life?" Tuck closed the door behind them. "You come to work, you hike alone, you show up for the rec leagues and through it all you're not really there. And you definitely don't talk about anything."

"I haven't had a lot to say."

"For three and a half years?" Tuck's pack joined Alex's and they began separating and cataloguing the extra ropes, shoestrings and miscellaneous matter that had been left behind. "I know Deanna's death was hard and I know her parents have put a lot of pressure on you to keep her memory alive. We're good." Tuck waved his hand between them. "It was just nice to see a sliver of the Alex I knew precancer. I kinda missed that guy."

"That guy and this guy are the same guy." Besides, it wasn't like he'd intentionally shut people out. It was just easier to get through the gray days after the funeral in his private bubble. And the longer that bubble was around him the harder it was to break through. After the call from the lawyer, the gray seemed to dissipate some. He wasn't sure he liked life outside the bubble, though, not if it kept his best friend talking about *feelings*.

Tuck tossed an empty canteen into a box and noted it on the paper. "That guy was alive. You've just been going through the motions. So, is she a hot baby mama, or one of those chicks with the sexy tats and piercings but an inability to make good decisions?"

Alex rolled the extra pack up and returned it to his own gear. "Paige is…" He beetled his brows. "Fine."

Tuck hooted and slapped Alex on the shoulder. "So we're talking one-hot-mama territory, aren't we? Is she single?"

He couldn't hold back the grin. At least Tuck was off the feelings subject and on to the physical. Physical Alex could handle. "You're an ass. And we didn't get that far."

"Do I detect a hint of hands-off in that sentence?" Tuck sat back on his heels, stacked the boxes and then stood.

Alex had no good response to that question. Besides, Tuck always had the ability to see right through him. From the attraction he still felt for the woman two days later he didn't think the wall he was trying to erect was quite thick enough to withstand the scrutiny. He picked up the boxes and shelved them in the storage area.

"It's okay, you know, if you like her." Alex shot

Tuck a back-off glance. In true Tuck form, he ignored it. "Dee wouldn't have wanted you to be—"

"Don't psychoanalyze me." Alex cut off his friend. Talking about feelings or how Paige looked in the abstract was one thing. Talking about Dee… Alex couldn't seem to talk to Dee anymore and he certainly wasn't going to talk about what she might or might not have wanted. "I'm not attracted to Paige." And maybe, if he repeated that to himself enough times, it would be true. "She's pretty but she's also the mother of the child I don't even know. We're barely acquaintances, much less anything more."

Tuck held up his hands in surrender. "Okay, got it. So when do you meet the kid?"

"Don't know yet." And damned if that didn't irk him, just a little bit. He got it. If a strange woman appeared on his doorstep determined to meet his kid he would react the same way. Even if there was a biological connection. But it still irked. He had a good job, no criminal history, a good family and friends. On paper he was perfect dad material, even if part of him worried he couldn't make a connection with the little girl. That somehow he would mess up her life.

Tuck didn't need to hear all that, though.

"We're having coffee to talk about it this evening." And just this morning he'd swabbed his cheek and sent the sample to the clinic.

Alex flipped the hours sign on the office door to

Closed and marked the time they would be back in the morning. He grabbed his keys from the hook behind the door and started for his truck. He'd let Paige lead the way. For now.

CHAPTER THREE

PAIGE SQUEEZED HER hands—hard—around her phone and then hit the delete key on her last text. The one that read Sorry, something suddenly came up. She couldn't do that to him.

To her.

The sooner she figured out what kind of man Alex Ryan was, the sooner her life could start forming the new normal it needed. DNA testing would take a few weeks, but if physical looks were anything to go by, she didn't need that confirmation. Kaylie was practically a miniature Alex. Still, she'd swabbed her daughter's cheek the night before and dropped off the strip at the clinic this morning. Maybe soon she could go to the grocery store without wondering if Alex would be buying grapes in the produce section or if her neighbors had figured out that there was more to the man sitting outside her house than met the eye.

Alex buzzed back that he would meet her there and before she could retype the blow-off message, Paige tossed her phone into her bag.

It was ridiculous, really, all the weird scenarios

that had played out in her head over the past two days. Since inviting him into her home, she'd had a nightmare that he fought her for custody, and then a made-for-TV dream about them falling in love and living happily ever after, complete with more tawny-haired, crooked-smiling kids in her house. Her fifth graders were studying a unit on the human body and Paige caught herself drawing Alex's image as the model for the male face.

Now she'd have to grade at least two dozen renditions of Alex's warm eyes and full lips. Paige sighed. This was not how a mature adult would react. A mature adult would hammer out the details of visitation through lawyers. The only lawyers Paige knew were friends of her parents, though, and she wasn't about to call that kind of drama into her life.

She could do this on her own.

Kaylie wandered in the door, dragging her Lalaloopsy backpack in one hand and her jacket in the other. "Hi, Mama." She tossed the light pack and jacket on Paige's desk, folded her arms and leaned against it. "Guess what we did today in circle time?"

Kaylie attended preschool at the small school where Paige taught. She pushed thoughts of Alex and joint custody aside to focus on the little girl.

"What?"

"We learned a new song about the days of the week. And I can teach it to you so you know, too.

Ready?" Paige nodded and waited. Kaylie snapped her fingers twice and then began singing to the tune of *The Addams Family* theme song, "There's Sunday and there's Monday…"

Paige watched her daughter, singing and snapping, and felt tears welling up in her eyes. He was going to love her, love her and want more and more time with her. Paige wasn't sure she knew how to share her daughter. Didn't know that she wanted to. She hurried around the desk and wrapped Kaylie in a tight hug. The little girl wiggled and pushed away.

"Too tight! And I'm not done yet." Paige released her, reluctantly, and Kaylie finished the song. "Think you can remember that?"

Paige nodded. "You are a very good teacher, sweetpea," she said mock-solemnly.

Kaylie looked at her expectantly.

"What?"

"Hug now." And she held out her arms. Paige wrapped her back up, hugging her tightly while Kaylie burrowed her head against Paige's neck, like she'd done since she was an infant.

It didn't matter how cute Alex Ryan was, Paige realized. It didn't matter that on paper he seemed like a good enough guy to be Kaylie's father. She couldn't drop her guard, couldn't let her attraction get in the way. Attraction as much as rebellion had led her down too many wrong paths in her youth.

There was the twenty-five-year-old who took

her to Texas over spring break when she was six-teen, and then an aspiring rocker who hit her. After that a football star who tried to turn her into a beauty queen, and the band instructor at her board-ing school. The one thing all four had in common was her parents' hatred of them.

It was the younger man—one of her father's students—whom she dated the year after earning her degree that had made Paige take a hard look at what she had been doing with her life. He ac-cused her of using him as an accessory when all her life she'd felt like the accessory her parents used to make their family seem perfect. Until that night she had floated from dead-end boyfriend to dead-end job, not using her degree, not practicing her own art, because at least when she was un-derachieving it annoyed her parents to the point they would call to tell her how much potential she was wasting.

That was when she took a substitute teach-ing job at the school, stopped looking for a new guy in every grocery aisle or bar and decided she wouldn't hedge her future on the chance her par-ents might approve of her, hell, might pay atten-tion to her, now.

She'd turned her life around, but she couldn't erase the memories of those mistakes. Paige couldn't allow Alex to be another in her long line of romantic misadventures, not when Kaylie could be the one hurt this time. She squeezed once more before letting Kaylie go.

"So, kiddo, Alison's picking you up tonight because Mommy has an appointment."

"But Auntie Al picked me up—" Kaylie beetled her brows and then snapped her fingers like she had when she was singing "—Wednesday. That's when she took me swimming."

"I know, and now it's Friday. But I have a boring, grown-up appointment and Auntie Al says she has a craving for pizza and maybe a princess movie. Sound like a good trade-off?"

"Two princess movies. Merida and then Belle, because they are the best princesses 'cept for Princess Amidala."

Paige laughed. "You'll have to talk that over when she picks you up, sweetpea. But I do agree with you on the Amidala-Merida-Belle thing." She glanced at the clock and realized Alison would be there in just a few minutes. She pulled Kaylie's class papers out of her backpack and ooh'd and ahh'd over her coloring and name-writing skills until Alison poked her head around the corner.

"Sweetpea! You ready for Princess and Pizza Night?" Alison came into the classroom, wearing tapered trousers and a tuxedo blouse with her long red hair wrapped up in a bun. She worked at a local winery in the HR department and always looked put together. Paige looked at her own pencil skirt and cap-sleeved shirt. At least she didn't have chalk on her butt today.

"Merida and then Belle, Auntie Al." Kaylie threw her arms around Alison's hips, hugging her. "And if there's time, maybe we could find Princess Amidala on Netflix?" She turned her hopeful gaze on Alison, batting her eyes.

Alison laughed and tousled the little girl's hair. "If you agree to a half-pepperoni half-cheese pizza, I could be persuaded to find an Amidala short."

Paige put Kaylie's jacket over her shoulders and strapped her backpack onto her back. "Bedtime is still eight o'clock, even though it's Friday, okay?" Kaylie nodded. Paige stood. "Thanks for watching her on short notice—again. Twice in one week, I owe you a girl's night."

"And you know I'll collect. So what's going on?"

Kaylie wandered across the room to the whiteboard on the wall and started drawing.

"I…have this thing." She hadn't told Alison about Alex's surprise visit that week.

Alison raised a brow. "Thing as in *D-A-T-E*?"

Paige shook her head, crossing her arms at the wrists and then shaking them. "No. Not even close. But not in front of her." She nodded at Kaylie, making smiley faces with the colored pens on the whiteboard across the room. They moved closer to Paige's desk and out of Kaylie's hearing range. "Thing as in *D-A-D-D-Y*."

Alison gasped and her expression turned serious. "He called."

"Nope, showed up on my curb and sat there like a stalker for going on two hours. Wednesday, just before you guys got back from swimming. Mrs. Purcell called me and then put 9-1-1 on notice."

"Mrs. Purcell. Sweet old biddie." Alison groaned. "Was he horrible and self-righteous about being a sperm donor?"

"No, he was calm and...normal."

"Normal is good."

"Normal might be his act. Especially with my track record."

"Don't do that. Don't talk about yourself like you're still the sixteen-year-old trying to get Mommy and Daddy to pay attention to you. We all act like fools when we're kids."

Paige glanced at Kaylie across the room and lowered her voice. "We don't all get arrested on prom night for TPing the superintendent's house."

"We don't all wind up with possibly the smartest, sweetest four-year-old, either." Alison hooked her thumb toward Kaylie, who was drawing lopsided birds over the smiley faces. "Remember, you're the one with the control here, so don't sweat it. Tell him about midnight feedings and the upcoming drama over losing her baby teeth. He'll run back to his home and forget all about you. And her."

Paige could only hope. And maybe dread. Because what did it say about someone that they didn't want to get to know a sweet kid like Kaylie? And what did her attraction to someone who could leave a child behind say about her? "I'll probably make it home before the second movie."

Alison gathered Kaylie's things before crossing the room to take her hand and start for the door. "Whatever you need. See ya." And they disappeared down the hall.

There was nothing left to do but drive to the next town and have coffee with Alex Ryan.

Thirty minutes later, sitting in the parking lot with her hands clenched around the steering wheel of her Honda, Paige decided she was being silly and childish about resolving this situation.

She had to go in.

Paige repeated that to herself twice more but her hands still seemed glued to the wheel, and not because Kaylie had "painted" it with Nutella a few weeks ago. No matter how much Paige scrubbed there was still a sticky feel to the wheel.

Alex's blue truck was parked five spaces down, between a low-slung convertible and a delivery truck. He was probably inside, waiting.

Paige blew out a breath as she summoned her courage. She peeled her fingers from the wheel and then dropped her keys into her bag. *Now go tell him what you expect.*

She pushed her long hair behind her ears and started toward the coffee shop. She ordered a half-caff skinny mocha and surveyed the room. Alex sat along the back wall, sipping his own drink. He had a black ball cap on the table, which matched the black tee with the Forestry Service logo over his chest. She could see jeans and hiking boots beneath the table. He must have come straight from work, like her. She smoothed her free hand over her hip and joined him at the table.

"Sorry, I'm a little late—"

He held up a hand, cutting her off. "No problem. It can't be easy, doing it all on your own. Babysitter problems?"

She nodded. Better he think she was waiting on the babysitter than building up her confidence to see him again. Paige sipped her coffee. "It isn't easy, not even when you have a partner."

"I know."

"I don't think you do. I don't think you understand the kind of unit Kaylie and I are. We don't need you to take on babysitter duties or chip in for her dance classes."

"Kids take dance classes at four?" His eyes widened at that. "I always believed stuff like that waited until school started."

"Some actually start at two, but that isn't the point. She might have gymnastics lessons, and at some point she'll probably need braces, or she might fall and break her arm. I'm a teacher, which means I get paid about two dollars an hour by the time you figure base pay against actual hours, but—"

"I never even thought about that," Alex interrupted. He twisted his mouth to the side. "Of course I can help with tuition or anything else. I have a decent health plan—"

"That isn't what I meant." Paige put her fingers to her temples. She was doing this wrong, all wrong. She shook her head. "What I meant was that we don't need your money. Whatever she wants I can give her. And what she needs isn't another part-time babysitter."

"But I'm more than willing to help out, however you need." He reached to his back pocket, and before he could pull out his wallet and offer her money for her mommy services—which would get him a quick smack on his hands—Paige kept talking.

"What I need is to know you're not going to disappear on her. And what Kaylie needs, or will need at some point, is a real father. Someone to teach her how to ride a two-wheeler and embarrass her when she goes on her first date. Those are things money can't buy. Attention can."

Alex tapped the tips of his fingers against the Formica tabletop. Nice fingers, Paige noticed. She clasped her hands in her lap, not wanting him to see the mess she'd made of her thumbnail throughout the day, worrying over how this night would go.

"Awful" had been her best guess earlier and that

was certainly how this felt. Not because of him. He was being perfectly nice, even if he'd been about to offer her a payoff like Mr. Nelson at the clinic. She was the one making a mess of it. Inadvertently insinuating he had to pay to see Kaylie. Throwing the chip she'd been feeling for the past few weeks down on the table. The chip labeled I Can Do This On My Own.

Finally, he sat back against the booth seat, spinning the plastic stirrer over the tabletop. "I don't have any expectations. And I know I can't replace you as Kaylie's anything. You've been there since the beginning. I'm the stranger who is biologically related but never so much as watched a younger sibling while my parents ran to the grocery store."

Paige had looked him up on Google during her free period but all she'd found was his wife's obituary and his picture on the Forestry Service website from when he was named Ranger of the Year two years before.

"You were an only child?"

Alex nodded.

"Me, too." So they had one thing in common. Well, other than Kaylie. "All my life my parents have jumped between complete indifference to me and total intrusion in my life. Their priority is what they want—for their lives and for mine. I know the pain she'll feel if you aren't willing to invest your time and energy into really getting to know her." She watched him closely for a moment.

His eyes were bright, his hands busy with the stirrer. A vein at his temple was pounding. She didn't want him to implode the life she'd built but she also couldn't just send him away. He was at the coffee shop because of a mistake, but he was also Kaylie's biological father. Paige tried to lighten the mood. "So coffee with the baby mama you never knew. Going well?" She sipped her coffee.

It took a moment but Alex laughed, a hearty sound in the quiet coffee shop. Paige looked around but no one paid any attention to them.

"Since I've never had coffee with an unknown baby mama before, I can honestly say I had no expectations. Listen, I told you the other day I just want to meet her. I know that sounds cavalier, like I'm going to give her an ice cream and then stroll away forever. I don't know how any of this is going to work. We barely know each other—" he waved his hand between them "—and we aren't friends. I was trying to talk myself out of knocking on your door the other day."

Paige sat back in her seat. She'd never imagined he would admit he had reservations about meeting their daughter. It wasn't the victory she'd expected, though. Instead of pumping her fist in a "whoop-whoop" she wanted to shrivel farther against the booth. God, it was like she was manic. *Yay! He doesn't want to meet her!* one minute and holding back tears because he didn't see what a gift Kaylie was the next.

"I kind of thought that."

"What I realized, just before you stepped out on the porch, is that I can't not be involved. Can't walk away. Drive away. I need to know her, as much as you'll allow. I won't push, I promise you I won't." The promise was there, in his brown eyes. In the tension in his shoulders and his thumb flicking against the stirrer.

"If you're not pushing yourself into our lives, if you don't know that you want to have a part in my daughter's life, just what do you want?" It was the question she'd been dying to ask for two days. The question that had brought on both the nightmare and the silly movie-ending dream.

"I'm not sure."

At least he was honest. "We can't be a replacement for the family you lost." The words were defensive so she gentled her voice. One thing she'd learned as a child was that histrionics didn't make the point. Solid, calm rationality did. "Fertility treatments are rough on couples. You lost your wife before they could really get started, and I'm sorry about that." She swallowed. "But no matter what you lost, Kaylie isn't the replacement part that will fix it."

"I know that, too." Alex bent the stirrer and then shoved it through the sip-spout of his coffee lid. "Whatever this is, it isn't guilt-ridden. I got over my wife's death a long time ago. I could have gone my whole life without knowing any of this, but I know. I can't turn back the clock, not on any of it. I can't forget that I have a daughter. All I'm asking for is a chance to get to know her. If not as her dad maybe as a friend?"

A guy who is a friend. It would be less intimate. Safer for Kaylie, certainly. In Kaylie's insular world friends stayed around forever, but maybe it would be simpler if they started with the friend card. For Paige, too. Friends had beer after ball games, not caviar by candlelight.

Then, because she didn't want to give him time to come up with an excuse, "Alison, the friend I mentioned the other day, and I have lunch every Sunday. This week it's at her house. You could come by. Meet everyone. It's informal. No pressure, and it's a familiar place for Kaylie."

Plus, it was less than forty-eight hours away. If this man wanted a relationship with Kaylie, he would cancel whatever plans he had. And if he didn't…better to understand his priorities now than later.

"Sunday." Alex crushed the empty coffee cup in his hands. "What time should I be there?"

CHAPTER FOUR

"I CAN'T BELIEVE you invited him," Alison hissed through her teeth as she picked up the bowl of potato salad and pushed open the back door with her hip.

Paige followed her onto the covered deck of the bungalow with a plate of condiments in one hand and a pitcher of sweet tea in the other. They started the tradition of Sunday dinners, switching between Paige's home and Alison's, after college. Sometimes friends stopped in. If Alison happened to be dating someone, he might stop by. Her parents were regulars since Kaylie was born, but they wouldn't be here today. One hurdle at a time, she decided, and Kaylie meeting Alex for the first time was a big enough hurdle.

"Scratch that, I can't believe he showed up. From everything you said."

Alex sat under Alison's maple tree with his large, muscled friend Tucker. It had seemed like an easy thing to invite him to the barbecue, a good way for him to meet Kaylie with few expectations and zero pressure on the little girl. Now that he was here, though, it was a different thing altogether. Because even though he seemed oblivious to the women on the porch and even though he wasn't pushing himself at Kaylie, he was there. Making her feel itchy and self-conscious. "I didn't say anything."

"And that was my point. When things are going well you talk, when things get hairy you clam up. It's been your MO since we were kids." Alison set the food bowls on the table and brushed her hands together. "So when you didn't give me a breakdown Friday and when you didn't say anything yesterday other than that you'd invited him, I figured the chances were slim he'd show."

"I tell you everything." Having brought out the condiments and tea, Paige knew there was nothing left inside until the chicken was ready, so she sat on Alison's bench.

Alison rearranged the bowls of food on the table as she was no doubt arranging her next words. "You tell me about things when you've already made your decision. And that's cool. I'm the friend, the supporter. The cheerleader. Not your priest or your mother."

Huh. Paige had never realized it, but Alison's words rang true. She did like to have her ducks in a row, so to speak, before telling anyone about her plans. Probably because if she didn't have logical, intelligent arguments for everything from a new bike to a new hairstyle as a child her parents automatically shot her down.

Had she done that this time?

"I never realized before now that I did that." Paige popped an ice cube into her mouth and then put her glass back on the table. "And I know. I was going to be strong. I was going to shut him down and insist that Kaylie and I were fine on our own." She picked her glass back up and rolled it between her hands. "I had this hope in the back of my mind that maybe he only wanted to make sure we wouldn't file for custodial support. But he isn't going away. He has a right to know Kaylie."

"He does. And you have the right to monitor those visits until you're certain where he's coming from."

"Park Hills," Paige said automatically. "I know, that's not what you were really asking. He's from Park Hills, works as a park ranger and lost his wife to cancer just before Kaylie was born. And if this isn't a supervised visit, I don't know what is."

"True enough. And the cute friend?" Alison indicated Alex's mountain of a friend sitting beside him under the tree. She flipped her head upside down, gathered her long red hair into her palm, grabbed the ball cap from the handrail and then slid her hair through the back opening. She waved a hand in her face. "Lord, it's hot out here for October. Seriously, what do you know about the friend?"

"You're terrible. My life is in turmoil and you're thinking about your next date?"

"Don't tell me you haven't noticed we've got two of the hottest men in St. Francois County in my backyard." Alison clucked her tongue.

Kaylie squealed from the swing set in the neighbor's yard, rescuing Paige from answering. Kaylie squealed again and Paige fisted her hands but managed not to run screaming into the other yard to protect her daughter from the swings. Kids played on swings every day, she reminded herself, and only rarely did they get hurt. Alex looked like he might run into the yard, too.

Helicopter parents, we're two helicopter parents in the making. For the past four years it was only her making sure Kaylie was safe in her crib, graduated from bottles to veggies, and didn't get an infection from a skinned knee. A small piece of her heart was glad she wasn't the only person watching over Kaylie now.

"I checked him out. He is who he says he is. He isn't crazy or an alcoholic and he doesn't have gambling debts." She took a fortifying breath. "I know my track record isn't great, but you have to admit most of the mistakes I dated were solely to get my parents' attention. But that is beside the point because we aren't dating. Not now and not ever. He's Kaylie's father and will eventually be my coparent. End of story." Definitely, definitely the end of the story.

"Well, he is quite dishy. And your Google search didn't return any obvious red flags." Alison sat back in her chair and folded her arms over her ample chest. She inspected the men in the yard as if they were paintings at an auction. "If you were actually in the market..."

"Which I'm not." Paige shrugged as if she hadn't spent most of the past three days remembering how the man looked in jeans and a fitted tee. Or wondering what he might look like in baseball pinstripes.

"For my money, though, Tall, Dark and Handsome Friend wins in the looks department."

"They aren't unattractive." Paige managed to say the words without her voice going into breathless territory but she couldn't bring herself to look Alison in the eye. The guys in the yard drew her attention again as they sat back in the lawn chairs listening to the Rams game on the radio.

"Pu-lease, don't tell me you haven't noticed Alex has a smile like a Hollywood star. Or that his body is taut without going over into veiny-muscle territory." Alison picked up her tea and drank. "And his voice is like sex on a stick."

Paige sputtered iced tea across the table. "Sex on a stick? What does that even mean?"

Alison waggled her eyebrows. "You know what I mean, and don't tell me you didn't notice."

"Did you spike the tea?" Alison shook her head. Paige mopped up the drops on the table, refusing to look her friend in the eye. "I didn't notice," she managed in an almost steady voice. "And my point was that he isn't a loser who donated his sperm and is now looking for some kind of validation. He doesn't have any dreaded diseases that might have been passed on to Kaylie. He's a normal guy who has been through a rough few years and had a kid dropped in his lap."

"Oh, no." Alison's voice dropped lower.

"What?" Paige blinked.

"You like him. Like, like him, like him."

The timer went off in the kitchen, saving Paige from having to answer Alison's statement but still she muttered, "I don't like him, like him."

Alison disappeared into the kitchen to finish barbecue prep and Paige turned back to the yard. Being grateful he wasn't a serial killer wasn't the same as liking him. Thinking he might be a good friend for Kaylie wasn't the same as thinking he'd make a good boyfriend. He seemed to be as nervous as she about dropping all this on Kaylie. Points for him. He had a steady job. More points. He looked good in Levi's. Extra bonus points.

Not that she'd really been looking.

He had a seemingly normal friend, which added to his points total. And slight overprotective streak aside, if Alison were truly worried about his motives she'd have given him her version of the Spanish Inquisition at the door and never let him set foot inside.

Then there was her private conviction that Alex Ryan was more than a commitment-phobe who would look for any reason to disappear.

Kaylie moved on to the sandbox, drawing her attention, and ran a toy truck over the wooden sides. Just a normal Sunday afternoon. Well, other than the incredibly distracting man sitting under the tree. He hadn't pushed himself at Kaylie, which was a relief. Her daughter liked everyone she met, but like many toddlers she needed time to warm up to most of them.

Paige watched him for a long moment as he listened to the ball game. Black baseball cap covering his tawny hair, tee stretched across his broad chest, faded blue cargo shorts that were slightly tight in all the right places. His eyes were a deep brown that seemed to turn to gold when the light hit them just right. He crossed his ankle over his knee and held the longneck bottle by his fingertips beside him.

It just wasn't fair for a man to have the tawny eyes *and* the tawny hair, not to mention the thick eyelashes and that little scar at the corner of his mouth that seemed to wink when he smiled.

His friend said something and his laugh cracked across the backyard, sending the butterflies in her belly into overdrive. It was a good laugh. A solid, confident laugh.

He turned and his intense gaze settled on her, pushing the butterflies to full-on panic mode. Alex smiled and tipped the bottle toward her before taking a drink. He turned his gaze back to his friend Tucker, but Paige had the unsettling feeling his focus was still on the deck.

On her.

It made the hairs on the back of her neck stand up. Made her sit a little straighter in her chair. Cross her legs.

God. She was not, repeat not, interested in the man as a...

Shoot. Yes, she was.

She needed to cap that feeling the way she capped the tubes of paint in her studio: tightly. Not just for her own sanity, either. Alison wasn't wrong about Paige's past romances.

She sighed. Men who either couldn't or wouldn't treat her as anything more than an accessory. Something to put on and take off as the mood suited them.

Paige never doubted her decision to have Kaylie as a single parent.

Not until the gorgeous man sitting under her best friend's tree had shown up on her doorstep. Well, curb.

Please, don't let him treat Kaylie like an accessory.

Alex pointed and Paige looked in that direction in time to see Kaylie climb up the rungs of the ladder and hurl herself toward the metal trapeze frame hanging from one end of the swing set.

Her breath caught in her throat for a moment that seemed to take too long. Kaylie sailed through the short space, tawny hair flying behind her, until her little hands caught the bottom rung and held fast. Her legs swung once more, twice.

Kaylie giggled as the trapeze swung crazily to the side. And then she fell, hard, down to the ground.

Paige was out of her chair like a shot and so was Alex. They started toward Kaylie but she got up, dusted off her rump and turned toward the house.

"Didja see me, Mama? I flew! I really flew!" She high-fived herself. "Good job, Kaylie, good job!" An enormous grin split her face and she turned to the ladder. "I'm'a go again. Watch this time," she ordered.

Paige stopped short of the swing set, Alex beside her, and watched as Kaylie climbed back up the four-rung ladder. She settled her feet, holding on to the sides of the swing set as she twisted her mouth to the side and looked intently at the barely moving trapeze.

"She'll be okay. She'll be okay." Paige whispered the words like a prayer. "Be okay. It's only three feet off the ground. Be okay."

Alex joined in, his deep, whispering voice combining with hers in the she'll-be-okay chant.

Finally, Kaylie pushed off the step and jumped toward the trapeze once more. Her hands slipped and she tumbled to the soft earth beneath the swings.

"Oh, no," Paige said, stepping forward. But Alex's hand on her wrist stopped her.

"Wait."

Who was he to tell her to wait? She couldn't wait. Her baby just fell three feet to the hard ground.

Kaylie stood up again, dusted off her behind and shoved her hair away from her face. She looked up at the trapeze as if it betrayed her and then stomped away from the swing set toward them. She beetled her brows, mumbling to herself and looking back to the swings.

Paige caught her daughter in her arms. "You okay, baby?"

"It wasn't supposed to move."

"What wasn't supposed to move?" Alex knelt beside them in the grass.

"The hand swinger. It was s'posed to stay still." She wriggled out of Paige's too-tight grasp. "I told it I'd come back later but only if it promises to stay still." Kaylie shot another glance toward the trapeze, swinging lightly in the breeze. "Only if it stays still," she enunciated each word in her angry, four-year-old voice and continued to Alison's deck. "I need juice," she called and pushed open the sliding glass door to the kitchen.

Paige put her hand to her heart. "She's okay. I thought I might have lost about a year off my life there for a second."

Alex chuckled beside her. "If you lost one,

I think I lost five." He angled his head toward the deck. "Can I buy you a glass of tea for your nerves?" he joked.

Paige shook her head. "I need more than tea after that."

"Anything for Supergirl's mom."

"Princess Amidala, thank you very much."

Alex put his arm around her shoulder and squeezed. Paige couldn't resist a lean-in, just for a second. A hint of sandalwood that she recognized as him tickled her nose and she forced herself away before she could turn her head into his chest and take a deep breath. They weren't friends, not yet. And even if they became friends, that was all this could be. She wouldn't jeopardize Kaylie's relationship with her father by starting her own relationship with the man. Alex's next words made her squeeze her eyes closed to repeat that promise to herself once more. Twice.

"And she's way more than okay. She's just about perfect."

Still, his words echoed in her mind.

CHAPTER FIVE

"I FORGOT TO call them." Alison closed the sliding door softly behind her, apology written all over her face. "And it was such a perfect excuse, too."

"They're here?" Paige took a step away from Alex, who was suddenly way too close for comfort. The butterflies took up residence in her belly again, but this time for an entirely different reason.

Her parents stepped through the door holding hands with Kaylie, who was chattering about her leap to the trapeze.

Angry with her choice at first, Hank and Dot Kenner were trying to build a solid relationship with Kaylie. They came to the Sunday barbecues, school events and birthday parties. Conversations centered around Kaylie, and most of the time Paige could forget that for the first twenty-four years of her life they were either absent or controlling her every move.

They were *trying* with Kaylie, Paige reminded herself, and that meant something.

Hank was tall and overdressed for a backyard barbecue, but then when was he not? Even during summer break from the university in St. Louis he wore the same checked shirts, bow ties and tweed sport coats that he wore to teach constitutional law to second-year candidates. Paige's mother, Dot, wore a geometric print dress with deep reds and oranges as the base colors. She focused her attention on Kaylie as she told the story of her leap from the swings. Afterward, Dot turned an accusing gaze toward Paige, who forced herself to unclench her hands.

"You let this child jump from a swing set to a trapeze?" She said the words as if Kaylie had been BASE jumping from the St. Louis Arch without a parachute.

Paige indicated the small swing set in the next yard. "No broken bones. Kids jump—"

Dot interrupted, gripping Kaylie's little hand tighter. "She could have—" her gaze dropped to Kaylie "—*B-R-O-K-E-N* her neck." She spelled out the offending word.

Kaylie squinted her eyes at her grandmother. "*B* is for *bat*. And *ball*. And *bunches* of grapes," she said, pulling her hand from Dot's grasp. She plucked her juice cup from Dot's other hand and wandered off, chattering about more *B* words. "And *bear*. And *bling*. And *br-r-ring* me a cookie," she said, giggling at herself.

Paige watched as Kaylie climbed onto one of the lawn chairs, crossed her legs at the ankle and sipped her drink. She really was the best kid.

"She didn't break anything, Mother," Paige said, keeping her voice calm. Level.

"It was irresponsible."

"It was childhood," Paige insisted despite the fact she'd had nearly the same reaction as her mother when Kaylie was midflight. But thinking something was different from wrapping her daughter up in bubble wrap for the next five years or insisting that she never swing or climb on a jungle gym.

"Okay, well, we have barbecue chicken coming from the oven in just a few minutes. I'll just run inside and grab a few extra place settings. Mr. and Mrs. Kenner, can I get you something to drink?" Alison said, in an attempt to ease the tension between Paige and her parents. Paige sent her a thankful glance. Alison had been caught between them for nearly as long as Paige could remember. Hank and Dot waved off the offer of drinks, but Alison kept going toward the sliding glass door. "You'll help me, won't you, Joe?" She looked at Tuck, who was drinking the last of his beer.

"Joe?" she said again. Tuck's blue eyes widened in surprise when he realized Alison was talking about him. "Could you help me in the kitchen, sweetie?"

"Ah, sure, sweetie." He straightened his six-foot-plus frame from the deck post.

The two of them disappeared into the kitchen, leaving Paige with her parents and Alex.

There was just no way to explain to Dot and Hank who Alex was without ruining Paige's plans. Paige's actions frequently met with disapproval from her parents. When Paige first decided to use a fertility clinic, they'd told her she would make her child abnormal. Their opinion had gradually softened as Kaylie stole their hearts, but Paige still saw flickers of condemnation in their eyes from time to time.

She was not telling her parents exactly who Alex was. Not now. Not when her mother was working her way up to a full-blown migraine after less than five minutes. Alex deserved better than a full-on Dot Meltdown.

Alex cleared his throat behind her and she realized she was standing between him and her parents like some kind of guardian. Maybe she was. Hank and Dot might be doing a good job with grandparenting, but they were anything but picture-perfect parents.

Paige motioned from Alex to her parents and back again. "Hank and Dot Kenner, this is Alex Ryan. He's a—"

"Friend," Alex interrupted before Paige had the chance to say anything else. Which was good because her mind blanked when she realized she had no idea how to introduce him. "Uh, Joe and I can't resist good barbecue."

Dot grabbed Paige's upper arm and turned her away from Alex. "You're on a date with Kaylie ten feet away?" Dot faux-whispered the words, as if Alex might be deaf as well as gorgeous.

"Yes, Mother, and we were thinking about going inside to do the dance with no pants—" she used her mother's least favorite sex slang despite feeling like a rebellious child for doing so "—and leaving Kaylie listening to the football game—so it's a good thing you're here to help out." Paige pulled her arm from her mother's grasp. "Of course we're not on a date. He's a friend. You know, a person with whom you talk and play on softball leagues with, and have barbecues."

"You play sports?" Her mother seemed dumbfounded by the idea. True to form, though, Hank was already bored of the conversation. He made his way to a chair at the head of the table and sat, hands folded in his lap, thumbs twiddling.

Paige sighed. "It's just part of the definition, Mom."

"Although I do play in a rec softball league during the summer," Alex added.

"You don't have to be sarcastic," Dot said, ignoring Alex completely. She pressed her fingertips to her temples. "I just never know with you, Paige."

Yep, full-blown migraine would be hitting any moment. Paige tried not to feel bad that she had caused her mother pain—again—but couldn't. She gently took Dot's hand and led her to a cushioned chair in the deep shade.

"I'll get you a cold cloth for your head, Mother.

I'm sorry." She motioned Alex to follow her inside. "I'm sorry." She whispered the words as soon as they were inside.

"For what?"

"I—" Paige wasn't sure what to say first. Sorry for not knowing what to call him? Sorry for that silly argument with her mother? Sorry she'd invited him here altogether? All of the above seemed like a good bet at this point.

"We all have crazy people in our families," he said and bumped his shoulder against hers. The tingle returned with a vengeance. "Your craziness is just a little closer than most."

Paige twisted her mouth to the side. She pulled a washcloth from a drawer and wet it in the sink. Alison and Tuck returned to the room, faces slightly red. "Where have you been?"

"I, um—"

"Alison needed some help in the, ah, basement," Tuck said helpfully.

"Alison doesn't have a basement." Paige wrung out the cloth before focusing on her friend. "You're the troubleshooter, remember? You keep me from saying stupid things to my parents and in return I buy you wine."

"She didn't take Kaylie's Flying Wallendas act well, did she?"

Paige shook her head and then shot Alison a wicked smile. "On the other hand she thinks you're dating Joe here, so there's plenty of fun dinner conversation in store for you. With the added benefit of her calling your mother once they're home."

"You didn't!" Alison's eyes widened to quarter size.

"Nope, she totally inferred it."

"You let her." Alison put her hands on her hips. "And after I cooked your favorite chicken for lunch."

"I couldn't let her think I was dating Alex, could I?"

"Uh, ladies, we kind of like being talked about, but not when we're actually in the room." Tuck spoke up from the kitchen counter. "And if we're dating, Alison, you should probably know my name isn't Joe. It's Tucker."

Alison blushed a bright red that clashed completely with her auburn hair. Tuck grinned at her and wrapped a strand around his finger.

"But you can call me Tuck."

"Back to the issue at hand." Alex spoke up from the doorway, where his gaze shot from the people on the porch to the little girl in the yard. "What do we tell them about me?"

"Nothing," Paige finally said after weighing her words. "You're a friend here for a barbecue. That's all anyone needs to know."

THE PANICKED LOOK on Paige's face made Alex want to march out onto the deck to order Hank and Dot to stop treating their daughter as if she were five, or an unwanted annoyance. But that wouldn't solve anything. He'd never gotten to fix the strained relationship he'd had with his parents because they'd died in a car accident when he was in college. Then Deanna had come along with her boisterous family and a home filled with love and encouragement. Knowing her family helped him make peace about his own.

Alex had no idea how to give the same peace to Paige and that made his stomach clench in a weird way.

Why did he want to tell them anything? Part of him wanted to scream from the rooftop that he was Kaylie's father. Watching her in the backyard had been a treat and after only an hour, she had already wound her way into his cold heart. But part of him wanted to keep his relationship with Kaylie a secret. Let it grow naturally without any preconceived notions or ideas. He had a feeling that if Hank and Dot knew he was Kaylie's father, Kaylie would also know before the day was out. He didn't have to have read a million parenting books to know this was not the way to spring a new relationship on a kid. Although he had read one. A long one Dee had picked out before she got sick; the author insisted children needed structure, unconditional love and encouragement. Mostly structure and authority, though. Nowhere did the book say a child's sperm donor should swoop into her life acting like Daddy Dearest within a thirty-minute time span.

"So we're just friends, for now, and leave the dating to Joe and Alison over there," he finally said. "Works for me."

Alex was tasked with carrying the additional place settings to the table while Tuck was given chicken duty. Paige and Alison filled glasses while Hank and Dot ignored the goings-on entirely. He might not have a romantic relationship with Paige, but he wanted to kick her parents in the shins to make them straighten up.

From what he could see Paige was the perfect daughter. He'd done some checking and learned she volunteered making receiving blankets for a charity hospital in St. Louis. She was a teacher and she was raising an amazing kid! How could her parents not see all the wonderful things about her?

She brushed against him as she took the last of the glasses to the table and a hot zing of pleasure rocketed from the light contact at his shoulder to his groin.

Eventually his body would get the message that his brain already knew: Paige was the mother of his child. She might become his friend. She was not going to be his girlfriend.

The table was quiet as they passed plates of food around.

"My friend at the gallery wants to know when you might have another piece for him," Dot said, her gaze intent on Paige. "There is a big show for local artists coming up at the end of the month, you know."

Paige took a bite of her salad and chewed slowly. "I'm focused on school during the year, you know that. My students need all of my attention."

"Paige, these offers aren't made lightly, dear, and they won't be made for long if you keep turning them all down."

"Is the painting in your living room for school?" Alex interrupted, sensing Dot was about to go on a tangent. "The white daisy?"

She shook her head. "That one is for Kaylie, actually. She wanted something pretty in her room. Didn't you?"

Kaylie nodded, her wavy hair bouncing around her shoulders. "I wanted something warm so when the snow comes after Christmas my room won't be so cold."

"The painting was beautiful. I don't know a lot about art, but I liked it." He had. It wasn't finished and he'd only caught a glimpse but the pretty garden in the painting reminded him of Paige. Her home. Herself. Pretty and interesting.

"Thank you." She mouthed the words across the table and Alex lifted his shoulder. Paige grinned and finished her salad.

"So you are painting, then?" Dot was like a dog with a bone and Paige rolled her shoulders, as if relieving tension. He could only imagine how her mother's nagging affected her but ordered himself to focus on the chicken, not the woman. "You have the chance to really make something of yourself, Paige. Teaching painting to uneducated children who don't understand Impressionism much less the Renaissance isn't using the talents you were blessed with—"

"I LIKE MY JOB, Mother," Paige interrupted before her mother could really get going. This was the same argument they'd been having since before Kaylie was born, and unlike when she was a child, Paige didn't need her parent telling her she was wasting her talents. As much as she liked painting she was no van Gogh. Besides, she liked teaching, and she had told her mother so. For the millionth time. "I like educating the children about art history, and I can see how their work changes with that knowledge throughout the year. Some of them are really good."

"But, sweetheart—"

"Mommy's paintings are the best in the school. I seen them in the library." Kaylie enunciated the last word. She had barbecue sauce all over her face and she turned a megawatt smile to Paige. Dot shot an annoyed look at Kaylie.

Alison scraped her chair back. "Who wants dessert? I know I'd love some chocolate cake." She looked around the table at the still-half-full plates. "Okay, chocolate cake it is. Kaylie, why don't you help me cut a few slices?" She held out her hand and Kaylie jumped up from the table.

"Can we cut them in shapes?"

"Sure, kiddo," Alison said as she slid the glass doors open. "We'll make cutout cake slices."

Their voices trailed off as she slid the door closed behind them. She refused to have the rest of this conversation before virtual strangers so Paige turned to the other side of the table.

"Tuck, Alex, could you give us a few minutes?" Paige asked and waited until the men closed the door.

"It's nice, dear, that you enjoy the school work," said Dot, a patronizing note in her voice that was the opposite of the slightly uncomfortable expression on her face. She seemed to bite her tongue for a moment.

"I like my job, Mother—"

Dot cut her off. "But the fact remains that your talent is above decorating school libraries or a child's bedroom. We only want what's best for you." She pressed her fingers to her temple again. "So stressful, wanting the best for children who don't listen. Hank?"

He nodded and stood, not saying a word.

"Think about what I said, dear. Your work could be hanging in a real gallery if you would only apply yourself."

Paige didn't trust herself to reply with the calm she'd perfected over the past few years. So she focused her attention on gathering the plates left at the table. A few minutes later, Dot and Hank were gone. The door slid open.

"And I thought my parents were disappointed when I decided to hike for a living," Tuck said. His flippant words had the desired effect. The ice chilling the backyard thawed and talk turned to football and Alison's work at a local winery.

Kaylie skipped onto the deck and finished her juice before running back to the swing set, certain the trapeze was ready for her this time. Alison gathered two serving bowls and started for the kitchen; Tuck followed with the platters of chicken, leaving Paige and Alex alone on the porch.

"I really did think your painting was good."

"Thanks." Her word was a whisper, and when she caught sympathy in his gaze she knew a hint of pain still shone through her green eyes. "I'm sorry about that. Alison was supposed to call them to cancel but she forgot." Paige tossed her napkin on her plate. "I should have been the one to call, but somehow they can still make me feel so small." She folded her arms over her chest.

"I've seen worse."

"No, you haven't."

"I changed my major from accounting to natural sciences my sophomore year. My dad was an accountant. His dad. My mother's brother. My parents thought I was turning into a hippie or something."

"Really?" Paige finally looked at him. Alex nodded. "I keep telling myself I won't do that to Kaylie. I want to be her support, her encouragement. Not a stumbling block to her happiness."

"Then you will be."

"How can you be so sure?"

"You're doing a great job, from what I've seen, so far."

Paige felt herself glow at the compliment. "Thank you."

Alex shrugged. He was quiet for a long moment, watching the little girl across the yard. He could see this becoming a normal part of his life. He'd always wanted family, kids. And, yeah, he thought that was over when Dee died, but maybe...

Kaylie climbed to the top of the ladder and squinted her eyes at the trapeze swinging lightly in the breeze.

Alex held his breath when she flexed her knees, still studying the handrail. Then she reached forward and jumped. Caught the handle, swung forward and back a few times, giggling madly across the yard. When the trapeze slowed, she dropped to the ground and circled back to the ladder.

"Good job, sweetpea," Paige called across the yard, clapping for the little girl.

Paige was right. The two of them were a unit. They didn't need him, not the way he suddenly seemed to need them.

"Would you like to go to dinner sometime? Just

us?" The words escaped before he could pull them back. Paige turned, green eyes wide. She swallowed and put her hand to her throat.

"Why? What?" Paige asked, her voice unsteady.

Even if he could, Alex didn't want to take the words back. He wanted more days like this one.

Maybe Paige and Kaylie were his second chance. Different from what he'd imagined, but second chances didn't come along every day.

Maybe moving fast was worth the risk. So he repeated himself.

"Do you want to go to dinner sometime? Just the two of us?"

CHAPTER SIX

PAIGE REACHED FOR her glass, took a slow sip of tea. Have dinner?

No, that was a bad idea, with a capital *B* and *I* for emphasis.

They were supposed to keep this friendly, get to know one another.

Still, her heart had leaped in her chest at his words, and she knew they were so much more than friendly.

Her reaction was similar to the ones she'd had toward her crushes in high school. The flying feeling that accompanied her wild trip to Texas over spring break; the excitement at seeing how her father's face practically glowed when he learned she was dating one of his students. Every single one of those situations had ended with a loud implosion and weeks of Paige picking herself up and putting herself back together.

Dinner was an exceptionally bad idea.

She finished her glass and, because her hands wanted to fidget, she set the glass away from her and then folded them primly in her lap. Squeezed her fingers until her knuckles turned white as a reminder to remain calm. Poised. Fidgeting was a sign of weakness according to Dot; weakness was not tolerated.

"Are you asking me out on a date?" She wished the words back but it was too late.

Alex slipped his finger around the middle of his glass, making a gap in the condensation on the outside. "Yeah, I am."

Paige looked through the sliding glass doors, but Alison was nowhere to be seen. For that matter neither was Tuck, and Kaylie was across the yard at the sandbox, having given up on swinging from the trapeze. No one to come to her rescue. No one to interrupt what was going to be a very uncomfortable conversation.

She cleared her throat. "Why?"

"Because you interest me. No one has interested me in…well, a long time." He squinted as he looked into the bright afternoon sunshine. "I want to get to know you. Dinner seems like a good option."

"I don't think that's a good idea. We barely know each other."

"That's how dating usually starts—with two people who don't really know each other but who want to get to know one another." He finished his tea. "I think it would be good if I knew Kaylie's mom a little better."

Kaylie was the perfect excuse to turn him down,

Paige decided. "I don't date, not really. I especially don't date men who have a connection to my daughter. She's just a little girl, she can't understand the emotions that go into dating—or stopping dating, for that matter."

"It's only dinner. A chance for me to get to know Paige, not just Kaylie's mom. A chance for you to understand Alex rather than the anonymous number on the sperm-donor sheet."

"We did that already. Coffee last Friday, remember? You know I'm a schoolteacher, I know you're a park ranger and we've already agreed that you'll start out as Kaylie's friend before we move to the more serious stuff." She had to remain firm on this. For Kaylie.

Maybe a little bit for herself. Because look how interested she was in him now and she'd only known him for a few days.

"One coffee date, and we never touched on your actual art. Your plans for the future. Mine, for that matter." Alex pushed away from the table. "I like what I know of Paige-the-Woman. I'd like to get to know more about her."

Oh, so dangerous. Getting to know the real Paige. Would that be the Paige who helped to plastic-wrap the police cruiser the night of the big ice storm? Or would that be the Paige who scored exceptionally high on her SATs only to choose art school over an Ivy League education?

Or maybe he'd like to know the Paige who used

men as a means of getting her parents' attention. She'd been living down Fun Paige's reputation for almost five years, since the night she broke things off with the law student and decided to change the direction of her life.

Most people didn't mention all the hell she'd raised as a kid. Most of them, even Mrs. Purcell, welcomed her back to the quiet community in the Missouri countryside just before Kaylie was born. She was grateful for the welcome. For their acceptance of her and of Kaylie. She would not jeopardize any of that for a date with Alex Ryan.

It wasn't that she didn't want Alex to live down her reputation. But she didn't want to see his face when he learned the kind of person she used to be. That she apparently still was, because the voice in her head telling her to go out on a date with Alex was Fun Paige. The Paige who acted first and thought about the consequences later. The Paige she'd promised herself she wouldn't be when she had her own family.

She couldn't afford to be that woman, not again.

Paige loosened her hands in her lap. It wasn't even that she thought her reputation would smear Alex's.

The problem was she didn't want him to know, period. She liked knowing that when he looked at her he only saw the woman she was now. There was no shadow of the girl she used to be. No past for him to dredge up and use against her.

For Alex there was only Paige-the-Mom or Paige-the-Teacher.

She wanted to keep it that way.

It was smarter that way. Smarter for her. Definitely smarter for Kaylie.

This was not the time to act impulsively but to come up with a plan and stick to that exact path.

Having a path and a plan was absolutely smarter.

Why did she keep repeating that to herself?

Paige tucked a strand of hair behind her ear and looked anywhere but at Alex, who leaned against the deck railing, feet crossed at the ankle, thumbs tucked into his back pockets. T-shirt taut over what had to be the best-looking set of pecs she had yet to see.

Nope, she was definitely not looking at him.

She had a plan: let Alex be Kaylie's friend, watch him like a hawk—not in that way, in a motherly way—and assign him to the "friends without benefits" category she assigned nearly every man she knew.

"Paige-the-Woman stays up too late, hates washing her car and is probably a little too indulgent with her daughter." She picked up Kaylie's plate, still filled with veggies but with barely a smear of barbecue sauce left, and gestured at it for emphasis. "This is about Kaylie, remember? Getting to know her, building a relationship with her."

"I'm not sure getting to know Kaylie precludes getting to know you. And, if you're worried about veggie intake, you could always make vegetables a game."

Paige laughed. "You read a parenting book, didn't you?"

Alex blushed, which made Paige giggle harder. He was cute when he blushed. And he crinkled his nose when he laughed along with her.

"I might have read one, but it had some good ideas." He followed her into the kitchen, carrying their empty glasses in his big hands. "You know, count the stalks of broccoli as the kid puts them in her mouth—"

"And wait for her to throw them up when she can't chew all seven at once?"

"Okay, that might work better on peas. But there's always the reward system."

Paige rinsed the plates, holding in the urge to shake her head or dissolve into another laughing fit. Alex didn't deserve that. He was trying. And parenting books weren't bad, per se, it was more that living with a toddler in the real world meant being a little more creative. "So you'd have me bribe my daughter with M&M's or a video game each time she eats her vegetables?"

"Reward, there's a difference."

"Tomato, to-mah-to." She finished rinsing the dishes and stacked them in Alison's dishwasher. "So, Kaylie eats her vegetables because she gets chocolate or something as a reward. To get her to finish her homework—"

"She has homework in preschool?" Alex asked incredulously.

"In theory." Paige scrunched her brows together. What was her point again? Right, the reward system. "To get her to put her dirty clothes in the hamper—better reference?"

He nodded and motioned for her to continue.

"—the reward is an extra fifteen minutes of television, and then she expects that same return with everything. But life isn't like that. We don't all get the fluffy unicorn at the checkout counter just because we put strawberries and apples in our shopping cart rather than chocolate-chip cookies and potato chips."

"She's only four, and it's only a way to get her to try something new."

"And then she's fourteen and then twenty-four, and then she's still living at home when she's thirty-four because she's never learned that there are things you do—like hold down a job and pay rent and buy groceries—even though you don't like those things." Paige huffed out a breath. "I'm not saying I have meaningful conversations about the benefits of vegetable consumption every night after dinner, and I have wavered when we're in the grocery store and she won't be quiet about a new package of cookies. But you're the new person. You have to be careful or she'll figure out the reward system starts and stops with you."

Alex scowled and then his expression softened.

"I didn't think of it like that. I just read the book and it made sense."

"The books always make sense until you're in the middle of a meltdown because your child was good walking through the aisles and wants one of those little plastic dolls at the checkout. And you say no." Paige shrugged. "Sometimes 'eat your vegetables' or 'no' or 'don't pick your nose' just have to be enough."

"And she'll eat her vegetables when she's ready?"

Paige nodded. "Or I'll make her a smoothie later with all her least favorite veggies juiced into it."

"Sneaky."

She pointed her thumb at her chest. "Mom. There's a difference."

"So about dinner—"

"I don't think it's a good idea."

Alex cocked an eyebrow and that smooth smile spread across his face, pulling the scar at his mouth until it disappeared. "If you have dinner with me I'll wash your car."

Paige laughed. "I already told you the reward method doesn't work." But she was tempted. Oh so tempted, and that was definitely a bad thing. Temptation had a way of wrecking her life.

"You said it doesn't work on four-year-olds. You're not four."

This time Paige blushed. The intimate tone of Alex's voice and the dark look that came into his eyes when he said the words were too much. Too interested.

Too daring.

He reached his hand toward her face and Paige backed up, her hip hitting the corner of the counter.

"No, I'm not four and—"

A crash from the pantry interrupted Paige's train of thought. She hurried across the kitchen, pulled open the door and gasped.

Alison and Tuck were wrapped around each other, kissing. Her hands were under his shirt, her ball cap on the floor and his hands forked through her thick, auburn hair. A couple of soup cans fell from the shelf when Tuck backed Alison up another step, joining the collection of canned green beans and packages of dried pasta already on the floor.

Alison opened her eyes and pushed against Tuck's broad shoulders.

"Um, hi," she said, putting an inch of space between them. "We were, uh…"

"Checking the expiration dates?" Alex's voice was filled with laughter at the twin expressions of embarrassment on Alison's and Tuck's faces. "Having a little dessert?"

Tuck took Alison's hand and led her into the kitchen. "Getting to know one another better," he said. "Not that it's any of your business."

Paige had seen plenty of kisses and she had talked about the dirty details of even more, most of the time with Alison. Something about this kiss was different. Maybe because Alex seemed to want to test the boundaries they'd agreed on just a couple of days before. Seeing Alison wrapped around the handsome ranger tied Paige's stomach into a knot. Made her clench her hands and take another step away from Alex.

Not that she was angry with Alison for kissing Tuck. She was single and unattached. He was most definitely kissable, from his full lower lip to the teasing light that never quite left his blue eyes. Paige wasn't a prude, for Pete's sake. Seeing Alison and Tuck wrapped around one another in the pantry made her wonder what it would be like to kiss Alex. To tease her tongue against that scar at the corner of his mouth. To feel his hands buried in her hair. On her body.

To trace her fingers against the thick muscles of his shoulders. To feel the strength of muscles not hidden by his tees and shorts at all.

"We just…" Alison trailed off.

Paige waved her hands in the air and pasted a smile on her face. She knew when Tuck said they were in the nonexistent basement that something was going on between the two. They were entitled to a little fun; both were consenting adults. "No need to explain." None at all. And she needed to get out of here because all she could think about was that game Spin the Bottle, and joining Alex in the pantry after her spin landed on him.

That was so not helping.

"Like Tuck said, it's not our business. I was just coming in to tell you thanks and I'll see you Tuesday, for girls' night." No need to go into Alex asking her out or why she couldn't want to go. Paige had to get out of the kitchen. Away from Alex. She waved and backed out onto the deck, calling to Kaylie that it was time to leave.

Neither Tuck nor Alison had a kid who could be caught in the cross fire should things go wrong. They could afford to flirt and be reckless.

She wanted to be reckless. That's what had her upset. Not that Alison was kissing a hot guy, not the reminder of what she might do if the situation were reversed.

She wanted their situations to reverse. She loved Kaylie, but there were times she did wish she didn't have to worry about babysitters or being quite so careful about people she allowed into her life.

Until three days ago, when Alex had shown up on her curb, she hadn't missed being single once since making her decision to create the family she wanted rather than wait to see if it happened on its own. Now it seemed she couldn't stop thinking about being impulsive.

"Paige," Alison called from the deck.

Paige grabbed Kaylie's light jacket from one of the lawn chairs and motioned her daughter to hurry. Then she plastered a smile on her face and turned back to her friend. "I expect details later," she said, waggling her eyebrows. "Full-on details," she lied through her teeth.

"I'll call you later," her friend said, concern etched in the thin line of her mouth, her eyes worried.

Alex stood in the shadows, watching Paige intently. She dared not look at him. Finally Kaylie wandered across the lawn and Paige directed her to the car. The little girl didn't fuss about leaving—score one for the non-reward-giving Mom. Kaylie accepted that when it was time to go it was time to go—the little girl waved to the adults still on the deck and picked a petunia from Alison's flower bed.

She buckled Kaylie into her seat and then offered a jaunty wave to the three watching her from Alison's front porch. *See? Nothing to worry about here. Nothing's wrong. I'm— Crap!*

The manual transmission stalled as she pulled away from the curb. So much for the jaunty wave.

All the way across town Kaylie chattered about the trapeze and seeing her grandparents and meeting her new friends, Alex and Tuck. Paige added a few "uh-huhs" and "reallys" to the conversation but didn't truly join in.

She was too focused on ignoring the pang in her belly.

The one that told her she'd gotten what she wanted—she had avoided a date with Alex Ryan.

Why, then, did she feel like she'd lost something?

ALEX PUSHED HIS shopping cart past a row of too-ripe bananas, choosing a bunch that was still mostly green and putting it under a loaf of French bread. He needed to hit the meat counter and then the dairy section and this day would finally be over.

Not that it had been a bad day. Three days after the barbecue, one week since he'd met her and Alex decided it was a Paige Day.

He paused at the end of the aisle, looking left and then right to decide which way to go. He usually shopped at the grocery store in Farmington, but the past three days he'd been assigned to St. Francois Park rather than St. Joe, and the market in Bonne Terre was closer. He saw the sign for the meat counter and headed that direction, plucking a box of snack cakes off another shelf as he passed.

Added benefit of shopping in Bonne Terre: he might run into Paige. If that happened it would really be a Paige Day, not just a Memory of Paige Day. She'd turned down his dinner invitation, but he chalked that up to the situation. First meeting with Kaylie. Tuck's attraction to Alison. Paige's parents. He had a feeling her parents had a lot to do with her insistence that they not go on a single date.

What they needed was a little unexpected contact. Something that wasn't set up around their daughter. The attraction he felt for Paige was... unexpected. Maybe slightly unwanted. But it wasn't wrong. He'd convinced himself of that during a hike on Monday when he couldn't get her out of his head.

He kept hearing her laugh through the wind in the trees. Felt the brush of her fingers against his arm. Saw the sad smile she'd offered him after her parents left the barbecue.

Even after the worst argument he'd had with Deanna, the one about going to the fertility clinic because she thought something was wrong, he'd been able to concentrate on the trails, his work. To get lost in nature and decompress for a few hours. He'd gone home that night and agreed to go with her to the clinic because whatever his misgivings, it was important to her.

Monday, he hadn't gotten lost in anything except his memories of having coffee with Paige, of the painting he'd seen in her home and holding her hand when Kaylie jumped off the swing set. Of his mouth going dry when Paige's gaze locked with his after they found Tuck and Alison in the pantry together.

That was the biggest distraction.

He'd wanted to kiss her then. Wanted to follow her home after she left.

Alex placed his order at the counter and then stepped back while the butcher wrapped everything up.

He hadn't followed her home because he knew what would happen. He would kiss her, probably

scare her off. She wouldn't go back on her promise to let him get to know Kaylie, but after only
knowing her a few days, Alex's priority was to get
to know the mother as well as the daughter.

To build a relationship with them both.

And wasn't that crazy?

After Dee died, he'd thought that part of his life
was over and that he was fine with it. How could
a strange woman and a little girl bring back all of
those emotions when he barely knew them?

Alex added the paper-wrapped pieces of meat to
his cart and continued down the aisle to the dairy
section, picking up a package of lunch meat and
a jar of pickles on the way. He spotted a sale on
macaroni and cheese in another aisle and stepped
away from his cart to grab a couple of boxes, but
his cart kept moving.

Alex raced after it but he was too slow and the
cart rear-ended a shapely body bent over the egg
case.

Paige dropped the carton of eggs and whirled
around as Alex squeezed his eyes closed and gri-
maced. So not the impression he wanted to make.

"Hey," he said, grabbing the cart and pulling it
away from Paige. "I must have nudged it when I
saw the mac and cheese sale."

Paige's expression morphed from annoyance to
mirth. She smiled at him. "You're not who I expected." She wore a pretty skirt with blue flowers
on it, a plain blue tee and a jean jacket. It was still

warm enough to wear sandals and he saw she'd repainted her toes a deep purple. He was staring, he realized, and focused his attention on her face.

He got a little lost in her green eyes and the soft tendrils of hair that had escaped her ponytail during the day. What had she said again? Right, not expecting him.

"Someone else likes to run you down with their shopping carts?"

She shook her head, checked the carton of eggs and placed it into her basket. "Not really. I just…" She shook her head. "What are you doing here, anyway?"

Alex picked up a gallon of milk and joined her as they walked toward the checkout stands. "Stalking you," he deadpanned.

Her eyes rounded and then she elbowed him. "You're terrible."

"I've been working at St. Francois Park this week instead of St. Joe. Couldn't face the drive to Farmington so I stopped here on my way home."

"No fast food? Pizza delivery?"

"You wound me." Alex put his hand over his heart, glad for the comfortable repartee they were sharing. Paige grabbed a couple of boxes of the discounted macaroni as they passed. "I do cook. I don't always rely on the kindness of near-strangers or fast-food restaurants for my meals, you know. You?"

Paige motioned him ahead of her in the checkout lane. "One of those parenting things. I didn't want to have debates over fresh grapes versus snack cakes or whole-wheat bread versus white. So I'm shopping solo." She placed a whole rotisserie chicken on the belt as Alex paid for his things.

"Nice. Sneaky, but nice."

"Mom, remember? There's a difference." She put a bunch of kale on the belt followed by plain yogurt and fresh berries. "I'm also meeting Alison later for a girls' night—manis, pedis and wine—to thank her for watching Kaylie last week."

"Busy night."

"When you find a babysitter, you take advantage of the time. You can't want to talk about mani-pedis or feeding my kid."

Alex paid for his things and then waited at the end of the line until Paige's were bagged and she had paid. "I like talking to you."

She shot him a sideways glance. "Because…?" She drew out the word.

"Like I said the other day, you interest me. What project did you start at school today?"

Paige blinked at the abrupt change of subject, and then seemed to relax. "My fifth graders are learning about Pop Art, which they assume means positioning ketchup bottles on a windowsill or decoupaging labels on a canvas."

They chatted about school all the way to her

car and while he helped her load her groceries, and then stood beside her hatchback as the conversation switched to talk about the parks. All very casual, just a conversation between friends, but Alex couldn't help noticing how the parking lot lights shimmered against Paige's hair or how the way she leaned one hip against the car outlined her long, long legs. She paused before getting into her car.

"You don't have to do this."

"Do what?"

"Make nice with me. Pretend you're interested in my class. Just because we aren't dating, it doesn't mean I would keep Kaylie from you."

Alex tilted his head. "That thought never entered my mind. As I said, I like talking to you."

Paige bit her lower lip. "But, why? I'm not… You don't…"

"You're not my type? I don't know you? True enough on the second. As for the first, I've never really had a type," he lied. He had had a type and it was all Deanna from the first moment they met—freckles and short legs and blond hair. Now it was all Paige, and that was unsettling. But the more he tried to push her from his mind the more firmly she seemed entrenched there.

"I was going to say it's too soon. But I kind of feel like I've been saying that for a week." The words were harsh but her voice wasn't. There was a question there, one he couldn't define. A curiosity.

He stepped closer and couldn't resist touching his finger to the soft skin under her chin. He felt the touch like a lightning bolt burning along his nerve endings and when he spoke his voice was deeper than normal. "I like you, Paige Kenner, and if all I get are these chance meetings at the grocery store, that is okay with me."

She wavered. Just for a second, but Alex was so focused on her he couldn't miss it. For one second, she leaned slightly toward him and her mouth opened just a hair. He could feel her breath on his skin, could smell her fruity shampoo and something richer, darker beneath that. Perfume, maybe.

He leaned in, pressing his lips to hers. Just the slightest touch, and then she straightened and opened her car door.

"B-broken record or not, it is too soon." She straightened her perfectly straight jacket and sat behind the wheel. "I won't change my mind, you know. Not because you just kissed me under the parking lot light or because we buy the same brand of mac and cheese or because you asked about my work."

Alex stepped back and flexed his hands against the cart handle as if that might ground him from the chemistry he was feeling. "I know."

"Us going on a date is too much pressure. It's too soon."

"Okay." He agreed because "too soon" was so much better than the never he got on Sunday.

CHAPTER SEVEN

"I DON'T GET HIM." Paige lifted her foot from the water tub at the base of the spa pedicure chair when the technician indicated. Alison, sitting in the chair next to her with a blissful expression on her face as the massaging backrest moved up her spine, didn't reply. "What does he want?"

Finally Alison opened one eye. "Sounds to me like he wants to go out with you. Would that be so terrible?"

Paige glared at her friend. Of all the times for Alison to stop playing devil's advocate in Paige's choice of men… "You're the one who reminded me a few days ago about my not-so-stellar past in the man department."

The technicians began painting their toes. Deep green for Alison and hot pink with a glitter top coat for Paige.

"Because I didn't want you to leap before you looked." Alison groaned as the apparatus hit her shoulders. "We have *got* to do this more often." She clasped her hands over her tummy and tilted her head to look at Paige. "Would it really be so terrible to have dinner with the man? He's Kaylie's father after all. It could be like a romance novel, two strangers with only a little girl in common."

Paige rolled her eyes. "I 'just had dinner' with the law student and two years later I was still using him. That is not romance-novel-heroine material."

"That was the old Paige. You're not that girl anymore. You're a woman, a great mom, but a woman, and I'm pretty sure having Kaylie didn't erase all the womanly needs we all have."

"That's part of the problem," Paige mumbled. The technicians led them to the dryer area and Paige busied herself with her bag.

"What?"

"Nothing." She pulled her credit card from her wallet and handed it over to the nail tech. "I know this is a complete overreaction." His kiss still burned against her lips. It was light and fresh. The whole situation was too pretty. *Daughter Helps Mom and Dad Fall In Love*. Definitely something that only happened in fiction. Reality was arguing over dance versus soccer practice, mortgage payments and who would clean up after dinner.

Or, worse, not arguing about anything. Not talking about anything. Putting a happy smile on your face in public and once the front door closed, going to separate rooms to live separate lives.

They had nothing in common, other than Kaylie. How could a relationship start with zero common interests? What happened when the chemical flame burned out and all that was left was a silent dinner table, separate bedrooms and separate lives?

She spent the first half of her life waiting for her parents to announce their divorce. Waiting for them to have a meaningful conversation about something. Wondering if it was her fault that her father spent more time with his students than with his family. She wouldn't put Kaylie through it, too. Sooner or later Alex would realize she wasn't the woman he wanted. It was better all the way around if they skipped over the part where he pretended she was anything more than the mother of his child.

"Paige. What?" Alison wouldn't give up, Paige knew. Her best friend was like a dog with a bone when something sparked her attention. And Alex's interest in Paige had sparked her attention.

Just like that barely there caress and kiss in the parking lot had sparked a fire she was still trying to put out.

"He kissed me."

Alison's eyes widened. "And?"

"And, I stopped it. It was just a moment, a bad-decision moment." *A moment I can't stop reliving.* She sighed. Now was not the time to spill that little secret to Alison. "So you had dinner with Tuck last night?" Talking about Alex's friend would distract Alison; talking about her love interests was usually a guaranteed distraction.

Not tonight.

"He's fun. And we're not talking about me, we're talking about why you won't go on a date with Alex—who is your type in every way, and who kissed you last night at the grocery store."

"It was more a peck than a kiss. And he's not my type." He was the opposite of her type: accomplished, employed. Nice.

"He is, and not just because he's handsome and has a good job."

The dryers switched off and the nail tech brought back her credit card. Paige signed the slip. "How about that glass of wine before I hijack our entire night with my obsessing?"

Alison stopped her as they exited the salon. "How about we keep talking it through until you know what you want to do?"

"This night is about thanking you for helping out with Kaylie, not getting all crazy about Alex Ryan." Paige started her car and pulled out onto the street. "Tell me more about that project at the winery with the students from Washington U."

"The project is on hold. Tuck is looking good. Why can't you date Alex?"

Paige sighed. "He's dangerous."

They arrived at the wine bar in a few minutes and were shown to a table in the corner. Paige ordered her favorite white but Alison chose a new local red.

"Keeping my eye on the competition," she said. "Here are my reasons to be on Team Alex on this one—you've been looking for a solid, dependable man your entire life. He stepped into the argument with your mom on Sunday, he still hasn't stopped ribbing Tuck about catching us in the pantry and he didn't stop Kaylie from being a kid. None of those are dangerous things."

"Having a decent job isn't the same as not being dangerous."

"It's the first step. You know he stood by his wife through cancer, and before that he was willing to visit a fertility clinic. Those are solid, stand-up things."

So he was solid. A stand-up guy. Committed. The kind of commitment it took to stand by when the one you loved suffered through radiation and chemotherapy. That kind of love didn't just go away, did it? Add one more reason to the Don't Date Alex List: How could he have gotten over that kind of love? And where did that leave her and Kaylie?

Paige shook her head. "No, it's better if I stick with friends, no benefits, not even a dinner now and then. That way he can concentrate on Kaylie and nobody will get hurt."

"Paige—"

"No, Al, it really is better this way. You know me. Before Kaylie I always took the leap at love before I looked to see if there was a net to catch me. Well, I'm looking now. I'm inspecting the net for frayed edges. I've messed up every relationship I've ever had, except for my friendship with you and my love for my daughter. Alex apparently had a marriage strong enough to withstand cancer. Those are two very big snags waiting to become a big, fat hole in the middle of the net."

Alison finished her drink. "Don't put all that on you. Yes, you made mistakes. But we've all been young and stupid. You never had anyone to help you pick up the pieces, not really. Dot would pile on the guilt and Hank would ignore you. You reacted to them and because of them, not because of something broken inside you."

"And what about Alex? We've both said it—he was committed to his wife. He sees Kaylie as a commitment, and that's great. But, Al, I don't want us to be the people he settles for because he can't have what he really wanted."

Paige pushed her glass away. She knew what she had to do to protect Kaylie and that was keep Alex strictly in the friend category. Look at how she'd reacted on the way home from the grocery store—smiling, singing along with the radio and imagining herself and Alex in the lead roles of a falling-in-love song. She was already so close to the edge with him.

In her heart, she'd always wanted Kaylie to have a father. Someone involved and interested in her life.

"It's better this way, better just being friends

and focusing our attentions on Kaylie for the next few months."

"And after that?" Alison crossed her arms over her chest and tapped her foot against the hardwood floor. "What happens when she's settled and Alex is a regular part of life?"

"Then this minor attraction will be old news. No big deal."

"Mmm-hmm."

The initial attraction would fade, Paige told herself. It always did. She just had to hold out until then.

THE ATTRACTION WAS still there. Alex shouldn't be surprised by it, but there it was. Again. He also shouldn't like it, especially when Paige was clear there would be no dating and definitely no kissing, but he did.

Alex watched through the floor-to-ceiling windows separating the entrance of the rec center from the pool area where Kaylie would have her swim lesson in just a few minutes. Paige had called earlier in the day to invite him along. He'd jumped at the chance and didn't examine too closely what he wanted—the invitation to watch Kaylie swim or to be closer to Paige.

Kaylie waved from the top step when she saw him and Alex couldn't stop the smile spreading over his face. God, how had he gone all this time without knowing about this kid who was part of him?

"Hi, Alex," she said in her little-girl voice. "Are you watching me swim?"

"Wouldn't miss it," he said and wasn't surprised to realize he meant it. "I was a swimmer, you know. But I bet you could teach me a few things." Somehow, after only one official meeting, the little girl had wound her way into his heart, leaving it less cold than before. Her mom, too, he admitted, as he watched Paige take Kaylie into the changing room. There was something about Paige that wouldn't let him go. Part of it was physical. There had been one woman since Dee. Two years before, after a night out with Tuck and the rest of his rec-league team. Two years was a long time. That had to be why he couldn't stop thinking about her. Why she was as high in his mind as the little girl he was supposed to be getting to know, but the physical was only part of it. The other part wanted to know about her. Her art, her favorite foods, favorite pastimes.

They were back in a few moments and Paige sat next to him on the bench. Kaylie joined the other kids at the side of the pool, laughing and giggling with her friends.

"Thanks for letting me know about this."

Paige shrugged. "No problem. I'm glad you made the time."

Alex mimicked her shrug. "No problem. I'll always make time for her."

Something flickered in Paige's eyes but was

gone before he could decipher it. He watched the kids at the side of the pool for a few minutes, uncomfortable in the silence. Which was weird. He'd never felt uncomfortable around Paige before.

He caught a couple of looks from the other parents around the pool. Wondering who he was, what he meant to Paige most likely, and then he understood the discomfort. She was the single mom. In a small, close-knit community like this, inviting him to a swim lesson was a big deal.

"I thought you might enjoy it. She loves to swim." Her tone was tense, and Alex felt responsible. Because what was tense about a mom taking her kid to swim lessons? Nothing, until you added a sperm donor to the mix.

"I used to swim." Maybe talking about something innocuous would dispel the tension. "Just summer leagues when I was in school, but it was fun."

The coach blew her whistle and one by one the kids jumped into the pool, sputtering as they came back to the surface to hold on to the side. Another instructor joined the coach and they started at opposite ends of the pool, helping the kids rocket away from the wall on their tummies. Reminding them to blow into the water like elephants, and reach their arms to the ceiling. When Kaylie's turn came she hesitated and Alex felt his hands clench. The instructor, a young girl with a long brown ponytail, encouraged Kaylie to kick away from the wall. Finally she pushed off, but instead of reaching her hands above the water, Kaylie pushed around in a doggie paddle.

"Big arms, Kaylie," Alex couldn't help shouting out, echoing the phrase the instructor used. Paige shot him a side-eye look but didn't say anything. Kaylie didn't change her stroke, just kept pushing around from beneath the surface. He called to her again. "Come on, Kaylie, you can do it."

The little girl looked over at him, forgot to paddle altogether and slipped beneath the water. She came up sputtering and shaking her head as the instructor caught her and held her up. Her tiny hands came up to her eyes and rubbed, then she shook her head and blinked her eyes open. The instructor said something he couldn't hear and Kaylie shook her head as they started back to the side, Kaylie on the instructor's hip as she walked.

"She can do it—" he began and stood up, but Paige reached out, putting her hand on his forearm and urging him back to the bench seat.

"Don't embarrass her."

He turned, dumbfounded. "I'm encouraging her."

"You just screamed at her from across the pool, distracted her and she inhaled a mouthful of pool water. What would you call that?" Her voice was quiet in the loud room, but he could hear the anger beneath the calm words. Alex sat, watching the little girl at the side of the pool, who was studiously not looking his direction.

When she probably needed to be since he was sitting beside her mother and she'd just inhaled pool water. But he wasn't wrong, darn it. It wasn't wrong to encourage her to swim correctly. Every other parent in the place seemed content to see their kids dog-paddling when they could be freestyling with just a little more effort.

"She wasn't reaching out of the water, that's important when you're learning to swim, isn't it?" Somehow it was important that Paige agree with him, which only made him more annoyed. Because her opinion shouldn't matter.

He was a swimmer, she was not an athlete. He might be new to the parenting game, but he wasn't new to the dangers of the water.

Paige focused on Kaylie, who rocketed off the wall again, this time on her back. And once more her arms stayed below the water instead of reaching above it. Alex clenched his hands, but didn't call out to her this time.

"You're doing great, Kay," Paige called when she reached the rope dividing the shallow from the deep water.

He saw the little smile on Kaylie's face when she heard her mother's voice. She didn't turn her head, didn't drop below the water. She did a semismooth turn and kept back-floating toward the starting wall. He couldn't not say anything, could he? All she had to do was push her arms above the surface.

"Reach, Kaylie, just a little higher. You're doing great," he added, not wanting to be accused of embarrassing her again.

Paige didn't look at him, but her next words were definitely meant for him. "Proper strokes are important, but this is a beginning class. The focus is on getting comfortable in the water, learning to stay above the surface, not racing a fifty-meter freestyle in under thirty seconds."

"It's hard to break the bad habits." He wasn't budging on this. Sure, he'd been wrong about the reward method for vegetables, but he was right about this. He knew it. It took the better part of his thirteenth summer to relearn how to breaststroke because of a bad instructor when he was little.

"She's four. She's not training for the Olympics in Rio." This time there was steel at the bottom of her voice. "And whether she was in training for the Olympics or not, you're here as a *guest*."

Alex took a deep breath. Two. Counted to five. What was going on here? He'd merely wanted to encourage his daughter to take swimming seriously, and Paige was acting as if he'd completely betrayed them both. "I'm trying to help," he said, but the words sounded angrier than he intended.

"No, you're trying to instill more by-the-book parenting on her. You can't reward kids into acting the way you want and you can't expect them to be perfect imitations, either. You were a swimmer. I get it. But you were a swimmer as a teen, not a toddler. There's a difference." She looked around, her face pale and her hands clenching the bench seat, white at the knuckles. "And we aren't doing this here. Not in the middle of her lesson. If you want to continue this discussion, we'll go outside. She's had enough embarrassment."

Alex looked around. Every parent in the pool area had their gazes trained on him and Paige, not the water. Not the kids. He swallowed this time, feeling like he imagined Kaylie had when she went under so quickly after he called out to her.

"I didn't mean to embarrass her. Or you," he said stiffly. He folded his arms over his chest and scooted back on the bench, determined to watch the rest of the lesson without saying a word.

How did it come to this uncomfortable point? He'd only been trying to help. Was it too soon to act like a parent? When could it be okay? And how the heck was he supposed to know what to say to the kid when everything he'd read was apparently wrong?

Once all the children finished their strokes, the instructors pulled out Hula-Hoops, submerging them partially below the water. He watched as Kaylie kicked away from the wall, buried her head in the water and stroked forward through the hoop.

Felt a glow of excitement when he saw the joy on the little girl's face as she realized she'd swum half the length of the shallow end. Paige called out to her, praising the effort, and Alex joined in. So what if her arms weren't straight and if she only reached above the surface a couple of times? His kid just swam, face in the water, for nearly ten meters.

Alex held out his hand to high-five Paige, but she kept her focus on the girl in the water.

It wasn't like this pre-Paige. He and Dee had agreed on parenting styles, had found the same benefit from the book she picked out when they first began talking about having kids. They agreed on parenting styles—stern, focused, but giving the child room to breathe and have their own opinions. That was what calling to Kaylie was about. Wasn't it? Trying to help her be the best she could be— that was how a parent acted.

Alex blew out a breath. If they were going to do this, really be coparents, they had to figure out a way to agree. Starting with an apology couldn't hurt.

"I didn't mean to embarrass her or step all over your toes."

"Is that an apology? Because she's the one who needs it, not me." Shoulders stiff, Paige kept her attention on the pool.

Alex wasn't so sure about only Kaylie need-ing the apology. "I'll talk to her after the lesson. I hope you can understand I'm new at this. Everything I know about kids I read in a parenting book over four years ago and then skimmed over again a couple of weeks ago."

She was quiet for a long time, watching the water as Kaylie submerged to pick up a rubber ring and then again when she held her breath for fifteen seconds. "You weren't wrong, technically," she said grudgingly. "Kaylie wasn't reaching up and over like she should have been."

Alex felt victory at the admission but it was hollow. Somewhere in the past few minutes having Kaylie do the stroke exactly right became overshadowed with her joy in being in the water. Joy he could see as clearly when she was underwater as when she was above it.

Paige shook herself and, when Kaylie left the water a moment later, held a dry towel to her. The little girl trotted off to the changing room and Paige turned back to him. "She'll have forgotten about this by the time we get to the pizza place. The coaches are taking the kids out because this is the last lesson of this session. I didn't mention it earlier because…" Paige sighed, shot a flustered look in his direction. "You could come. If you want." Her words were as stiff as his back against the cement-block wall.

"I'd like that."

Because damned if he didn't want to smooth over the rough edge he'd just created.

PAIGE WATCHED ALEX from across the crowded pizza parlor. He was talking with one of the other dads, as if they'd known one another for years. Like that same parent hadn't been giving them the side-eye from the second Alex ordered Kaylie to swim like an adult and promptly sent her daughter underwater. She'd wanted to dive into the shallow depths to save her but that would only have embarrassed Kaylie more. Until tonight, she'd been one of the standouts in the class.

How had she missed that Kaylie did more dog-paddling than swimming? And why did it suddenly matter? A small part of her wanted Alex to be so impressed by Kaylie's swimming that he would have to… What? Applaud Paige's skills not only at single-mothering but at swim coaching? She wasn't the coach. When she and Kaylie swam it was more about fun than perfect strokes. And Kaylie wasn't so much embarrassed by him calling out to her as shocked when the water went up her nose.

It was Paige who was embarrassed because suddenly every eye in the place was on her. On Alex. And she could see them putting two and two together and getting four. Sperm donor four.

The intensity he showed over Kaylie's swimming was one more reason to keep him on Friend

Beach, no matter how his faded Levi's outlined his long legs or how yet another black tee stretched tight across his shoulders. Tonight was only the first in what was sure to be a long line of differences between them. Paige believed in discipline but she also believed children had to be free to make choices, to voice opinions. To be heard. After Alex's outburst she was sure he believed in discipline but was not as sure about the choice-making, opinion-voicing part.

How had she missed the intensity? It was there in the watchful stance, his gaze that was never still. Even talking to the other father, his attention swiveled between the man, Kaylie in the ball pit, the waiter delivering drinks.

Her knees went a little weak at the picture he presented—strong, tanned body and wicked smile. Focused and attentive. She tried to swallow but her mouth was dry.

The other parents mingled, chatted up the coach and other instructors the way Paige should be doing. Instead she was wedged behind the "Dance Dance Revolution" machine. She knew everyone inside the building, had attended preschool programs with some, had worked on a fund-raiser for the local hospital with others. She'd invited Alex because she didn't really have a choice, not after mentioning the party to him at the pool, but that didn't mean their differences had to ruin her night.

Kaylie called Alex over to the ball pit, laughing as she showed him how she swam under the balls. He smiled and said something to her. Paige's belly clenched for an entirely different reason this time. Because already her daughter was becoming attached to her father. Another reason to keep things friendly between them, Paige told herself. Because Kaylie deserved to have a dad.

What if someone noticed the resemblance between the two?

No, she would not obsess about what anyone thought about her inviting Alex to this event or to the lesson before; he had every right to be there and the reason why was nobody's business. Tonight was about celebrating Kaylie's accomplishment. Paige was proud of her daughter.

And incredibly annoyed at herself because she should be casually chatting with Alex—with anyone, really—instead of hiding in the corner behind the dancing game.

Her phone bleeped in her hand, making her jump in the shadows.

Do you have the party under surveillance?

Alex. She couldn't stop her lips from smiling. When they'd arrived she'd mentioned making a quick call once she had Kaylie settled in the ball pit. Just her luck, he noticed her in the corner, not using her phone. He sat with his back to the table, elbows perched on the edge, not looking in her direction, but she couldn't help the feeling that all of his attention was on her.

The thought made her toes curl inside her zebra-striped flats.

I'm an art teacher, not a cop. I was just looking for Alison, she said she might stop by.

She saw that wicked smile flicker over his face and wondered if he saw through her lie. Alison had better things to do than chaperone a nondate between Paige and Alex. He texted back.

Not avoiding me?

No.

Her hands shook as she typed out another lie. She hadn't technically been avoiding him; she was avoiding the distraction of him. There was a difference. Right?

I figured you could find me.

Too late, she realized how that sounded. Like she was playing hard to get.

She wasn't playing, not hard to get, anyway. The game she was playing was much more dangerous because a week after meeting Alex her hard-and-fast rules about dating were beginning to wither away. She had to get used to being around him without feeling her stomach going all floopy or reaching her hands out to touch him. Paige looked at it as an inoculation—seeing Alex in crowded places and with a built-in time limit would lessen his magnetism.

That was her plan.

Not that it seemed to be working because, crowded room or not, her attention was on him.

I was blinded by your light when you opened the door five minutes ago.

God, so he knew just how long she'd been wavering behind the dance game.

That was just the sunset.

And then, for good measure,

Where are you and I'll get Kaylie from the ball pit so we can eat.

He looked in her direction, caught her staring at him. Cocked his head to the side to let her know he'd caught her.

Third table on the left. I ordered half-cheese, half-supreme deep-dish.

Paige's mouth went dry. Alex never looked away, not while he sent the last text, and not when she stepped out of the shadows. He only watched her, eyes dark, lazy smile on his full lips.

His presence pulled her forward, which was probably a blessing because staying hidden in the corner would convince him that she wanted him. That she was weakening in her resolve.

She wouldn't weaken, not after his actions at the pool and not because she was attracted to him.

"Mama," Kaylie called from the ball pit. Her wavy hair was still damp from the pool. She wore jeans and a bright yellow T-shirt with a cat printed on the front. "Did you see me count to fifteen in the pool?"

"I already told you I saw it all." She veered off her path toward Alex to focus on her daughter.

Kaylie blushed. "Just making sure."

Paige wove her finger through the mesh to massage the little girl's wet hair. "Great job, Kay. I'm proud of you."

"Watch!" Kaylie held her nose and disappeared under the balls. She started counting, her voice muffled by the pit, and popped back up when she hit fifteen, spraying balls in every direction. "It's harder with water but I can even do it without holding my nose."

"Great, kiddo." Paige squatted down to be on eye level with her baby.

"Watch again!" Kaylie took a deep breath and pushed out her cheeks until it looked like she had two of the balls in her mouth. Paige cringed at the thought. Kaylie disappeared into the pit again and when she popped up said, "I'll show you in the water when we go swimming this weekend, 'kay?"

Paige gave her a five-minute warning before turning to Alex. She set her bag on the table. He held a chair out for her and the butterflies beat against her stomach walls once more.

"I appreciate your asking me to come here tonight, especially after I messed up Kaylie's freestyle."

Paige waved a hand. "She leveled up, and she's already forgotten it. Why don't we?"

When the waitress came by, Paige ordered a soda. Then, because she was desperate to keep the conversational ball rolling, she asked him about the park assignments.

"Back to St. Joe for the rest of the week and then, once we hit November, it will be one park each week on a rotating basis. Winter is our slow time of year."

"Not many people want to camp in the cold and snow, I imagine."

"Not a lot. Maybe I'll take you camping in the spring. You could bring your art supplies." He waited a beat. "I wouldn't mind having a Paige Kenner, the original, in my house."

She eyed him for a second. "Are you flirting

with me? Or just trying to make me forget about our little disagreement at the pool?"

He widened his eyes in mock surprise. "Me? Neither. You were clear in the grocery store. Friends, no benefits. Plus, you already said the pool thing was forgotten."

Paige didn't believe him for a second, but she also didn't want to turn into the shrew who always found fault. "In that case you should know my camping skills are nonexistent. Kaylie would love it. Any chance she might see Big Foot?"

Alex laughed. "Not in our parks. From what I understand he likes to stay in the Pacific Northwest."

Paige relaxed against her chair. This could be okay. Talking to Alex, making plans. Like they'd known each other longer than a week. Like they might be actual friends one day. Friends without attraction buzzing between them. He finished his drink and she found herself mesmerized by the up-and-down motion of his Adam's apple as he swallowed.

Okay, maybe not exactly friends, but that was what the flu-shot theory was about. A few more meetings like this and this weird attraction would be gone.

Or at least under control.

They were quiet for a few minutes. Kaylie squealed in the ball pit, laughing and playing with several other kids. The waitress delivered the pizza and refilled their glasses. Kaylie meandered over to the table. "Just cheese, please, Alex," she said, holding the plate in her little hands. He put a slice on her plate and she looked at him expectantly.

"More?"

"Cut it up," she said and plopped the plate on the table before him. He raised an eyebrow at her. "Please," she added and then grinned. "I forgot."

"I've got it." Paige cut the slice into bite-size pieces and pushed the plate to Kaylie's seat across the table. The little girl picked it up and then started for another table, filled with her friends.

"Hey, where are you going?" Paige asked.

Kaylie stuffed a bite of pizza in her mouth. "Kids eat with kids here, Mom," she said and continued to the smaller table with her friends.

Paige's tummy clenched and she turned her attention to Alex.

"Pizza's great," he said around a bite of food. "Are we supposed to be insulted that she would rather eat with her friends than us?"

"I think we are. She's never done that before. Tonight is for you two. I'll call her back."

Alex shook his head. "Don't. Let her play. We talked earlier, at the ball pit."

"Are you sure? I can—"

"Paige, it's okay." He reached across the table and stilled her hands with his, and a zing of attraction buzzed along her nerve endings. "We talked about going slow. If you force her to eat at the table because I'm here, it will bring up more questions. So let the kids eat with the kids and we'll make this table adults only."

The bite of pizza stuck in her throat at the vision that brought on and she coughed. Took a quick sip of soda and then took another bite. It tasted like rubber in her mouth. The more she chewed, the bigger the piece seemed to grow. Finally, she forced it down with another drink and pushed her plate away. She would eat when she got home.

Or maybe never.

Alex watched her while he finished his first slice and then reached for another. Just like a man not to notice tension thicker than Chicago-style deep-dish pizza, she thought.

"You look nice," he said.

"This is not a date."

"I'm not allowed to notice a beautiful woman sharing a table and a pizza with me?"

"You're supposed to notice the mom with the four-year-old attached to her hip."

"You've raised quite the independent four-year-old. I've been around you two twice now, and she's never been the hide-behind-Mom type." He finished another slice of pizza. "And those aren't mom-jeans you're wearing."

The zinging feeling along her nerves turned to a pulse that made the hairs on the back of her neck stand up. Paige tried to push the feelings back. "Alex—"

"When I was Kaylie's age, my mom wore denim jumpers and clogs. When I was a teenager, most of my friends' moms were into the jogging-outfit thing. My wife wore all kinds of things, and that kept me from noticing any pretty moms in my vicinity. And now I've met you, and the jeans might be casual and the top covers everything nicely, but I can't help noticing the shape of your body underneath."

Paige swallowed. Her flu-shot theory was imploding fast. She tried to push back against the heat in her belly, but couldn't. Excitement at his words warred with the cautious voice in her head, telling her to stop his train of thought and turn it around on the tracks.

"I don't know how to respond to that," she said finally. "You're here to get to know Kaylie and… please, can we just keep it at that for a while?"

"Why?" The word was harsh, as if torn from his throat, but the look in his eyes…it wasn't angry or annoyed. His tawny eyes were curious, maybe a little hurt, and that nearly did her in.

Paige stiffened her spine. "Because of her." She pointed across the room, to the little girl at the small table laughing with her friends, ignoring the pizza on her plate.

"She seems well-adjusted to me." He lowered his voice and leaned closer to her across the table. Paige couldn't stop herself from leaning in, too, just for a moment. "We should have dinner, and not in a crowded pizza place with our daughter a few feet away."

She had to make him understand but didn't know how to do that without either telling him every mistake she'd made in the past or every fear that had cropped up since he'd stopped on her curb. Neither could happen. "There is a lot that can go wrong in a romantic relationship. I've seen them implode in so many ways and I…I just think, for her sake, it's better if we don't get involved."

"We're already involved."

"You know what I mean." Paige clasped her hands in her lap, refusing to reach out and touch him. Feeling the warmth of his hand against her own that first day had nearly been her undoing. She didn't think she could take another touch, even an innocent one. "We can be involved as her parents. But we aren't just a man and a woman without any strings. She is a big string."

"And once her relationship with me is on firm ground?"

"Then we'll be friends and we'll celebrate her birthdays and we'll figure out a holiday rotation. You won't even remember when you thought I looked good in these jeans."

Alex cocked his eyebrow. "I'll always remember how you look in these jeans." He touched her chin with his fingertip, just as he'd done in the parking lot. The touch burned but Paige was careful to keep her expression neutral, to not pull away.

"For now, I'll agree with you. I'll focus on getting to know Kaylie."

"You'll see that I'm right."

"And you'll see that I am," he said.

That was the problem, Paige admitted. She was afraid she would start seeing things his way.

ALEX TURNED RIGHT at the stoplight out of habit. The gates were usually closed by now, but they remained open, as if inviting him inside. Maybe this time he'd be able to talk to her. Maybe she could help him figure out why Paige was the first woman in more than three years who made him feel.

He didn't want to feel. Didn't like the turmoil that spawned in his belly when her eyes went dark. Didn't like feeling as if they were on different pages when it came to Kaylie.

Hated that even when they were on different pages, he still wanted her. How messed up was that? He and Dee were always on the same page, it was part of what he loved about her. That, and how she filled out everything from his old T-shirts that she salvaged as nightwear to the one-piece bathing suits she wore at the lake in the summer. He closed his eyes tight, trying to pull an image of Dee, any image, to his mind. He caught the fleeting sound of her laugh as he pulled through the gates and rounded the curve.

He pulled to a stop before her gravestone and

sat there, remembering Dee's laugh but seeing the ghost of Paige's image before his headlights.

His hands gripped the steering wheel, but he didn't reach for the door handle. Couldn't.

How could he tell his wife he was having these feelings for another woman? He hadn't told her about the one-night stand after the softball tournament. Couldn't tell her about Kaylie.

Wouldn't tell her how he felt about Paige. She was not a woman he should date, not now. Probably not ever. He'd been in love. Had had the storybook wedding that still gave him hives. Survived his partner's death.

He opened his mouth to tell Dee he loved her, but the words wouldn't come.

He couldn't lie to her, and while he did love his wife, what he felt for Paige was…different.

Alex sighed.

He put the truck in Drive and wove his way back to the entrance where the night watchman was just closing the gates. Waved as he drove through and continued on to the big house in Park Hills.

Sometimes life as an adult just sucked.

CHAPTER EIGHT

LATER THAT WEEK, Alex pulled into the driveway to his in-laws' farmhouse and stopped the truck. The white-frame house looked exactly as it had for the past ten years: green shutters, wide front porch. Sue Parker had placed pots of red and orange chrysanthemums on the steps for fall and leaves were finally starting to drift down from the elms in the front yard. Off to the side, the doors to John's equipment barn were open; he was probably in one of the fields this morning.

Sue exited a side door, wicker laundry basket in her hands, and began hanging clean sheets from the line in the yard. She wore faded jeans, a pink hoodie and Crocs on her feet. Taking advantage of another Indian summer day, Alex mused.

It was so familiar. A few years ago, Deanna would have been sitting on the seat beside him, chattering about nothing important. He rolled his shoulders.

Reluctantly, he put the truck back into gear and continued down the lane to park under a big elm tree. He got out and zipped up his light jacket.

Sue poked her head around the line of sheets and smiled.

"Alex. This is a surprise. I didn't expect you 'til tomorrow." She wrapped her strong arm around his middle in a tight hug. "But I'll take it. We don't get to see enough of you lately."

As if he hadn't been here last Saturday or the one before that…or the five hundred before that. It had been their custom, when Dee was alive, to spend Saturday afternoons with her family. He'd kept that tradition after she died because he was used to it. At first, it was comforting to be around people who understood and were content to talk about their own grief, distracting him from his own. Once the scars of Dee's death began to heal, he simply hadn't figured out a way to stop coming here every week. Besides, they needed him.

John ran a tight ship, but there was always room for one more set of hands to change the oil in a tractor or help Sue hang a new wallpaper border.

Sue pointed out the mums on the porch and then linked her arm with his. "I picked Deanna's favorite colors this year. They're pretty, don't you think?"

Alex nodded his assent. They were pretty and the fact that chrysanthemums had been Dee's least favorite shrub didn't matter. Telling her mother would just be mean.

"What's John up to today?" he asked as Sue led

him inside and set him up with a cup of coffee and a plate of cinnamon rolls left over from breakfast.

"He took one of the four-wheelers out to the corn field. You know, you should go out with him sometime. Like you used to. He'd like that."

He'd hate it, but again Alex kept quiet. John liked his quiet days in the fields, whether he was planting or harvesting or cultivating. He would return to the barn with the big machines and then take out one of the four-wheelers to look over his work. Making small talk was never on John's agenda.

"Maybe sometime. I was hoping I'd catch him at the house today, talk to you together."

"He should be back anytime." Sue sat beside him, eyes wide, hands suddenly trembling. "Why? You're okay, aren't you?" Her gray-streaked hair was pulled back in a ponytail, and little bits of her bangs had escaped to fall over her forehead. The crow's-feet at the corners of her eyes seemed to deepen and her voice grew shaky. "You're not sick?"

"No, not at all." Alex reached across the table, drawing her hands into his and patting them until she relaxed.

Sue took a deep breath, released it. "Then, what?"

"I have some news. It's good news, but I wanted to tell you both together." He'd hoped John would keep Sue calm. She had a tendency to overreact.

"You're moving. Oh, Alex, you can't leave St. Francois County." She plucked a paper napkin from the holder on the table and wiped the corners of her eyes. "Of course we only want the best for you, but leaving St. Francois? It's too soon. All the grief books say you shouldn't make any life decisions for at least five years after a death—"

"No, it's not that. I'm not leaving. I like living here, I love my job. I'm not moving away." He reassured her and tamped down a flicker of annoyance. The grief books didn't say anything about five years being a magical date for moving on. Some mentioned a year, and some said you would know when it was time to make a change.

He hadn't been ready when the lawyer called. Had been hesitant until the barbecue last Sunday.

Had been certain after the pizza party Thursday evening.

It was time to move on. Admitting it made him feel itchy. Unsettled.

Afraid, a little. Because he'd been so certain that part of his life was over. Gone with the finality of Dee's casket lid closing.

Now a little flicker burned in his chest when he thought of playing with Kaylie at the pizza place. Of maybe taking her to a swim lesson or two and not freaking her out. Watching her at a swim meet in a few years.

The flicker of heat turned to a blazing bonfire when he thought about Paige.

Turned to an all-consuming guilt when he saw the worry etched across Sue's chubby face.

He clenched his fists. Moving on was scary. He didn't want to hurt Sue or John. He didn't want to forget Dee, but apparently he didn't have any control over that. She was still there, at the fringes of his memory, but the sharpness of his memories had dulled. It didn't hurt to even look at the picture on his mantel. It hadn't for a long time, if he were truly honest.

He knew he couldn't keep living this shell of a life. Tucker was right, he had shut everything down for the past few years. Let life wash past him without really feeling the newness of spring or the full heat of a Missouri summer. Maybe he hadn't dealt completely with Dee's death, but he was dealing now. Shutting doors that should have closed already. Opening doors that might bring him out of the dark place where he allowed himself to hide.

Engine noise echoed faintly through the open windows and Alex looked out as John drove into the yard, parking just outside the big barn. He straightened his hat on his head and then caught sight of Alex's truck in the yard. Looked toward the house and hesitated before starting inside.

John let the screen door slam behind him and before saying a word made his way to the sink to wash his hands. His jeans were marked with dirt and he was careful not to brush up against the Formica counter while he poured a cup of coffee. He took a towel from the drawer and put it between his hip and the counter, still not saying anything. He was never one to chatter, but his silence made Alex nervous.

"Alex came out to talk to us, honey," Sue said. A look of relief passed over John's face, and Alex wondered what caused it. He joined them at the table.

Alex didn't know where to begin. He'd had a speech planned out, but the words escaped him. All he could see were their broken faces that last day at the hospital. All he could feel was the weight of John's hand on his shoulder the day of the funeral. Guilt, as strong as the day he'd packed Dee's things into boxes for Goodwill, washed over him.

This was wrong. He couldn't do this to them. Couldn't tell them he had a child when their child was gone forever.

No, he had to tell them. Before one of their friends spotted him with Paige or Kaylie and told them. It was his responsibility. His obligation. They were the closest family he had left.

He cleared his throat and started with the lawyer's phone call.

Sue interrupted almost immediately, her voice high-pitched and watery. "You and Dee have a—"

"No, no, we didn't. We don't." He started over. "Dee got sick right after the first implantation, remember? The clinic was supposed to have destroyed my sample, but they didn't. I have a child. A four-year-old little girl named Kaylie."

John shifted in his chair, his usually booming voice quiet. "That's…great, Alex."

"But Deanna has barely been gone that long." Sue placed her hand in John's on the tabletop. "How did they find out?"

"New computer system, inputting old records. It really doesn't matter." He waited a moment for the news to sink in. The ramifications of what having a toddler meant. They had to know he couldn't turn his back on his daughter. "I've met with her mother and we're moving forward. She agrees that I have the right to know the little girl." Sue's face was as white as the sheets hanging on the clothesline, and Alex placed his hand over hers and John's before continuing. "And I wanted you to hear, from me, what is going on. So you wouldn't be blindsided if one of your friends saw us and mentioned it."

Tears streamed down Sue's face and she didn't bother trying to wipe them away this time. "I guess you won't want to see us anymore, now that you're moving on with your life. I knew it had to happen. I just didn't expect it to happen so soon, Alex." She offered him a weak smile.

This was what he'd been afraid of. Sue thinking everything in his life pre Paige and Kaylie would be thrown out. From the moment of Dee's diagnosis, Sue thought the worst. She completely shut down after the funeral and when he took the boxes to Goodwill, she picked them up and stored them in her own attic. Sue couldn't let go of Dee. Alex knew coming here would snip another thread between them, but keeping them in the dark was not an option.

There had to be a way for all of them to coexist, he just had to figure out how.

"Now, Sue—" John began, but Alex interrupted, choosing his words carefully.

"I'll admit I may not make it out here every weekend, but I have no intention of cutting either of you out of my life."

"You say that now, but what about Thanksgiving dinner? Christmas? You should be with your family. Which one will it be?"

"I don't see this as an either-or." Alex took a breath. "You were Dee's parents, but you became mine in so many ways. You are my family and that isn't going to change just because I can now check the 'Father' box on school forms."

Sue pushed away from the table and a moment later Alex heard her footsteps on the stairs.

He blew out a breath. "I didn't mean to upset her, John. I'm sorry."

John shook his head. "It isn't your fault. Losing Deanna... It changed her. I'll talk to her, make sure she understands where you're coming from." He finished his coffee. "Bobby from the feed store saw you having coffee with a strange woman in Farmington last week. Told me about it."

Alex heard the question he hadn't asked. "That was Paige, the mother."

"Bobby says she's pretty. What does her husband think of all this?"

More than pretty, but there was no reason to tell John how Paige made his pulse race. It would be cruel. Besides, he might want Paige, but so far he hadn't been able to breach her defenses. Best to steer clear of that mucky conversation.

"She isn't married. No boyfriend, just her and the little girl. I'm going to be spending a lot of time with them both," he couldn't help saying. Like maybe his statement was readying John for another announcement. "It's platonic between us. We haven't told Kaylie—that's the little girl's name. Paige and I agreed it was best to start out as friends."

John nodded and got up to refill his cup. He offered a refill to Alex, but Alex shook his head.

"I'll make sure Sue is okay with all this. Don't take her tears too much to heart, you know how vulnerable she is."

"I do. It's why I came out today."

"It'll help her if you keep coming out, from time to time. Not every week, you've been doing that long enough." John chuckled and then sat back down. "You're a good man, Alex. You were a good husband to my daughter and you've been like a son to me. But if you keep coming here every week, where will you find the time to become a father in your own right? No, you take a little time away from us."

Relief washed through Alex. He may have botched the conversation with Sue, but he felt like he'd turned a corner with John. Progress and little steps, he told himself, but he couldn't stop a hint of sadness from clouding the moment. Alex's relationship with John had always seemed easy. He wasn't letting go of John, he reminded himself, he was making room for another relationship to build.

"I don't mind helping out around here, especially if it helps you out."

"Down the road, if it's okay with the mother and the little girl, I think we'd like to meet her." He frowned. "We'll never have grandkids." His voice broke and he cleared his throat. "It might be nice to hear a chattering little girl's voice around here sometime."

Alex swallowed and reached across the table to rest his palm over John's fist. It wasn't exactly a blessing, but maybe acceptance was the next best thing.

Fifteen minutes later Alex pulled into his own driveway and stared at the beige-and-brick house. The shrubs along the front walk needed a trim and there were no fall flowers to catch the last rays of sunlight. Two neighbors had colorful flags in their flower beds; he had a bare flag post.

The house looked like it always had but instead of welcoming him inside, he felt apart from it. As if he didn't belong there. Which was ridiculous. It was a great house and close to work.

Just restlessness, he decided. It felt like he was waking up after a nap that had lasted too long.

He flipped off the ignition and grabbed the mail from the box on his way inside.

Tossed the junk in the trash can and slipped a couple of bills into the computer table drawer in the corner of the kitchen. White cabinets. Marbled black granite countertops. White tile floor. Stainless-steel appliances. The kitchen he'd helped Dee design just after they were married. The place he'd spent so much time in before she died and so little now that he was alone.

Alex plucked a banana off the tree on the counter and took a bite.

Restlessness, hell.

He hadn't lied to John; his relationship with Paige was platonic, but damned if he wanted it to continue to be that way. When she was in the room, he didn't feel like the widower, the man left to make sense of death. He was Alex again. Just Alex. Just a man who knew how to be on his own.

And who knew he didn't want to be alone any longer.

PAIGE SHRIEKED AS Kaylie cannonballed into the water at the rec center pool on Saturday. It was just the two of them this morning, and she was glad for the time alone. Not that she minded sharing the pool with other parents, but sometimes it was nice not to worry about being too loud or splashing too much.

Kaylie tugged on her swim shorts from under the water and waved as Paige looked down. The little girl began counting on her fingers. One, two, three… Just as she had done for Paige—and for Alex—the other night at the pizza parlor.

Alex. Why did thinking of his name automatically bring his face to mind? The twinkle in his eye or that devilish smile? Because she was losing it. He wasn't a good bet, not in the long run. Not for her.

No, he didn't seem to be like any other man she had ever known, but Paige had no illusions. He'd never have given her a second glance if she wasn't part of Kaylie's package deal.

Still, if she allowed him to get close to her, she would tell him all her secrets. Then he really would only be in her life because of their daughter. He would see that she had changed, but straight-arrow types like Alex Ryan didn't take chances with broken targets.

Paige took a breath and submerged, too, holding the air in her lungs and locking gazes with the little girl as they both counted. Maybe a little oxygen deprivation would push thoughts of Alex out of her head for good. Kaylie hit fifteen, pounded her feet against the pool floor and rocketed back to the surface.

"Good, right?" Kaylie kicked her little legs, treading water.

"Amazing, kiddo," Paige said, pushing wet hair off her face and laughing with her daughter. "Now show me a back float."

Kaylie doggie paddled to the side, put her feet and hands on the wall and then rocketed back. A spray of water caught Paige square in the nose and she sneezed. Kaylie kicked and pushed her arms up and down the way she'd been taught, reaching up as if she might touch the ceiling. She made it halfway across the pool before she had to stop. Paige caught the little girl in a hug, holding her while she caught her breath.

"That was the best yet, sweetie," Paige said, dropping a quick kiss on the crown of her head.

"Can Alex come swim with us sometime?"

Paige swallowed. She'd known this moment would come. The moment Kaylie began thinking of Alex as her friend, and not just a new person who might or might not want to play. She forced the words past her clogged-up throat. "Sure, kiddo, but he might be busy."

Kaylie kicked around in the water, holding on to her swim board. "Alex told me he was a swimmer like me. He'll come."

Probably he would, and that was a whole other issue. One Kaylie didn't need to know about. She picked the kickboard from the side of the pool and handed it to Kaylie. "I'm sure he'll try. Go play for a little bit. No more tests."

Kaylie balanced on the board and swam off, under the close scrutiny of the lifeguard, to push little boats around the shallow end of the pool.

Paige pulled herself out of the water and dried off, still thinking of her daughter's newfound attachment to Alex. Paige sighed. From the moment they'd pulled out of the pizza parlor's parking lot, it had been how Alex talked to her in the ball pit, how Alex was a swimmer, how she'd shown Alex how good she was by leveling up. Alex, Alex and more Alex until Paige wanted to scream every time her daughter brought up the man that still consumed her thoughts.

Would it be so bad to admit she wanted him? To cave and go on a date with the man? They did have Kaylie in common, after all, and they had chemistry.

She gave Kaylie a two-minute warning and watched as she gathered the little boats, setting them near the entrance steps where the lifeguard could collect them.

Good idea or bad idea, she had to do something about these feelings. She liked the man, probably a little too much. In the past she'd have run with the attraction and worried about picking up the pieces later. She didn't want to pick up any pieces, not now. Not when life was finally going her way. Nice job, good friends. She couldn't remember the last time one of the church ladies looked at her sideways, like she'd been caught singing in the choir with her robe tucked in her pantyhose.

Her parents… Well, Dot and Hank might never fully support her but at least most of the time they were pleasant. They loved Kaylie.

Why mess all that up?

Her phone bleeped. It was Alison.

How about ice cream and a movie tonight with the princess?

Paige didn't have to debate. Ice cream and movies with Alison and Kaylie would keep her mind off her attraction to Alex. Plus Alison could read her like a book and would somehow know, if Paige begged off, that it was because of the handsome stranger who was now such a big part of her life.

She texted back a time and suggested a recent animated movie Kaylie wanted to see. Then she called Kaylie out of the water, already planning how to keep the conversation off Alex and on Tuck.

A few hours later, Kaylie picked up the DVD box for the twentieth time. "Are you sure Auntie Alison is coming over?" She plopped down at the kitchen table, resting her chin in her hands and focusing her puppy-dog eyes at Paige.

"Positive, Kay, she'll be here around four. Which is just enough time for you to help me clean up this watercolor mess."

Kaylie halfheartedly swiped a paper towel over a bit of blue but it only served to spread out the paint, not pick it up. Paige sprayed more cleaning solution over the counter and scrubbed.

"And you're sure we'll have time to watch the whole thing before bedtime?"

"Absolutely. Plus, it's Saturday night, which means you can stay up a little later."

Kaylie sighed. "I just don't think there will be enough time."

"If you help me clean up the time will go faster."

Kaylie swiped at the drips of colored water on the counter again. "I guess."

Paige bit her lip to keep from smiling. Her daughter had the martyr act down to a science. Not that she gave in to it, at least not very often.

The front door opened and Kaylie squealed, tossed her soiled paper towel in the bin and rushed for the front of the house. Paige finished cleaning the counter and was just putting the supplies away when Alison and Kaylie returned to the kitchen. Kaylie plucked the DVD off the counter and hurried into the living room to put it in the machine.

"You do realize we're watching the movie from the comfort of our sweats tonight?" Paige said, frowning at her purple sweats with "Pink Panther" emblazoned down the legs. Alison wore skinny black jeans and wedge-heeled sandals with a striped sailor top, and had her hair pulled back to cascade down her back.

"I have a date later."

"Don't let us hold you back." She wasn't hurt, not really. Not because she was Alison's predate entertainment.

After all, Paige had been the one without strings at one point in her life. Had focused all her energies on the man by her side until things blew up and Alison picked up the pieces. She had the strings now; her job was to be a good friend. Tuck was a good guy, like Alex, but unlike with her and Alex, there was no reason for Alison not to go after Tuck.

Alison waved one hand as she hung her leather jacket in the hall closet and sat at the counter. She lay down a manila folder and pushed it across the top. "Please. The cool kids don't date until after eight these days. I've got time for a movie with my favorite kid and my bestie first."

Paige eyed the folder. "What's this?" Paige asked as she filled glasses with ice and tea for them. Kaylie had a juice box already open on the coffee table.

"Ehh, we'll talk about it later." She hooked her thumb toward the television as the opening credits began to trumpet from the speakers. "I don't think the kiddo can wait any longer."

Paige laughed. "Ice cream now or later?"

"Later. We can't keep the princess waiting."

The three of them settled onto the couch, as they had done since Kaylie was a baby, but Paige couldn't keep her mind on the animated dragons and princesses. She kept thinking about camping, a pastime she'd never truly understood, and waking up in the early dawn hours to paint the sunrise.

Kaylie, focused on the on-screen battle, didn't blink when Paige rose to get popcorn. Alison followed her back into the kitchen.

"What's up?"

"Nothing. Just distracted, I guess." Paige reached into the cupboard for oil and popcorn and then dug the popper from the lower cabinet. The setting sun glared through her sliding glass doors and Paige drew the blinds closed. Soon it would be dark almost before she and Kaylie returned home from school. She wondered how the parks system worked during the colder, shorter days.

She would need to figure out a Halloween costume in a couple of days. She wondered if Alex liked to dress up.

Then pushed images of him dressed as a hunky Roman soldier or a bloodsucking vampire from her mind.

"Work?"

Paige shook her head. "Alex."

"I had a feeling."

"How are things going between you and Tuck?"

"Fine. He's funny and he knows how to kiss. We'll see how things go." Alison grabbed a grape from the bowl on the counter. "How are things between you and Alex?"

Paige glanced into the living room but Kaylie's attention was focused on the movie. "He asked me on a date. Again."

"I know."

"How do you know?"

Alison grinned. "Apparently men talk about the women they're interested in as much as women talk about men. Who knew?"

Paige's cheeks burned. "He talks about me?"

Her friend nodded. "Talks about you. Loses his train of thought. Apparently he's quite smitten."

"It's because of Kaylie."

"It's because of you. When he's talking about Kaylie he's focused and excited about dad stuff like riding bikes. Makes sense. Tuck says when he talks about you he gets lost, stares into space a little. Good, right?" Alison popped another grape into her mouth.

Paige shrugged. It felt good to hear, but that didn't solve the problem of all the other relationships she'd imploded in the past. Her track record wasn't stellar, and there was so much to lose. A few days buried in a pint of ice cream wouldn't heal the wounds of a breakup with Alex, she knew. And he wouldn't hurt Kaylie, she was certain of that after only knowing him for a week, but if they dated and it didn't work, how awkward would it be to have him picking up Kaylie on a Friday night?

Then there was the other problem.

The what-did-Alex-see-looking-at-them problem.

"Maybe you need a hypnotist." Alison's words broke through Paige's funk.

"I need a what?"

"A hypnotist. You know, 'Every time you hear the number four you'll quack like a duck.'" Alison intoned the words. "But in your case you won't quack like a duck, we'll just block out your entire past."

"Not funny." The first kernels of corn began popping. "I don't want to forget my past. I just don't want it to mess up my present."

"From where I'm sitting, it already is. You have to take a chance, Paige." Alison filled a glass with tea from the fridge and returned to the counter. She pushed the manila folder to Paige. "I have it on good authority that Alex Ryan isn't a felon, had a solid three-point-five GPA in college and owns his own home."

Paige reached for the folder but drew back, putting her hands in her pockets. "You had him checked out?" She finally read the file from the fertility clinic last night so she knew the basics. How much more could Alison have found?

Alison shrugged. "I had some potential employees to vet. Throwing in one extra name to Google was no big deal."

"Of all the crazy, scheming…" She reached for the folder but pushed it away at the last moment. "What does it say about him, anyway?"

A burning smell drifted to Paige's nose and she grabbed the popper, unplugging it and dumping the ruined corn into the kitchen sink.

"What's going on out there?" Kaylie called, still focused on the movie.

"Nothing, sweetie, just making popcorn."

She twisted around on the sofa. "Can we have extra butter?"

Paige nodded and Kaylie returned her attention to the princess and unicorn on the screen.

"What it says is that Alex Ryan is a good guy. He might eat cookies in bed, the investigator didn't go that far, but he's had exactly three citations—all speeding violations and all from his college days—and he's never been fired from a job. He grew up in Park Hills, played baseball, football and swam in the summer. He volunteers with a kiddie rec league now, plays on a couple of leagues through the winter months."

The second round of popcorn finished and Paige took a bowl into the living room.

When she returned to the kitchen, Alison picked up the folder and held it out until she took it. "And any fool can see that you're attracted to him. Your radar isn't wrong this time Paige. You have to trust it."

She popped a few kernels into her mouth and

chewed. It would be so easy to go on a date with him. Throw caution to the wind, just for one night.

But it wouldn't end with one night. Whether they fell in love or could barely stand one another, for at least the next fourteen years he would be an integral part of her life. They would plan birthday parties together, attend parent-teacher conferences and school plays. And then there was college and Kaylie's wedding. As awkward as it was to deny the chemistry between them, it would be so much worse if they dated and failed at a relationship.

What if she and Kaylie were just part of the package ripped from him when his wife got cancer?

Paige riffled the edges of the folder but didn't open it. Because the words on the page didn't matter. It didn't even matter that her best friend had the man checked out. What mattered was what she thought of him, and what Paige thought was that he was dangerous. Dangerous to her peace of mind. Dangerous to the woman she wanted to be.

Dangerous, dangerous, dangerous.

The movie ended and Kaylie asked to watch it again, as she usually did with movies she liked. Paige sent her into the bathroom and then reset the DVD, still thinking about what Alison had said. Nice guy, nothing blatantly off about his past, although he certainly had one—a wife, her extended family, death. More obstacles to think about.

Once Kaylie was settled with more popcorn and

juice, Paige returned to the counter where Alison finished her bowl of popcorn.

"Ice cream sundae?"

Alison shook her head. "I have a date, something you should be having, you know."

"Al…"

Alison held up her hands in surrender. "Okay, I won't push." She picked up the folder and stuffed it into her bag. "By the way, your mom called my mom and I've been fielding my own version of 'why are you dating a park ranger?' for the past week."

Annoyance washed over Paige. Of course Dot called Alison's mother; it was what Dot did. If something upset her she dealt with it by upsetting someone else. Kaylie's trapeze jump coupled with Paige turning down another gallery request and the two strange men at the barbecue set her mother off. Alison's mom was laid-back about most things but not her only daughter's dating habits. She wanted Alison married off with babies on the way, and Paige felt terrible Dot was making things tenuous between Alison and her mom.

"I'm sorry. I've been so distracted with Alex I didn't even think about my mom calling yours. See, it's another reason to avoid him. I'm not a good friend when guys start distracting me."

"Please, this is a little more than an infatuation. I get the pressure. He's Kaylie's father." She hopped off the high chair and then took her jacket from the hall closet. "And this is not me pushing, but if you wanted to invite Alex to lunch tomorrow, it's okay with me. It might be good for you, to see him on your own terms. In your own home." Alison started for the door. "At least think about it. If you make spaghetti Bolognese I'll bring dessert. Or we could cancel and make it just the three of you."

Paige walked with Alison onto the porch. "I'll call you in the morning. To let you know."

Alison left and Paige stayed on the porch, listening to the sounds of the epic battle from Kaylie's movie filtering through the house. She was thinking about asking him.

And that was a whole new set of problems.

CHAPTER NINE

ALEX'S EMAIL PINGED from his computer at the workstation in his kitchen. He turned down the stove burner and put a lid on the pan filled with rice pilaf. He had emailed Paige earlier, pictures of the boxes he and Tuck stored away the week before and a few images of the two of them leading a Boy Scout troop into the forest last spring. Along with the pictures he wrote,

So you don't think I sit outside the park office in a lounge chair, tanning all day.

Emailing her was an impulse he couldn't deny. After spending Friday morning with Sue and John, and then being unable to settle into his own home that afternoon, he'd gone to the park. Hiked the equestrian trail at St. Francois and then detoured down Mooner's Hollow, his favorite area inside the wilderness. The entire time he'd wondered if Paige would like the hike. If she would find something to paint.

If he would kiss her when they reached the

secluded overlook that only the most experienced hikers knew about. Thinking about kissing Paige led him off-trail and he'd wound up on the back edge of the park on acreage that butted up against private land. An old cabin sat in the clearing, the roof falling in, and it added a haunted air to the area. Sad. He took a picture with his camera phone and thought about sending it to her; he settled on less personal pictures of him with Tuck and the Scout pack, starting their photo email exchange.

He stirred once more and then wiped his palms against the legs of his sweatpants. Wondered if Paige was wearing another pair of ripped jeans or if she was in something more comfortable. Pushed that image away because thoughts of Paige and something more comfortable were making him incredibly *uncomfortable* below the equator.

His email pinged again as he sat at the desk. Paige's reply held two images: one of her at her college graduation, dated six years before, and another dated on the first day of school this year. She wore a painter's smock and her hair pulled into a high ponytail. The kids gathered around her all wore paint-stained T-shirts several sizes too big, but his focus was on her, in the middle of the mass of kids with a huge smile on her face. She wore a skirt that barely reached her knees and under the smock a fitted tee hugged her torso, outlining her breasts. Definitely not like any teacher he remembered from elementary school.

Not even like the TAs he'd had in college.

So, you see, I am old enough to be a teacher, she captioned the photos. But I don't wear old-lady support shoes.

Alex's gaze skimmed the image again, looking for Paige's feet. She wore strappy blue sandals and the heels made her legs look like they went on forever. His mouth went dry and he reached for the water bottle on the cross-stitched rooster coaster.

She might have the diploma and the classroom, but she was still like no teacher he'd ever had. He emailed back, telling her as much. A quick estimate based on the college picture put her age at twenty-nine, give or take. Not that much of a difference from his own thirty-two. For the first time in a long time he didn't feel twice his actual age. Didn't feel he had to exhaust himself at work to face the long hours waiting in this house.

Most of his memories here, the hard ones at least, were stored in the attic. Boxes filled with pictures or souvenirs he or Dee had picked up during vacations to Branson or the Texas coast. Still, not all the memories could be boxed. Deanna chose the backsplash with roosters painted on the tiles; she picked out the cookware and utensils. He'd picked the fifty-five-inch television and leather sofas in the family room beyond the kitchen. He still didn't understand the functionality of the mountain of tiny throw pillows on the couch. They were uncomfortable at best and a pain in his ass to move out of the way at worst.

Still, sometime in the past three years, no, the past week, the house stopped seeming like a testament to his relationship with Dee and just his home. He pushed the teaspoon of guilt that tried to spill into his heart away. This was his home, and it wasn't as lived-in or homey as Paige's place, but it was comfortable. It was his life and if he found someone that brought in the light again, that had to be okay.

Didn't it?

Are you flirting with me, Mr. Ryan?

Her return email jolted him out of his reverie.

Alex pushed away from the desk, telling himself it was time to stir the rice. But it wasn't. It wasn't even a ploy to keep her guessing about him.

He had promised himself he would just be Paige's friend while they figured out the Kaylie situation. But being her friend was a moot point when he couldn't even take a hike without thoughts of her distracting him into getting lost.

Okay, not lost, but off-trail to the point that it was simpler to hitch a ride back to the parking area with a local farmer than to try to walk back.

Convincing himself they could be friends had only been feasible before he'd spent time with her. Talked to her. Flirt-emailed with her for the past hour. Before he'd run her down with his shopping cart and spotted her hovering behind a video game at the pizza parlor with those big green eyes focused on him. Whatever she'd been thinking that night couldn't have been platonic. Not with the kind of heat she'd thrown his way from the darkened corner.

This was uncharted territory for him. Dee had been his friend before their first date. None of the girls he'd dated before her had been serious, but all of them had been friendly with him before he asked them out. Alex couldn't think of a single person he'd felt this attracted to without that person being his friend before his feelings changed. It wasn't just because of Kaylie, either. Alex liked Paige, and he wanted to be a good dad to the kid but he wasn't fooling himself into thinking that they could meld into a typical married-with-kids family overnight. Or, if they did become more than friends, that it wouldn't blow up like so many marriages. Hell, he shouldn't even be thinking about long-term commitment at this point.

But Alex couldn't tell her any of that, not without making her think he was a complete lunatic, so he stirred the rice and then tossed a steak onto the broiling pan before sending her the picture of the old cabin that he'd taken that afternoon.

Beautiful! Where did you find it?

He described the area and, not wanting the connection with her to end, asked what they were doing the following afternoon.

I'm always amazed at the places I've never seen when I've lived here nearly my whole life. We're having lunch tomorrow, my place, want to come?

Alex couldn't stop the little jolt to his heart at her words. And he knew it wasn't the date he wanted, but it was another step forward.

What should I bring?

Her reply seemed to take hours but Alex knew from the counting down of the kitchen timer it was less than a minute.

Just bring yourself, should be a nice afternoon.

Warmth spread through his body. A big step forward, and he didn't know why the abrupt change in her tactics, but he also didn't care. They still weren't dating, but inviting him to her home, for a

family dinner was a big deal. Tomorrow he would
see her again. Spend more time with his daughter.

The computer pinged again.

I asked you a question earlier and you didn't
answer. Were you flirting with me?

His heart pounded in his chest and he admitted it was pounding more for Paige than from the
thought of seeing Kaylie. He could say no; she
probably wanted him to say no. The last thing he
wanted was for her to think he was pressuring her
about going on a date. At the same time, he refused
to lie about what he wanted. It went against the
grain. He wasn't perfect, but Alex prided himself
on being open and honest with his friends.

The timer went off, giving him more time to debate his reply. Deny the flirtatious tone and keep
things friendly? He removed the steak from the
broiler, put it on a plate and then put the plate in
the microwave to keep it from overcooling. Or he
could roll the dice on the fact that she'd invited
him to another Sunday lunch and admit to it. He
took the pilaf off the burner and turned off all the
stove switches.

Alex returned to his desk and wrote, I believe I
am before hitting the send button.

With no ticking timer to keep track, he watched
the clock on the wall move through the slowest

three minutes of his life. This was it, then. He'd taken things too far, too soon. Finally, his email pinged. He didn't even pretend not to triple-click the mouse so he could read her message.

See you tomorrow.

Tomorrow. It was quickly becoming his favorite word.

By nine Sunday morning Paige was a nervous wreck. She pulled a pair of capris from her closet and then shoved them back inside a moment later. It was lunch, for goodness sake, lunch. Casual. Her home turf. Why was this so hard?

Flu shots. Innoculations, right? Today Alison, Tuck and Kaylie would provide the buffer so she could keep her focus on not being attracted to Alex. For the fifteenth time she thanked her lucky stars that she edited that last email from the I think I like that response to his admissions of flirting to the more innocuous See you tomorrow. And once more blasted Reckless Paige for pushing him on the flirting subject at all.

Because he was anything but casual. Alex was soft caresses and stolen kisses and flirting via email. It was also dangerous and no matter how many things she distracted herself with she couldn't stop thinking about him. Case in point, she hadn't uninvited her mother to lunch today after Alex had accepted her invitation last night.

She needed more time to prepare the lie, anyway, Paige thought as she dialed the number. A last-minute cancellation was so much easier than a long, drawn-out conversation. Her mother answered on the second ring.

"Hello, Mother."

"Paige, what a surprise."

Nope, the surprise was coming in a few minutes. "So how was your morning?"

"How is any Sunday morning, dear? Quiet. We attended mass last night and this morning I've been watching the birds in the wildlife area across the way. Your father is watching one of his news shows."

"Oh, that's nice." And blah. Like so many Sunday mornings from her childhood. "Mother, I was calling to tell you that we're canceling lunch this week. Alison, uh, isn't feeling great. I'm going to make her some chicken soup and take it over." If there was one thing Paige had learned in her twenty-nine years it was that the more details the better where Dot was concerned.

"I hope you aren't taking Kaylie over. You don't want her getting whatever Alison has."

"I'll take care of it, Mother. I just wanted to call before you left."

"That was very considerate."

And wasn't this the stiffest conversation they'd

had in months? "We could have dinner later this week. If you'd like?"

"Oh, sweetheart, it's only one lunch. We will see you next week. But do tell Kaylie hello."

Sure, because what every four-year-old wanted from their grandmother was a secondhand hello.

"Have you given any more thought to the gallery showing? The deadline is coming up at the end of the month."

Paige lightly tapped her head against the wall. "No, Mother, I've been swamped with work and Kaylie's swim lessons."

"Paige, they will not keep asking if you keep declining." Dot's voice sharpened.

"I know, Mother."

"This isn't because of that man, is it? The one who came to the barbecue last Sunday with Alison's new *friend*." Her voice was flat, condemning.

"No, Mother, it has nothing to do with Alex. I have a job, you know. A daughter I'm raising on my own—"

"And whose fault is that?" her mother's voice accused.

Paige ignored the interruption and continued on. "I have responsibilities that I can't blow off for a week to come up with a painting for—" she cut off the words *for a friend who is doing you a favor* and instead said, "a gallery that might already have a full showing."

Dot clucked over the phone. "You're too talented

to think like that. Just consider sending your plans to the gallery. I know you won't regret it."

"I'll consider it, Mother. I'll talk to you soon." Paige hung up before Dot could really get going.

Her talent was hobby work, wasn't that what the last gallery owner said before he realized Paige was around the corner from him? He backtracked fast enough, fawning over Dot Kenner's daughter, but the damage was done. Dot called in a favor to get Paige's work into the gallery. It had nothing to do with talent.

She blew out a breath to shake off the conversation. Dot was never going to change, and there was nothing Paige could do about it.

"Sweetpea, how about a bike ride before lunch?" She found Kaylie on the floor in her room playing with her dolls.

"Can I ride the big bike and not my old trike?"

Paige gave Kaylie a new two-wheeler with training wheels on her birthday. She still rode both, but preferred the big-girl bike. "Definitely. Grab your tennies."

She readied Kaylie still thinking about the conversation with her mother. Maybe that wasn't such a bad thing. Obsessing about her mother's inability to accept Paige's life choices might be a nice distraction from obsessing over the handsome father of her child.

"AND SO ALEX is sprawled on his belly over the side of the cliff when a fox comes out of its den, howls, and the cat jumps out of its fur, digs its claws into Alex's arm and is off like a shot." Tuck finished the story, cracking everyone up. Kaylie, eyes as round as quarters, took it all in.

"Did you save the kitty?" She turned to Alex.

"I'm not sure how much was me and how much was the cat's fear of the fox, but it made it back to its family." The he pointed to a thin white scar on his wrist. "But it left its mark."

Kaylie traced her tiny finger over the crooked scar and Paige found her own fingers itching to follow the line over the bone in his wrist to the underside of his arm.

Had something similar happened to cause the scar at his mouth? she wondered. Had he been trying to rescue a bird or was there a freak storm and he'd been caught in it, forced to break into that old cabin from the picture he'd sent, and had a splinter from the door caught his lip?

Get a grip, Paige. In her mind, he was now Indiana Jones wearing a superhero's cape. It had taken until the moment his truck pulled into her drive to stop her annoyance at her mother and for her to give in to Alex's brand of distraction. Watching him with Kaylie. Listening as he and Tuck traded friendly insults and then broke into peals of laughter.

Even now, as she watched them from the kitchen sink, father and daughter were talking about nothing important. Her heart clutched at the sight. She

172 THE DAUGHTER HE WANTED

might be completely overreacting to the man but Kaylie was taking him in stride. Asking questions about his work and then telling him about her school. Most of the things she knew about him were because of Kaylie's questions. She knew he preferred peanut butter and jelly to bologna, that he preferred blue Powerade and that his eyes crinkled when he laughed. He was fanatical about swimming.

He caught her studying him and offered Paige a smile. Her belly flip-flopped and she pretended interest in the already-clean saucepan in the sink. God, the more she was around him, the more her body seemed to be training for the Olympics.

She finished the lunch dishes while Alison tucked leftovers into plastic containers and put them into the fridge. Tuck refilled glasses and Alex entertained Kaylie with more of his park adventures. A little piece of her wondered if it could always be like this—friends having a meal, talking about nothing. Tuck slid his hand over Alison's hair and Alison shot him a smile.

No, their little group wasn't just friendly. Alison and Tuck were obviously involved in more than a couple of casual dates. Alex wasn't just Kaylie's friend and based on practically every conversation they had he didn't want to be just friends with Paige.

But she needed to know that she and Kaylie

weren't substitutions for the family he'd thought he would have four years before.

A glass slipped from her hand and shattered against the stainless-steel sink. Alex was out of his chair and across the room in a heartbeat.

"I'm okay," she insisted but Alex still took her hands in his, examining them for cuts or pieces of glass in her skin. Heat drenched Paige from the contact and she pulled away.

Wanting Alex was...like breathing lately. Thoughts of him interrupted her work at school, distracted her when she should be working on Kaylie's painting. Paige wiped her hands on the dish towel and then grabbed the rubber cleaning gloves from the under the sink to start cleaning up the mess.

"Dang it, I loved that glass." She didn't know how she would replace it. Alison had picked up the painted frog glasses in Mexico a couple of years before.

Alison held up her hand. "I volunteer to hop down to Playa Maya to find another set. She's okay, right, Alex?"

"I'm fine—" Paige began, but Alex took her hands in his again, inspecting them once more.

Finally satisfied she wasn't in imminent danger from glass shards, Alex put the rubber gloves on his own hands and began picking up pieces of glass. The pink gloves should have looked odd on him, but they didn't. Instead, the pink seemed to accentuate the size of his hands, the strength of his wrists. Paige swallowed and looked away. But her gaze was drawn right back to the man at the sink, cleaning up after her.

"You don't have to do that. I made the mess."

He shrugged and plucked the last big shard from the sink before pushing some of the smaller pieces together in the middle. "Happy to help."

Kaylie parroted, "Happy to help, happy to help," in a British accent she'd picked up from a morning cartoon.

Okay, then. Paige grabbed the dustpan from the closet and set the edge so Alex could sweep the tiny pieces into it. Tossed them into the trash and then her gaze clashed with his again. She was mesmerized by his hazel eyes. Wanted to know what he was thinking. He pulled one pink glove from his hand and then the other and Paige licked her lips. Time seemed to stand still as he looked at her over the bin. Alex swallowed, his Adam's apple sliding down and then back up.

The back door closed and the sound was loud in the room. It snapped Paige out of the trance she'd been in. She dumped the pan into the trash and turned away. Three shadowy figures played on the deck outside: Alison and Tuck distracting Kaylie from the tension in the room. How she wished she could be four and oblivious. But she was twenty-nine and Alex was the biggest distraction she'd come across in ages. She needed to put some distance between them.

"We should go. I have papers to grade and I'm sure Alison and Tuck would like some adults-only time."

"This is your house."

Right, her home. Her hands flexed at her side. God, she was losing it. "I meant—"

Alex reached for her and Paige forgot what she was going to say. She knew she should shake off his hand but she didn't want to.

All the reasons they were a bad idea were still in her head. In her heart. But she was tired of thinking about all the different ways this could go wrong. Tired of wondering when she would mess this up. She'd changed, damn it. She wasn't looking to Alex to make her life complete or to get her parents' attention. And as much as she wanted Kaylie to have a father, a real dad kind of man in her life, Alex was more than that.

He was funny and handsome and smart and she liked him. Until he'd come along it had been easy to ignore the men who flirted with her. Simple enough to assuage her physical needs on her own. He was here now, showing her all the ways she'd been missing out—on someone to laugh with, someone to light that fire in her belly.

No, she didn't know how he really saw her, saw Kaylie.

Maybe it wouldn't be so bad if she took just one

step forward, to see if that fire and that laughter could grow into something more.

She turned and linked her hand with his. "So you were flirting with me. In email."

"Seemed like the safest bet." His deep voice rippled along her nerve endings, his hand light against hers. "Every time I tried to in person you shut me down. A man can only take so much rejection."

Paige grinned. "Something tells me you've done your share of rejecting."

Alex shrugged. He looked at their linked hands. "So is this a 'yes' to a date?"

"This is a strong 'I'm thinking about it.'"

He raised an eyebrow. "Not the right answer."

"It's the answer you get today." Her voice was nearly steady when she said the words. Thank goodness.

"Then I can't wait for tomorrow."

CHAPTER TEN

IT WAS THE best answer Alex had had so far. And who cared that they'd barely texted between Sunday and today? It'd been four long days when he'd been busy wrapping up end-of-the-season paperwork at the parks, anyway. She had school. He'd had a video chat with Kaylie on Wednesday after her swim lesson and the little girl had showed him the whale picture she'd finished during preschool. She told him she wanted to be Snoopy for Halloween but was worried they wouldn't find a Sally or Lucy outfit for Paige. Which sent him online to find one. He'd found Snoopy, Sally, Lucy and a Charlie Brown costume. Added all four to the shopping cart because he didn't know if Paige liked Sally or Lucy, and then had them express shipped.

He didn't really expect to have a long, intimate conversation with Paige after she sent Kaylie off to brush her teeth, but it had been nice talking about her day. Nicer still when she blushed when he complimented the paint-speckled tee she'd been wearing. The very thin tee that left very little of her upper body to his imagination.

God, the mind was a horrible, terrible, so bad, very good thing.

A truck pulled into the parking lot and the shorts-wearing deliveryman stepped from his truck with several packages in his arm.

"Figured you were working today and I'd save you the trip to the distribution center." Ron Cherry had been Alex's favorite wide receiver in high school. He'd blown his knee out his sophomore year in college and come back to St. Francois County. His two boys were on Alex's rec team last summer and were both talented athletes.

"I forgot to change the shipping address again, sorry about that." Alex signed for the packages and set them on his desk.

Ron waved and returned to his truck.

Tuck returned from his hike around one of the shorter trails and pointed to the packages. "You didn't order a decade's worth of beef jerky again, did you?"

"No. Halloween costumes."

"You hate Halloween."

"I don't hate it. It just seems odd that some adults need to have costuming and makeup to have a good time." Actually, it was more that costumes and alcohol seemed to steal every inhibition from every person in the world for one night.

Alex prided himself on his control, and watching other people willingly give it up made him twitchy.

"So you're going to the party at the Low Bar this year?"

Alex shrugged and before Tuck could question him more, his cell buzzed.

"You should go, you know."

Alex tuned Tuck out so he could read the message.

I hate to ask at the last minute, but my babysitter just bailed for this afternoon and I'm supposed to chaperone a lock-in for the third-grade girls. Any chance you could watch Kaylie? Just for a couple of hours?

"Yes!" It was another small victory but one he would take. Paige was reaching out to him.

"Sweet. I asked Alison last night. You should bring Paige."

"What?" Alex shot back a quick yes to Paige and then put the rest of the paperwork in his desk drawer for next week. "You asked Alison what?"

"About the Low Bar Halloween party. You should bring Paige."

"I don't do bar parties, especially not adult dress-up bar parties." Alex shook his head. He'd never gone barhopping on Halloween, not even in college.

Tuck folded his arms over his chest. "Damn,

you act like you're eighty. You just said you were going."

"No, I didn't." Had he? Alex felt like he was in a bad Abbott and Costello routine only instead of baseball they were talking about costuming.

Tuck grabbed one of the packages. "You have a costume."

A costume that would get him laughed out of the bar. Not that he went there often, anyway. "I'm not going to the Low Bar on Halloween night. Those are…something else."

He couldn't very well tell Tuck he'd purchased four Halloween costumes and might not need any of them. He waved his cell phone. "That was Paige, she needs me to watch Kaylie for a couple of hours tonight."

"Okay, so the Halloween party is off the conversational radar." Tuck turned the chair on the opposite side of Alex's desk around and leaned his arms over the back as he sat. "So this is good. A step forward and all that."

"Yeah. A step forward." One that Alex was determined not to mess up. He typed "babysitting games" into a search engine and waited while three million results were returned. No way he could go through that many. He narrowed the search to games for four-year-olds but that only culled the list by a few hundred thousand. "What do four-year-olds do?"

Tuck shook his head. "I've been around her as

much as you have. She swings, plays in sandboxes. Although outdoor activities are probably out." He pointed to the window, where the first drops of rain hit the glass. "I'm thinking you need board games."

Alex switched from search engine to online store and typed in "board games." Monopoly and Old Maid seemed like good bets so he made a mental note to stop by a department store on his way home.

"You liked Monopoly when you were a kid, right?"

"As much as I liked any board games, sure." Tuck shrugged. "She'll probably want to be the shoe. Girls love shoes."

They'd play a game, maybe have dinner. No problem. He had this in the bag.

"So how are things between you and Alison? Costume parties? That's a big step," Alex said.

"Things are good. Did you know she's the HR rep for the winery outside Farmington? Smart and funny and looks."

"Until you decide she's also clingy and annoying." Too late, Alex realized he said the words aloud. "Dude, I'm sorry. I didn't mean that. She is charming and funny and smart."

Tuck waved a hand, dismissing the insult. "She's different. I like talking to her. She doesn't call me twenty times a day to say she misses me or to ask if I like chicken better than steak." He was quiet for a long moment. "I think she might be the whole package."

"Really?" After only a couple of dates? Alex couldn't believe it. It usually took Tuck five to seven dates to decide if a girl was pretty, much less that he wanted to spend quality time with her.

"Really."

He could hear the sincerity in Tuck's voice. And who was he to judge? Since he'd met Paige all of Alex's preconceived notions about attraction and chemistry were out the window. She turned everything upside down and he'd barely even kissed her.

A few hours later Alex knocked on Paige's pretty pink door with the Monopoly game in one hand and a bag filled with a card game, raw vegetables and dip in the other. Paige pulled the door open and raised an eyebrow at his packages. She wore track pants and a hoodie with a pink top underneath. Gray, pink and neon-blue sneakers were on her feet and her hair was pulled back into a ponytail. She looked adorable.

"Thank you for coming. I can't believed the babysitter bailed, and taking Kaylie with me is out because she had a slight fever this morning. She's fine, it broke around noon, but the school has a policy about fevers and school-sponsored events. Alison is coming to our rescue for the overnight. She should be here after work and you can go back to your evening." She spoke nonstop, as if afraid she might forget something if she slowed. Paige eyed the game and the other bag. "Usually babysitters only bring themselves You won't need all this."

"I've never been a babysitter before. Decided I should come prepared."

She peered inside the bag and bit the corner of her mouth. "Broccoli, carrots and sweet peppers. Nice combination. But she won't eat any of it." She led him into the kitchen and set the bag on the counter. Kaylie curled up with a tablet computer, playing something. "Kaylie, Alex is here until Alison gets off work. Best behavior, okay?"

The little girl didn't say anything, just kept tapping away at the screen.

"Kay!" Paige raised her voice and Kaylie's attention shot to the kitchen counter. A smile stole over her face.

"Alex! You're gonna sit on me!"

Paige shook her head and laughed softly, the sound tickling the hairs on the back of his neck. "Am I supposed to sit on her?" he asked in mock sincerity.

"Kaylie-speak. She's taken to shortening as many words as she can lately. But if she gets out of hand, sure, sit on her. Metaphorically speaking."

Kaylie, out of hand? Alex didn't think that was possible, at least from what he'd seen so far. He had games and snacks. This night was going to be a piece of cake and he said so.

Paige raised an eyebrow but didn't contradict him. She turned her attention to Kaylie. "Five more minutes and 'Angry Birds' is done, got it?" The little girl nodded and then started tapping at the screen again. Paige checked her watch and grabbed her bag off a nearby chair. "Alison should be here by six. Text me if anything explodes in the meantime. I really appreciate this."

"Momma, wait!" Kaylie's little footsteps clattered down the hall and she threw her arms around Paige's hips. "I'll miss you." Paige hugged the little girl close.

"I'll miss you, too. But Auntie Al has a lot of fun stuff planned and I'll see you for breakfast in the morning, okay?"

Kaylie pecked a kiss on Paige's cheek. "Mmm-kay. See you in the morning." And then she ran back down the hall. Alex heard a soft thump that had to be Kaylie landing on the couch.

"There's a twenty on the counter for pizza. Thank you." She held on to the doorknob but didn't move.

"You're welcome. I'm glad you called. It means a lot."

She waited another moment. "You know, Monopoly is a little, uh, advanced for four-year-olds. Maybe just color? Everything you'll need is in the hall closet."

"I'll let her be the shoe." Doubt clouded Paige's eyes so Alex pushed on. "What little girl doesn't like buying stuff?"

"Yeah, but—"

Alex touched her hand and her car keys jingled. "Go, you'll be late. We'll be fine. It's only a couple of hours, right?"

"Okay, well, text me if you need anything. I'll talk to you soon."

And she was gone.

Alex looked into the living room at the painting of the daisy. A small house had been added to the background and it looked remarkably like Paige's home. He ran his finger over the side and smiled. Painting Kaylie's own house onto the canvas was a nice touch. He wondered what other surprises Paige had in store for their daughter.

In the kitchen, Alex grabbed a bottle of water from the fridge and asked Kaylie what she wanted to do.

"Play 'Angry Birds,'" she replied, never looking up from the game. "Do you like 'Angry Birds'?" She reclined against a couple of pillows, feet on the couch and knees pulled up. The tablet rested against her legs and she tapped the screen.

"Never played it." Alex checked the clock. At least five minutes had passed since Paige left. "Your mom said five more minutes, kiddo. You should turn it off now."

"After I finish this level. I have a red-bird bomb and a chicken bomb to set off next."

Seemed like a good compromise so Alex left her to the game and set up the Monopoly board on the kitchen counter while he finished his water.

He glanced at the clock again. At least ten minutes had passed.

"Kaylie, time's up." He used his most firm voice,
imitating the tone he remembered his father using
often when he was growing up.

"I don't have three stars yet. I need three stars."

Alex walked to the sofa as Kaylie used her last
bird-bomb and started the level over. "It's time to
turn it off, kiddo." Alex reached for the device but
Kaylie pulled it away from him.

"I have to have three stars. It's not done 'til I
have three stars." She hit the play button, took aim
with a yellow bird and tapped the screen to let it
fly. Two monkeys and a wooden stick house were
taken out. Interesting game. Alex settled beside
her, giving her a hint for the next bomb. Another
two monkeys and a cement house dropped this
time, along with a pineapple. "We got the treasure!" Kaylie's voice squealed across the room.
She high-fived Alex and loaded another bird into
the slingshot.

This time the last of the wooden houses fell
down and the last monkey fell over, leaving two
birds with nothing to hit. They'd won the level.

Kaylie bounced on the couch, tablet held high
over her head. "I won, I won, IwonIwonIwon." She
bounced a few more times and then flopped down
on the sofa. "Let's get more pineapples!" she said,
her voice lowered into a growl. Alex reached for
the tablet and she jerked it away from him. "No!"

"Kaylie, it's time to stop. You have three stars and it's time to stop." Alex used his dad voice again, but it didn't work.

Kaylie grabbed the tablet and scooted off the couch. "No, I want pineapples. More pineapples."

What did that parenting book say? Kids needed limits. This was the limit. It was past Paige's five-minute mark, she'd finished the level and gotten the three stars. "Kaylie," he began.

"I need more pineapples!" Kaylie yelled, little hands fisted around the tablet.

Alex kept his voice steady but the blood was pounding in his ears. He didn't want to be the bad guy but he also wanted to be obeyed. What was it Paige had said that first day? Kids had to learn there were things they had to do—like homework and jobs. Well, there were also things they had to learn not to do. Like throw fits. "No."

Kaylie pushed into a corner of the sofa, the tablet pulled to her chest like a shield. "More pineapples," she said, this time in a quieter voice and with tears in her eyes. Okay, so Paige made this look supereasy.

Alex took the tablet from her and put it on a high shelf while she sniffled about pineapples and treasure. He could handle it.

Hadn't he talked a drunken hiker back to the campground just a few weeks ago? And didn't he deal with angry, didn't-understand-how-RVs-worked city dwellers on at least a weekly basis during the summer months? He'd graduated at the top of his college class. Hell, he'd managed just fine when Dee was so sick she couldn't stomach the smell of fresh fruit in the house. He could deal with a four-year-old's tantrum.

"Why don't we play a different game?"

"I was *playing* a game. I want 'Angry Birds'!" Kaylie folded her arms over her chest and kicked her foot against the sofa once more for good measure. Where had the sweet, funny little girl he'd known for the past two weeks gone?

"I brought Monopoly and Old Maid." Alex kneeled down before her, offering a perfectly sound solution, at least in his opinion. He ignored the sweat rolling down his back and the panic he could feel clawing its way from his chest. He could handle this. "Which would you like to play?"

"I'd like to play 'Angry Birds,'" she said, in the calm Kaylie-voice he recognized.

"We're not playing video games right now. It's time for something different."

"Then I want a snack."

Alex took a breath. "I brought veggies and dip or we can see what's in the fridge."

"I like dip."

Alex breathed a sigh of relief. That hadn't been so hard. A little uncomfortable, but to be expected. No one liked to be told no. He pulled veggies and dip from the bag on the counter, and then read Paige's note about tableware and glasses. Kaylie picked up the serving spoon he'd set down, scooped half the container of dip out and plopped it mostly on her plate, then raked her finger through it and tasted.

"Yum. Good snack!" She devoured a little more dip while Alex dished a couple of carrots, broccoli and a sweet yellow pepper onto her plate. She pushed the veggies off. "Don't like those."

"Broccoli's good." Alex dipped a stalk and took a bite. Kaylie wrinkled her nose.

"Broccoli trees grow in my mouth. Yuk." And she dipped her finger into the dip again before licking it off.

Okay, lots of kids probably didn't like broccoli. He hadn't liked it until he was a teenager. No big deal. "How about a carrot?"

"Too crunchy." She dipped her finger again.

"A yellow pepper?"

Kaylie shook her head and her curls bounced around her face. "Pepper makes me sneeze." And she directed a fake sneeze toward the veggies.

Alex held back the chuckle threatening to escape his throat and dipped a pepper, took a healthy bite. "That's a different kind of pepper. These are sweet." He held one out. "Try it."

She shook her head furiously. "No. Don't like it."

"Just one bite?"

Kaylie clamped her lips closed and pushed her

plate across the table, straight into the dip she'd dumped onto the counter.

"How about some juice?"

She shook her head.

"A cracker?"

Another shake.

"You said you were hungry. You can't just have dip." Alex placed his hands on his hips. And then quickly shoved them in his pockets. Nineteen-fifties mom he was not.

"I'll play 'Angry Birds,'" she said and was off the stool in a heartbeat. She sprinted for the shelves and started to climb, but Alex reached her before the shelving unit could topple over on her. Heart beating fast, he spun away and set her on the couch.

"No 'Angry Birds.' No tablet. You've had enough screen time."

"I didn't scream."

"*Screen*, not *scream*." Alex sat on the coffee table so he could look directly into the little girl's eyes. "Mommy said no more tablet. So no more tablet. Do you want a snack? Or do you want to play a game?"

"You're not Mommy."

No, he wasn't. He was barely Daddy at this point, and she didn't even know that. "I'm a friend and Mommy left me in charge until Auntie Alison gets here."

"Auntie Alison will let me play," Kaylie said

in a wheedling tone. Yeah, he wasn't falling for that one.

"Nice try, kid. No tablet. No 'Angry Birds.' How about we play Monopoly?"

"Movie?" she asked hopefully.

"Nope. No screen time."

She wrinkled her brow. "I don't know what that means."

"It means no TV or movies and no video games."

She thought for a second. "Read a book?"

"Sure, what do you want to read?"

Kaylie pointed to the high shelf. "Biscuit books."

"I like Biscuit. Where are your books?"

She pointed to the shelf and offered him a sweet smile and nearly batting eyelids. "On the screen."

Alex bit back a smile. Precocious little terror. When Kaylie got an idea into her head, she didn't give it up easily. "How about an actual book? From the shelf?"

She sighed. "Okay, we'll play a game. Go Fish?"

Finally, something he knew. "I brought that game with me, too."

They were just finishing round two of the game when the house phone rang. Alison's name displayed on the ID pad as Alex picked up.

"If you're calling about dinner, I have no idea. So far Kaylie's polled for doughnuts and cupcakes."

"Who is this?" Alison's voice was creaky over the phone line and Alex's senses went on alert.

"It's Alex, what's wrong?"

"Flu. Or maybe that old wives' tale about never eating shrimp from a vending machine is really true." Alex heard a hoarse cough over the line and then the sound of retching. He shivered and held the phone away from his ear. "How did I call your number instead of Paige's?"

"You didn't. I'm at Paige's. The babysitter canceled at the last minute, so I'm filling in until you get here. Only I'm thinking it's best if you stay home." Kaylie pulled on his T-shirt hem and pointed to the fridge.

"I want juice."

Alex grabbed a box of apple juice from the fridge and handed it to her. Kaylie wandered back to the table and started dividing the cards according to color as she sipped through the straw.

"No, it's okay, I'll take some more Pepto and be there in ten minutes—" she began.

"Alison, go to bed. Pour a glass of ginger ale and keep sipping it all night. You don't want to dehydrate."

"You're a good guy, Alex Ryan. My investigator was right about you." Another round of retching and then, "Paige is a lucky girl. Tell her I said so." She hung up the phone and Alex looked at it for a long minute. He wasn't positive but that sounded like a compliment.

Alex placed the phone back on the hook, watched it for a long minute. Investigator? Tuck had told him Alison was the HR rep for the winery. Had she used her contacts to look into his past? He tried to be angry but couldn't. She was looking out for her friend and he couldn't blame her for that. Plus, he could have a little fun with Paige over it when she was home. He watched the phone for another minute before deciding not to call Paige about Alison's illness. She probably had enough on her plate with the preteen drama at the lock-in. He had this under control. He turned back to Kaylie as she placed the last blue and pink cards in their appropriate piles, a finger of dread crawling up his spine. He barely survived the past ninety minutes, could he make it through an entire night?

"Well, kiddo, it's just you and me tonight. What do you say we think about dinner?"

She cocked her head to the side and her wavy hair tumbled over her shoulders. "I want to eat dinner, not think about it."

Alex grinned. He pushed the weakness away. He conquered the video game tantrum. Paige called him to fill in, which meant she trusted him. He could make it through a single night. He was the dad.

CHAPTER ELEVEN

PAIGE PULLED INTO her drive, rubbed her dry eyes and then gave in to exhaustion—just for a moment—and laid her head against the steering wheel. The last of the third graders had knocked out somewhere between four and five this morning, which wouldn't have been so bad. But pre-knockout, there had been girl drama. There was Emily, who forgot to mention her lactose intolerance until after scarfing down two extralarge slices of pizza, and then Analeise, who decided she wouldn't talk to anyone wearing a ponytail. That included most of the girls and both chaperones. Dealing with her had been a treat. But it was over. The last of the parents had been at the school at seven-thirty. She'd done her teacherly duty and for at least another month she could use it to avoid things like bake sales and play rehearsals.

She took a breath, promising herself the biggest cup of coffee she could make—shoot, she might just drink straight from the carafe—followed by as many Cokes as she needed to get through the rest of the day without screaming for help.

Well, the coffee wouldn't make itself. She spotted mail peeking from the box on the porch. She forgot to bring it inside last night. Paige trudged up the walk, plucked the envelopes from the box and started for the back porch as she thumbed through the notices. Cable bill, bank statement. An envelope from the clinic, probably telling her what they already knew: Alex was Kaylie's father. She was too tired to deal with any of it right then so she pushed open the back door and dropped the mail onto the little side table. When she turned back to the room, Paige stopped dead.

Alex and Kaylie snuggled on her small sofa, Kaylie's head wedged between his armpit and the oversize cushion. He had one arm thrown over his eyes and the other across Kaylie's back. Her little girl feet barely reached to his knees and his legs hung over the too-short end. Both had their mouths open and were snoring softly in the quiet room. Her heart clutched at the sight. If they'd been a family, a real family, how many times would she have seen this very thing?

Would Alex have been the kind of dad who let an infant nap on his chest? Would he fall asleep telling bedtime stories?

Paige toed off her shoes and put her bag on the counter before crossing the room barefoot to turn off the bright blue TV screen. She watched them, again, for a long moment. Yeah, he'd have been that kind of dad. Would be from this point forward because it was the kind of man he was. Giving, attentive, committed. She swallowed.

Gorgeous in a rumpled tee and jeans.

She still had no clue what this situation was for Alex. Were she and Kaylie replacements? Were they the accessories he'd been missing since his wife died? Or was this something else, some new thing that he was interested in and would tire of later?

She'd been the accessory for her parents and this didn't feel like that, not even a little bit. Still, she hadn't realized she'd basically turned into her parents with the law student until she'd broken his heart. She didn't want to break any more hearts. Didn't want her own heart broken.

Or Kaylie's.

Then again, could this be that something new and shiny that would grow into a solid, sustainable relationship? The three of them. Together. A tiny piece of her desperately wanted to believe that.

After only a couple of weeks she was tired of trying to figure out what might happen. Why not just go along for the ride? She'd picked herself up before, she could do it again. Could protect Kaylie from the romantic fallout if that happened. Somehow.

She curled into a corner of the love seat and lay her head against the back. She'd just watch them until they woke, and then send Alex on his way. Coffee could wait just a few more minutes. Her eyes drifted closed.

PAIGE WAS HALLUCINATING. Exhaustion had taken over and she was losing it completely. It was the only explanation for why she smelled bacon in her living room. The only rational one, anyway, because she certainly wasn't cooking anything and there were no bacon fairies.

A light sizzle-and-pop sound met her ears. Okay, smell hallucinations were one thing. Hearing hallucinations something else entirely. Paige forced her eyes open but that only made the hallucination weirder.

Kaylie sat at the kitchen counter drinking chocolate milk and cutting bright pieces of construction paper. Normal enough.

Alex wore Paige's pink-and-red floral bib-apron—the one she used when she worked with watercolors rather than oils—and stood over the stove. He also wore the pink umbrella hat she'd bought Kaylie last summer at the concert under the St. Louis Arch.

Definitely not normal.

Paige sat up and shook herself, blinked a few times, but Alex still stood over her stove, spatula in hand, wearing her favorite apron with the umbrella hat on his head.

"What do you think, Kay?" He'd picked up her nickname for their daughter, and hearing it from his mouth made her stomach go wonky. "Are we cleared of rain for the morning?"

Kaylie hopped off the high chair and put her

hands on either side of her pressed-against-the-glass face. The day looked bright and sunny from where Paige sat.

"Nope, it's raining crocodiles and skunks out there." She climbed back onto her chair. "How's the grub?"

Alex lifted several pieces of bacon from the skillet and then poured the excess grease into a stoneware coffee mug before cracking a few eggs into the pan and stirring. Scrambled eggs, Kaylie's favorite. The lump in her throat that had been there since she'd seen them dozing on the sofa threatened to cut off her airway. He cooked. The man cooked and wore silly clothes for her daughter. Paige cleared her throat and swallowed hard against the tears clogging her throat. She wouldn't cry, not because she was overtired. Not because Alex cooking in her kitchen was completely new yet seemed as normal as the sunny October day outside her little house.

"Morning, Mama." Kaylie spun around on her chair. "We're making you breakfast."

Paige moved into the kitchen. "Good morning, kiddo." She squeezed the little girl to her side. "How was your night?"

"We played games and watched movies and Alex didn't let me play 'Angry Birds' very much but he did teach me to make a house from my Go Fish cards." She finished cutting the shape of a daisy from a piece of construction paper and then glued it to another sheet filled with a house, a boat and some wavy-cut lines that were likely grass.

"Nice picture."

"Thank you. It's our house, I'm making it for Alex so he doesn't forget."

"I'm sure he'll love it." There was that lump again, this time in her chest. She hugged Kaylie close and then turned to Alex as he scooped eggs onto plates. "Where is Alison, by the way?"

He handed her a plate. "Probably lying on her stomach in the middle of her bathroom. She called last night with either a bad case of the flu or a bit of food poisoning. So I stayed with Kaylie."

"You should have called me." Paige reached for the phone and dialed Alison's number but there was no answer. She hung up. "I would have come home."

"And leave the other chaperone solo? It was no big deal."

"Yes, it was. I hope it wasn't too trial-by-fire."

Alex shook his head, but before he could say anything Kaylie rejoined the conversation.

"I still have to draw all of us. The boat isn't ours but Alex says he likes to fish so I added it in," she said. "The house has windows shaped like stars, because I like stars, and the flowers are daisies because you like daisies. So the boat is because Alex likes to fish. And he says he'll swim with us sometime, Mama. Neat, huh?"

"That's great, sweetpea." Paige was still trying

to take in the very family-like picture Kaylie and Alex made in her kitchen. Where was the anger? The annoyance? She poked around but found nothing except the lump in her chest that meant she was in way over her head. Her daughter was falling in love with her father. Paige couldn't be angry about that.

Just go with it, Paige. Encourage the bond. He's not the kind of guy to run out on a kid.

But was he the kind of guy to drop a woman like a bad habit? She didn't have an answer for that.

"Kaylie, why don't you push the papers down the counter so we can eat? You can finish after."

"I'm not hungry," she said and glued another daisy to the paper. "I'll just have milk."

"You'll eat first," he said and put a plate in front of her.

Kaylie clenched her jaw and stared at him for a long minute. Paige waited for the explosion. Kaylie wasn't much of a breakfast eater, and she definitely had ideas about finishing projects before eating or bathing or even going to the bathroom. But the explosion didn't come. Kaylie pushed the papers across the counter and picked up her fork. Paige blinked and couldn't stop the smile from spreading across her face.

How had he done that?

"Well done." Paige accepted a plate from Alex. "Nice hat. Most men would look silly wearing a hot-pink umbrella on their head but you make it work." Alex pushed the hat off his head and set it on the counter, a sheepish grin on his face.

"We were exploring before breakfast," he explained.

Paige waved a hand. "No worries. I've been known to wear tutus and tees for backyard tea parties. Breakfast is usually a battlefield here."

He lifted a shoulder and then took a bite of his eggs. "We have an understanding."

"And?"

"I wear silly hats and play games and she follows my instructions when the time comes."

"Good luck with that when you're cooking something other than scrambled eggs and bacon." But she didn't want to harp on their differences, not when she'd had ten minutes of sleep in the past twenty-four hours. And not when he'd just experienced his solo parenting gig. "How did the veggies and dip go last night?"

Alex smirked and shook his head. "About as you'd expect. We ordered cheese pizza."

Paige took a bite of bacon and closed her eyes as flavor assaulted her tongue. "You can handle a kid and you can make breakfast. Are you sure you're a park ranger and not a nanny in disguise?"

"What's a nanny?" Kaylie piped up, talking around a mouthful of eggs.

Alex chuckled. "Like a babysitter, only a nanny lives with the family. And, no, I've never been one. I've picked up a few cooking tricks over the years, though. Mostly with breakfast food. I make a mean waffle."

"Why not a nice waffle?"

Paige giggled. Alex chuckled. Kaylie looked from one adult to the other, a baffled expression on her face.

"It's a figure of speech. He means that his waffles are really good."

Alex bent to pick a couple of paper scraps from the kitchen floor, the move outlining his butt and making Paige's mouth go dry.

Kaylie shook her head as if the adults in the kitchen had lost their minds. She pushed her plate away, announcing that her tummy was full, and then took her papers to the coffee table.

"Literal kid."

Paige nodded. "Very literal, although by the end of the day she'll have tried that expression out on at least three inanimate objects." They finished breakfast in companionable silence. Paige yawned and pushed her plate away. "That was delicious, thank you, but you didn't have to cook us breakfast."

"I figured a night with fifty eight- and nine-year-olds deserved a decent breakfast. You look tired." There was concern in his voice and it nearly did her in. But he'd been here all night, even if she was still considering how fine he looked in the rumpled tee.

Paige swiped at her hair and wiped her eyes

with the back of her hand. "Nothing a little coffee can't fix."

Alex gathered the plates and began rinsing them in the sink. "Sleep would be better."

"I'll catch a nap when Kaylie has her quiet time this afternoon." She yawned again and then snapped her mouth closed.

Alex leaned against her counter and shoved his hands into his pockets. "We had a couple of moments, but she's a great kid. Smart and funny and mostly easy to please. Why don't you go upstairs and catch that nap now?"

Paige shook her head and leaned back in her chair, needing a little space from the man taking up too much room in her kitchen. Looking too cute in a floral apron, jeans and bare feet. "I'll be fine, and you've done enough. Go home. I'll drink a pint or two of coffee and sleep like a baby tonight." She couldn't hold back another yawn.

Alex pulled her from her seat and started for the stairwell, holding her hand. It felt nice to let him take the lead and she really was too tired to make much of a fight about it. "I made it through the past sixteen hours relatively unscathed. Kaylie's no worse for the wear. Take another couple hours and get some sleep."

Bed did sound wonderful. An image of her snuggled against Alex as Kaylie had been when she walked in the door popped into Paige's mind. She shook herself. *Nope, not going there.* Holding his hand was one thing, snuggling up quite another. But sleep… The room seemed to waver before her and Paige leaned against Alex. Just for a second, until she got her equilibrium back, she promised herself. But his arms were warm and his chest solid. Paige let her eyes drift closed and inhaled, smelling the sunshiney smell that was all him.

"Are you sure? I've made it through tired days before."

Alex took off the apron and held up his hand. "Scout's honor. I have nothing else going on today. Get some rest. I don't want to see you back down here before noon."

Paige stepped onto the bottom step but her foot slipped and she landed smack against Alex's shoulder again with an "Oof."

He scooped her up in his arms and started upstairs.

"I'm fine," Paige protested but he just kept going up, up, up, forcing her to clamp her arms around his divine shoulders. Their faces were mere inches apart and the part of her body held firmly against his muscles sizzled once more. Paige swallowed. At the top of the stairs Alex stopped.

"Which way?"

It took Paige a second to understand what he meant and then she pointed down the hall to her bedroom. "I can walk."

He didn't listen and Paige didn't push. She was too tired and it felt too good to be in his arms, even after that embarrassing slip on the steps. They crossed the threshold to her room and Alex put her down and then sat beside her on the soft pink-and-brown comforter. He reached over and pushed a lock of hair off her forehead.

Paige was caught by his gaze for a long moment before finding her voice. "Thank you for breakfast."

"My pleasure." His voice was low in the room. "Thanks for calling me yesterday. It...meant a lot." He trailed his index finger along her hairline. Paige didn't push him away. She was caught, mesmerized by his gaze. Fascinated once more by his full lips and the little scar at the corner of his mouth.

"Alex."

He rested his hand against the mattress and Paige pushed her back against the headboard. "Paige."

"Th-thank you, for staying."

Paige didn't know if she swayed forward or if he leaned in but in the next moment his lips were against hers, moving slowly. Tasting, as if she might be the sweetest fruit. Paige reached her hands to his neck, feeling the smooth skin there and playing with the hair at the back of his head. She didn't care. Not about his motives or what might happen down the road. For this moment she only wanted to feel him against her. To enjoy a moment when she was Paige and not also Kaylie's mom.

She refused to feel guilty about that, and slanted her lips more fully against his, opening for him. This was so much more combustible than the kiss at the grocery store. Alex's tongue slipped inside her mouth and Paige inched forward, wanting more.

Maybe it was more to the point that she was tired of insisting she didn't want or care about him. She did. A lot. Cared about the man he seemed to be and the way she felt when he was around. The way he seemed to complete their family unit, but more than that, the way he made it okay to be a woman as well as a mom.

Alex cupped his hand around her head and pulled gently on her ponytail, slipping her hair from the band. His tongue played against hers for a long moment and then he pulled back.

He sighed and rested his forehead against hers. "I shouldn't—"

Paige shook her head and pressed her finger against his full lips.

"Don't. Don't say you shouldn't have kissed me. I leaned in, the same as you. I'm tired but I'm still in control of who I do or don't kiss."

Alex pressed a swift kiss to her forehead and stood.

Not wanting him to see just how affected by the kiss she was, Paige waved her hand toward the door. "Now get out of here so I can have that nap."

And regain a little equilibrium. God knew, she was going to need it.

ALEX COULD SENSE her presence as she stepped off
the last step and came into the living room. She
had changed from the navy-and-green tracksuit
and tee to a black-and-pink version. No shoes on
her feet, so he could see her pretty purple-painted
toes. That mass of hair was loose around her shoulders and Alex closed his eyes, remembering how
she'd looked in her room when he'd kissed her.

He pushed the thought away. Kaylie was playing
the game on her tablet—again—and Alex was putting together peanut butter sandwiches for lunch. It
felt incredibly weird and yet right to be in Paige's
kitchen, talking with Kaylie and waiting for Paige.

But he shouldn't have kissed her, not when she
was exhausted. He would apologize once Kaylie
was distracted with lunch.

He held up a sandwich. "Want one?"

"With fluff, please." Paige nodded and then
poured a cup of coffee. "Thank you. For filling
in last night and for staying this morning. I actually feel more or less human now." She sipped and
closed her eyes. "You didn't have to do any of it,
so thank you."

Okay, so apparently they weren't going to talk
about the kiss. Just as well with Kaylie in the room.

Alex called Kaylie over for her sandwich, and
once she was settled on the couch with the game
and lunch he said, "I was happy to do it. It gave
me some time to hang with Kaylie, see how things

work when you're not just a friend at lunch but the person in charge."

"Sometimes being in charge isn't all it's cracked up to be." There was a note in her voice, something he couldn't quite name that unsettled him.

"Maybe. And maybe the newness is still coloring my vision, but even the minor meltdown she had over her game wasn't that terrible."

"Minor meltdown?"

"You gave her five minutes, she wanted to finish her game and then she wanted to get three stars." Paige nodded, as if she knew exactly what he was talking about. Because she'd experienced it firsthand, no doubt. Alex took a water bottle from the fridge and drank. "How do you do it?"

"Do what?" She watched him over the mug as if she was waiting for something. Alex wondered what that something was.

"Make it look so easy. I'm exhausted after eighteen hours. You've been doing this for four years. She's a happy, healthy, smart kid. She listens, and she wants things her way but she doesn't flip out when things don't go the way she wants. How do you do it?"

Paige sat down, relief evident on her face. "I made a choice, and promised myself I wouldn't make the same mistakes my parents did. And, you know, single motherhood doesn't leave a lot of alternatives to doing it all yourself." She laughed but the sound was slightly brittle.

"It can't be easy."

"I just… My whole life I've been told what to do and how to do it and no matter what I did—or didn't do—it was never enough." Her eyes rounded and Paige put her hand over her mouth. "I didn't mean to say that. I make them sound so terrible."

"I've met them, remember? The perfect parents from *The Brady Bunch*, they aren't. So how did you turn out to be so Marcia?"

Paige shook her head. "Oh, no. Marcia was perfect. I'm so not Marcia." She chewed on her lower lip for a moment as if she wasn't quite sure what to say. "They weren't abusive, and maybe they didn't know how to add a child to their lives and still be the people they wanted to be. So I was shuffled around and trotted out for family photos or big university luncheons. I promised myself on that first visit to the clinic that if I became pregnant I wouldn't do to my kid what was done to me. I'd listen and I'd parent but she would know why things happened. Why bedtime is at seven and why we eat vegetables as well as fruit. My child would know he or she was wanted and not just an accepted responsibility."

"You make it sound so simple."

"Anything but. And she doesn't always like my explanations or rules, but we get through." Paige shook her head and then leaned her chin into the palm of her hand. Her hair swished forward and a lock fell across her face. "At the end of the day, no matter what else has happened, it's just me and her and a bedtime story. Hugs and kisses. So even if things didn't go her way, she knows that I love her. I have to believe that's been enough." She waited a beat. "These questions, is this your way of telling me you don't want to move forward?"

He caught the note that time: wariness. That he might walk away or that he might stick around. He studied her face as he said, "Not even close. I want more, and I hope that doesn't freak you out." There it was. A flash of relief. Alex let out the breath he'd been holding.

"Will it freak you out if I say it freaks me out?"

Her green eyes were wide and open, a stream of emotions running through them. Fear and excitement and nerves and something else he couldn't quite put his finger on. He had a feeling the same emotions were showing on his face. "Maybe a little. Maybe freaking out isn't all that bad in this particular situation. We seem to take parenting differently. You're calm and encouraging where I'm intense and probably a little loud. That's going to be weird, at least for a while." He looked past her to the little girl on the sofa happily blowing up cartoon monkeys and stick houses. "I'm sorry I kissed you that way, upstairs. I wanted to, but you were tired and I should have—"

She held up her hand. "I already told you not to apologize about that. I kissed you as much as you kissed me. And I hear even married couples have different approaches to parenting now and again. You might even have disagreed with your wife."

Alex rolled that thought around in his head for a moment. It was Dee who'd picked out the parenting book, just like she'd picked out those ridiculous rooster tiles that he could only now admit he didn't like. Dee who was the cheerleader in high school. He'd mentally put Dee on the swimming bench beside him the other night and admitted she would have reacted the same way Paige had when Kaylie went under.

Paige pushed away from the counter. "I'm sorry, I shouldn't have mentioned…her."

Alex was quick to reach out to her. She held his hand for a split second and continued across the kitchen to pour tea into a glass. "No, it's okay. She isn't an off-limits subject, I just realized I've been carrying around conversations she and I had about potential future children as some kind of gospel truth when they were just conversations. Talking about what might happen or how we might approach a situation." She watched him closely as he talked. How did he make her understand? "Like you said at that first barbecue, there are theories and then there is the reality of being in the middle of a meltdown when every rule or idea you thought you had is out the window."

Paige stood with her back to the counter. "We don't have to always agree. We just have to be able to talk. About her. About whatever might be happening between us." She motioned her hand between them. Alex mimicked her stance against the other counter, shoving his hands into his pockets once more because it seemed the only way to keep them from reaching for her. And what Paige needed now wasn't physical connection.

"I'm not sorry I kissed you, and I'd like to do it again sometime when you aren't exhausted and half asleep." He hooked his thumb toward the living room. "I don't know how we do this without disrupting her life, at least a little bit."

"And yours." Her voice was quiet in the kitchen, the wariness back in her expressive green eyes. "You're going from widower to father and whatever else this is in the span of a little more than a week."

"And you want to know if I'll feel the same in another month or two or a year?" Hell, so did he. Because as much as he liked being with Paige and Kaylie, when he went back to the house in Park Hills he wasn't alone. Dee was still there, in the kitchen she decorated and the furnishings she chose. In the empty flower beds and the boxes in the attic he hadn't been able to give away. Alex swallowed. But even in Dee's house he could see Paige, sometimes more clearly than he could see his wife. That scared the bejesus out of him.

What happened when he couldn't see or hear Dee at all any longer? Would Paige and Kaylie completely overshadow the good years that had come before them?

Part of him hoped they would, because when they were around the crushing grief he'd felt for the past four years wasn't there. Part of him wanted to keep Dee alive, as alive as she had been on the day that picture was taken at the lake. Because those days were real. Those days mattered.

"I can't tell you how I'll feel in a week or a month or ten years from now. I can tell you that right now this scares me. I've been Dee's boyfriend, husband and now widower for almost half my life. I'm not sure what it means that I'm moving away from that man, away from her." He took a breath and charged forward because if he didn't say this, all of this, now, he might not say it. Ever. "But I like the man I am with you and Kaylie more than when I'm Alex-the-Widower. I want to be more than him. If that's all right with you."

Paige gulped and he watched the muscles in her neck work for a long moment. "I like the woman I am with you, more than I've liked myself in a long, long time."

"Then maybe that will be enough," he said, the hopeful note in his voice sounding high and unlike him.

"At the end of the day, no matter what happens with us, I'll be here and she will also have you. We have to trust it will be enough." Paige reached across the open space, tucking her hand in his. "Are you doing anything today?"

Alex hesitated. Saturday was a day he usually spent with Dee's parents, but just last week John told him to take some time. It would be harder on Sue, but it was already past noon. She wouldn't expect him so late.

Somehow that didn't make him feel better. A trickle of guilt pressed against his shoulders. Sue and John needed him, needed to be listened to and understood. Paige caught his hesitation and plunged forward.

"It's okay. I want to drop some chicken soup off for Alison, and I thought we could take Kaylie to the park for the afternoon. October has been warm so far, but the cold weather can't be far away." Paige gathered the dishes from the counter. "I've held you up long enough. You should go, get started on your weekend plans or—"

"The park sounds great," Alex interrupted. Before another wave of guilt could crash down on him, he continued. "I didn't have anything planned but grocery shopping. I hate grocery shopping."

She turned back to him, relief evident on her face. Like he might have passed a test of some sort. No, that was wrong. Paige wasn't the type to test. She was open and honest. The kind of woman who spoke her mind and expected everyone else to do the same. Maybe he should tell her about John and Sue rather than lying about groceries.

Paige sent Kaylie upstairs to grab shoes and a jacket and then followed so she could change. Alex didn't know why she needed to. She looked more than fine to him in those black yoga pants and the stretchy tee with her feet bare and her hair loose around her shoulders.

No, he didn't need to tell her about Deanna's parents. They were his responsibility, not hers. And today was their first full day as a family. Not a lunch or a dinner and no Alison or Tuck to provide that friendly barrier.

This was not the time to rock the boat. This was the time to enjoy the rolling waves and sunshine pouring down from the sky.

PAIGE LEANED AGAINST the headboard as she turned another page in the book. Tonight she and Kaylie were reading Dr. Seuss. Kaylie pointed to the words on the page as she read the last line. Paige squeezed her close and then got up to place the book on the shelf.

"I had fun today, Mama," she said with a yawn.

"Me, too. Prayers, please." She leaned her shoulder against the doorjamb and listened as the little girl said her prayers. "Good night, sweetpea," she said and turned off the overhead light. Kaylie pushed a button and circling stars filled the darkened room from the plush night-light on the bed.

"'Night, Mama." She yawned again and settled

farther into her pillows. "Tell Alex good-night for me, too."

Paige closed the door softly and drew in a slow breath. Tell Alex good-night. Why was she playing with fire like this? She leaned against the door and closed her eyes. He seemed like such a good guy but there were so many things she didn't know. So many things she wanted to know. So many reasons to not go down this path. She looked at the closed door beside her. So many reasons to continue on this path, too.

Because today seemed like a preview of what life might be like if she allowed Alex all the way in. Playing with Kaylie in the park. Exchanging a few heated looks over peanut butter and jelly sandwiches. Knowing there was someone downstairs waiting for her, if she'd just start walking. Under every friendly smile from Alex and beneath each incidental touch Paige felt more than friendship. More than what she imagined mere coparents felt for one another. That tug of attraction she'd been fighting for the past two weeks was stronger than she realized and while Alex was busy talking and laughing with Kaylie, Paige was busy watching him. Feeling his eyes on her from time to time and wondering what it meant.

Okay, so not wondering as much as getting butterflies in her stomach because she knew when a man was interested. Alex hadn't been subtle. He also wasn't pushy. When she said no to a date he backed off. Still, she could feel him watching her when they were together and the feeling was just a little bit addictive.

It made it hard for her to keep her head and think about Kaylie, put her daughter's needs before her own. Maybe that wasn't such a bad thing. She put her fingers to her lips, remembering the feel of him against her that morning.

She wanted to do more than put her arms around his neck and hang on. God, she was jumping in too fast. They barely knew one another. She'd kissed him. He'd kissed her.

She wanted to kiss him again.

Yes, he'd dropped everything to be a fill-in babysitter the night before, made sure she got a nap this morning and then spent the rest of the day playing house.

No, not playing house. It was more than that. More than a man filling a few boring hours with a kid and her mom. It was…

Paige couldn't name it exactly so she settled for "more" and pushed away from the wall. She could stand up here in the hall all night or she could go downstairs and have a relevant, succinct conversation about what this was. She walked through the kitchen and onto the back deck where Alex sat on a lawn chair before a low blaze in the fire pit. The sharp ends of three skewers were in the flames, melting off the last remnants of marshmallow from the s'mores they'd made after dinner. He lifted his beer and drank, the movement sure. Strong. Paige forgot to breathe for a moment as she watched him.

Moving fast or not, everything he'd done from the moment he'd first come to her home told her that Alex was different. More than a widower. More than a single guy. He was trustworthy and a hard worker. What she had learned since was that he was funny and dedicated and too handsome for his own good. A good kisser. No, she didn't really know anything about his personal life other than his work and the fact that he was a widower, but that would change. He didn't know very much about her life, after all, and it didn't seem to slow him down.

Paige pulled the skewers out of the flames to cool so she could wash them later and then, with nothing else to distract her, sat in the chair next to Alex.

"So Alison tells me you had me investigated."

Paige choked on her iced tea, sputtered trying to come up with something to say. All that came out was a squeaky "It was all Alison."

He smiled and the scar in the corner of his mouth made her stomach do another barrel roll. She really had to get that to stop before her organs were on permanent anti-loop-de-loop medication.

"And what did you find out about me?"

"That you once got a speeding ticket."

"And?"

"And you played football, along with the swimming, graduated from college with honors and have been up for several promotions over the past few years but haven't taken any of them." She didn't know why she said all that. He didn't know she'd read the full report before giving it back to Alison and hoping it disappeared forever. Why didn't she shrug and say she hadn't read it?

"Anything else?"

Because if they were going to start something, she decided, it might as well start with honesty. Otherwise what was the point?

"You've never been arrested. For anything, not even as a kid." He watched her for a long moment and she couldn't tell if he was really angry or mildly amused. It was too hard to read him in the dark. Who was she kidding? It was hard to read the man in the middle of the afternoon in the bright sunshine. "And you don't have a middle name."

"Mmm. Alison is very thorough, I see."

"Are you mad?"

Alex shrugged as if he were investigated all the time. "Tuck insists she's a good egg. I figure she was just looking out for you. But if you have any other questions, you could just ask."

There was one question she was dying to ask, something the report didn't tell her about him. "What do your parents think about all this?"

He looked at her across the fire. "About you and Kaylie?" When she nodded he said, "If they were alive, I think they'd be shocked and maybe a little worried. But they would come around."

His parents were gone. Hers weren't the Norman Rockwell–painting type, but she couldn't imagine them not being around. "I didn't realize… I'm sorry."

"It happened a long time ago. Car accident," he explained. "And since we set the precedent for comparing our families to sitcom perfection, they fell somewhere between the parents from *Roseanne* and *Married...with Children*, but they were good parents."

They watched the sky for a few minutes and then Paige asked, "Are your parents why you're so willing to give up your life to be Kaylie's dad?" It was so much simpler to talk to him when there was darkness all around and a fire between them. Easier to focus on the flames.

"I don't look at it as giving up my life. I look at it as taking it back." He was quiet for a long moment before finishing his drink and taking a breath. "I miss my wife but I'm not the grieving widower. Haven't been for a long time. As horrible as cancer is, it does give you time to adjust. Say your goodbyes and come to terms with death. I kind of forgot how to be Alex in the middle of all that. You and Kaylie are helping me find him again, but you're not replacements for Deanna or the kids we might have had. If that was on your mind."

Add mind reader to his slate of talents. Was

she that transparent? Probably. Paige didn't want to know but she couldn't stop herself from asking, either.

"Can you tell me what we are, then?"

He was quiet for a long moment, peeling the label off his bottle and twisting it around in his hands. "Different, I guess." He kept twisting the bottle, watching it closely or looking into the flames, but not at her. As if he couldn't. Paige bit her tongue so she wouldn't demand a better answer than that. Because she couldn't just be along for the ride, not this time. "I don't think I can define you. Either of you. Not yet, anyway. I can tell you I haven't felt like this in a very long time."

Paige swallowed. Maybe that was enough of an answer. For now, anyway. Because, really, they'd spent a few days together, run into one another at the grocery store. Had a disagreement at a swimming lesson. Maybe it was enough that they were both unsure what any of this meant.

"Me, either. Actually, I haven't felt like this, ever." There was one more question she wanted—no, needed—to ask. "What was she like?"

"Dee?" The flicker of pain in his eyes was stark even in the dim of the firelight and it made her stomach sink. The pain was gone in an instant, swallowed up by an emotion Paige had to define as love. And that made her tummy squeeze. He loved his wife. She couldn't blame him or dislike him for that. If he still loved his wife, what could he feel for either her or Kaylie?

She was mostly wondering about what he could feel for her, she admitted to herself. Because people loved wives and husbands as well as children all the time.

"She was short, blond, had freckles. We grew up in the same school, but didn't start dating until we were in college. She was a terror to drive with and a genius at saving money. She worked at a bank in Farmington." He cleared his throat and set the bottle aside, finally looking at Paige with sincerity in his gaze. "She would have loved Kaylie. She would have been awed by your connection to her."

Paige wasn't sure how to follow that up and the fire was burning down, so she picked up the cover, put it over the dying embers and then walked to the railing to lean out and look at the stars. She picked out Orion's Belt and the Big Dipper and focused on identifying as many other constellations as she could. Anything to stop thinking about the other woman. How was she going to compete with a perfect memory? Alex joined her at the railing.

"I don't think she would mind. Not me being Kaylie's dad. Not me getting on with my life. I don't even think she would mind if you and I…" He trailed off.

"Dated?"

He shrugged. The quiet and the dark urged

Paige forward, until they were side by side, shoulders touching.

"Kissed again?" she asked.

Alex put his hand over hers, like he had so many times over the past couple of weeks. Touching her, not pushing. Letting her lead the way.

Paige's heart beat a little bit faster because this time, instead of a sizzling spark of attraction, there was a slow burn that seemed to push from her belly and through to her fingers and toes, magnifying where his hand covered hers. Burning a little hotter where her jeans-clad thigh touched his. It wasn't going away, this attraction between them. And there was no guarantee it wouldn't burn out and scorch her heart.

She had to lighten the moment. Had to make whatever happened next about them and not about his memories or her insecurities. "Which do you like better, afternoons fishing on the river or evenings watching the stars come out?"

"Stars, with fishing coming in a close second."

"Chocolate ice cream or vanilla?"

"Peanut butter, actually."

"A rebel. Okay. Why did the chicken cross the road?"

He was quiet for a long time and then he shifted his hip against the railing so he could look at her. "Because you were on the other side."

Paige's heart skipped a beat at the intensity in his eyes. *Just breathe,* she reminded herself, *just breathe.* "Okay," she finally said. She threaded her fingers with his and then put his arm over her shoulders and leaned her head against his chest. He'd made it clear what he wanted but he hadn't pushed. This was her decision.

She wanted to get to know him better. Not just because she could still feel his kiss or because she wanted him. Because he'd dropped everything to come to her rescue last night. Because he understood how terrifying it was to watch Kaylie take that leap from the swing set to the trapeze, but he'd let her do it. Because, even though they weren't completely in sync where Kaylie was concerned, she thought maybe they could be.

Alex settled her against his strong chest. "Okay?" he asked, his voice seeming to rumble through her body.

"Do you want to have dinner Wednesday night? Just you and me?"

CHAPTER TWELVE

ALEX FOLDED A clean pair of jeans and a polo into his duffel, along with his boots. Work should be relatively slow, but Wednesdays were great for scouting along the trails. He didn't want to wear his work gear to pick up Paige that evening, though. He tossed bodywash and a towel in at the last minute and then hopped in the truck as the first full rays of sunlight lit up the Missouri sky.

Her questions still stuck with him. Just what were she and Kaylie to him? Not a distraction. He'd passed the point of needing to be distracted from what his life was, without Dee, a long time ago. And not a replacement, either, because if he wanted a replacement he'd have chosen someone who looked and acted like Dee.

A few heavy, gray clouds hung low in the west as he pulled onto the highway. They might see rain before the day was over, but for now it was a perfect, crisp morning. He turned the heat up slightly.

His cell rang and he looked at the readout.

Sue. The call he'd been dreading. Alex hit a button and spoke.

"Hey, Sue, good morning."

"Alex, it's good to hear your voice." Her voice was weak, a little crackly over the line and not because of bad cell reception. This was one of her bad days, Alex guessed. "I'm calling because I need your help and John isn't here. Could you swing by the house on your way to work?"

Not really, not when the farm was fifteen miles in the opposite direction.

"Please, I only need a few minutes," she added and her voice wavered across the line once more. Alex rapped his head lightly against the side window. He wasn't being fair to Sue. Yes, he told the Parkers about Kaylie and Paige, but he could have called to officially cancel Saturday. Or made an effort to visit them on Sunday.

He could have called them from work on Monday.

He didn't do any of those things because he'd been too busy thinking about Paige. Reliving the silliness with Kaylie. Hoping with every fiber of his being that last weekend was the first of many more to come. He swallowed. Moving on with his life didn't make him a bad person.

Leaving behind the people who loved him, though, made him an ass.

Alex checked behind him but there was no traffic on the road so he pulled a U-ey and headed toward the farm. "I'll be there in a few minutes, Sue. Is everything okay?"

She didn't say anything for a long time and then "It will be. Soon enough. I'll see you in a few minutes." She hung up the phone before he could reply.

When Alex pulled under the oak tree in the side yard and shut off the truck's engine, nothing looked normal. A few pairs of John's jeans hung on the clothesline and the barn doors were open so John was already out in the fields for the morning, which was ordinary enough. But there were five other cars parked in the yard that he didn't recognize. He stepped through the back door and into a flurry of activity.

Weak and sad on the phone, Sue was bustling around the kitchen and pouring coffee for an army of her friends, who were eating coffee cake, laughing and arguing over dates. Dates for what?

"Sue?" Alex crossed into the kitchen and everything stopped.

"Alex, you made it!" Sue pressed a hot cup of coffee into his hands. "I thought you might have forgotten about us this morning."

Forgotten what? Alex squinted his eyes, looking for any sign of strain around Sue's eyes or mouth. She appeared normal. Her eyes might be a little shadowed but he had a feeling that was from the makeup she rarely used. She wore a long skirt and a pretty purple top with flat shoes on her feet. Last week there were threads of gray throughout her dark blond hair but today it was highlighted and tamed into a sleek bob. She wore the earrings and necklace Dee had given her that last Christmas. He had to be missing something but for the life of him, Alex didn't know what.

"I didn't forget. Busy morning." He played along, not wanting whatever was going on here to pitch into the overly dramatic. "What did you need my help with?"

"The girls are helping me with a Christmas present for John and we wanted your opinion, remember?" Sue ushered him to the table where her friends made room on one of the bench seats. Alex sat, feeling like he'd missed something.

"We were talking about that silent auction, you remember, when you and Dee were still in high school?" said Mrs. Grady, who wore a bright yellow tracksuit jacket with a neon-green tee.

Mrs. Briggs chimed in from across the table. "I still say auctioning off you kids was the best idea. Fall cleanup and helping the elderly get ready for the holidays. But they—" she motioned to the rest of the group "—insisted auctioning off kids was a bad idea."

Well, when she put it like that… Alex bit back a smile. "We did bring in several thousand dollars for the new stadium with those autographed footballs and baseballs from the St. Louis teams," he said.

Mrs. Briggs poo-pooed his memory. "What the older people around here need is help. Help putting up decorations, getting all the leaves mulched. Who needs a stupid old football?" She paged through the mass of pictures on the table, not waiting for an answer. "Oh, Sue, what about this one? This would be perfect for the cover, don't you think?"

Sue picked up the image—a picture of Dee before she got sick—from the scarred Formica. Sniffed and passed it to Alex.

It was the picture he still had on the mantel, and seeing it brought back a host of memories. They'd been on John's boat at Pomme de Terre for the weekend, fishing. Dee leaned forward in the picture, laughing at something he'd said—what was it that he'd said? Alex couldn't remember. Even in the black-and-white snap he could tell her eyes were the bluest of blues, that at the end of summer her hair was nearly white-blond. The freckles over her nose stood out in the frame and her hand was at her ear, tucking a lock of hair away.

Alex swallowed. Why was he not feeling anything? No, it wasn't that he didn't feel anything, because the love was still there. His fingers traced her jaw and he could almost feel the softness of Dee's skin. It wasn't that he felt nothing, it was that the feelings weren't weighed down by grief and pain now. Alex mentally poked at his heart. A tinge of sadness, but the overwhelming grief that usually took hold when he saw pictures of his wife was gone, replaced by familiar memories.

He slid the snap across the table. "It would make

a fine cover," he said, still probing for something. Some emotion that he understood, that made sense to him. "What kind of book are you making?"

"A remembrance book. Pictures of John and Deanna from the beginning until...until she got sick." Sue whispered the last word as if the weight of it was too much to speak aloud. "You don't like it." Sue's face was crestfallen and she picked up the picture, tracing her finger over Dee's face.

Mrs. Briggs stood and put her arm around Sue's shoulders, hugging her tightly. And still there was no grief over his late wife. He felt sadness for Sue's loss but that loss didn't seem like his, not any longer. At least, not like it had a year or even a month before now.

"It is perfect, Sue-sy, he likes it." Mrs. Briggs shot Alex a look, imploring him to say something.

He reached across the table, unsure what he could say that would make Sue feel better. He swallowed. "It's a fine present. I might have a few pictures in the attic you'd like to use."

"See, Sue? Alex thinks this is perfect," Mrs. Grady joined in, adding her arm around Sue's shoulders, which were beginning to shake.

And then the pain started. Not because of Deanna or the present but because he was hurting Sue. Just because he was ready to move forward didn't mean everyone around him was in the same place. Alex took Sue's hands in his and squeezed.

"Dee would love it."

And while he wasn't living in the past anymore, he wouldn't shut Sue or John out, either. He thought about his date that night with Paige. She had enough family drama from her parents without dealing with his in-laws, too. He could do this, keep his past on one side and his budding relationship with Paige on the other. People did it all the time.

He wouldn't throw Paige or Kaylie in the Parkers' faces.

He wouldn't add more drama to Paige's life.

He just needed a little separation.

ALEX WAS LATE. Paige paced to the front window and looked up and down the street once more, feeling like a clone of Mrs. Purcell as she peeked through the curtains. The street was quiet and for the first time the absolute silence grated on Paige's nerves. Where were the skateboarding kids? The teens out for a pleasure cruise in Dad's car?

Thunder rumbled in the distance. Inside where they should be, that's where.

Her cell chirped and she looked at the picture of Kaylie back-floating during swim practice. Arms pushing up toward the ceiling. Alex had lain in the backyard, pretend-swimming in the grass less than a week ago, showing her how to reach up and around with her arms. She was getting so good, and part of that was because of him. No, she wouldn't have called out the way he did, not with that kind of intensity in her voice, but that didn't make him wrong. Not exactly. Just different, and wasn't life supposed to be about accepting differences and learning to live with them? Alex had taken his share of differences on the chin—losing his wife, learning about Kaylie. And yet he still wanted to move forward with her.

Paige went over the instructions for dinner and bedtime with the high school girl who babysat Kaylie on the rare evenings Paige had to work late. The two settled into the couch with the tablet and a new game. She looked out the window again.

No blue pickup parked in front of her house.

The grandmother clock in the living room chimed the half hour. Should she text? Call? It didn't seem like Alex to be this late.

She wiped her palms on the linen legs of her trousers and tucked her hair behind her ears for at least the twentieth time. Maybe she should pull it back...

Paige picked up the phone and then put it back down. She would not call and demand to know where he was, it was silly.

People were late all the time. A honk sounded at the curb and she hurried to the window. Alex.

He jogged up the walk and rang the bell, an apologetic look on his face.

Paige put on her best Disappointed Teacher expression and teasingly said, "You're late." Her stomach growled and Alex grinned.

"You're going to love dinner." He crooked his arm and Paige slid hers through. "I'm sorry," he said as he handed her into the truck. "Paperwork."

"No problem, I was only joking." She hadn't been about to melt down, not at all. Just a friendly joke to set the mood. Alex seemed to buy the lie. He slid behind the wheel and drove them out of town. "Are you and Tuck still working on end-of-the-season spreadsheets?"

He cut a glance in her direction. "How did you know what we were working on?"

"I have my mysterious ways."

"Tuck told Alison?"

"So maybe my ways aren't so mysterious. At least she didn't have a private detective watching you." Alex laughed at that. "What do spreadsheets have to do with rangering?"

Alex explained about visitor numbers and funding, making his job sound much more regimented than the hiking, suntanning and fishing he'd told her about before. She knew he'd only kidded her about the tanning, but this part of his job seemed almost…clerical. It didn't fit with the vibrant, outdoor guy she'd come to know.

"We used to have a secretary who took care of all that while we did the ranger thing. Budget cuts." He shrugged. "At least it puts my accounting background to good use." He pulled onto the interstate road.

"Where are we going?"

"St. Louis."

"But it's a Wednesday." She had school in the morning, an alarm that would sound by six so she could wrangle Kaylie out of bed and get cereal into her tummy before the mad rush to the elementary school. The thought of spending a long evening with Alex was nice, though. An entire evening of adult conversation, some light flirting. Maybe another kiss or two.

She could always double up on the coffee and go to bed at the same time as Kaylie the following evening.

"And a date is a date no matter what evening it falls on. I thought about taking you to the Low Bar or maybe the Chicken Hut in Farmington." There was something else in his voice, some emotion she couldn't quite put her finger on, but that made her think tonight wasn't just a flirting, kissing, first-date kind of thing. Then that note was gone and he was just Alex. "But seeing as we're adults with a kid and all, I thought real food and atmosphere were called for."

Paige's belly did a little flip. Strange note in his voice or not, the way his voice rumbled over the word *atmosphere* pushed her worries to the back of her mind. "And we're going to find that atmosphere at…"

Alex grinned. "You'll see in about forty minutes. How was school today?"

He kept her talking and Paige was grateful. The

more she talked the less nervous she was about what they were doing. Going out. On a date. Kaylie had a babysitter, and Alex hadn't yet mentioned their daughter. This was definitely a first date. Which was why the weird anticipation/nervous energy she felt was so off. She'd been on her share of first dates. Maybe not any with these kinds of implications, but in the grand scheme of things a first date was just that and if things didn't work out…

No, she was not going there. She was staying in the present and thinking about tonight. Not tomorrow or the next day or ten years from now. It was a beautiful Wednesday evening in October and she was twenty-nine for another ten days. That was enough.

As they drove along the interstate the changing leaves caught Paige's attention. She pulled out her phone to take a couple of pictures. They weren't great but she could work with them for a school project with her older students or maybe come up with a finger-painting plan for the kindergartners.

Traffic slowed as they drove closer to the city, and as they topped a rise Paige drew in a breath. St. Louis at night was breathtaking, the glowing streetlights like the intricate string of fairy lights she'd hung in Kaylie's bedroom last year. A million cities around the world probably looked just the same, but for her St. Louis was the best. Brilliant spotlights lit up the Arch in the distance and as they crossed over into downtown she saw two old paddle wheel boats carrying diners up and down the Missouri River.

Of all the places her parents had taken her on vacations, and even when she'd been away at boarding school nearby, St. Louis was the place she thought of when life got to be too much. She rolled down her window just a bit and under the smell of car exhaust she smelled the grass and the river.

Fall in Missouri. It was home.

Alex pulled to a stop before a small bistro near the Arch, handed his keys to the valet and helped Paige from the truck. A hostess in a smart black dress showed them to a table overlooking the river. She had been to nicer places, primarily as a tagalong with her parents, but the combination of view, lighting and Alex paled the other places.

"This is too much." Her eyes widened. She hadn't meant to say that aloud, but the words didn't seem to faze Alex.

He looked over the menu, chose a wine and when the hostess disappeared said, "I promised you atmosphere."

"A promise of atmosphere doesn't mean you have to waste an entire paycheck on one dinner." But it was certainly a lovely way to spend an evening. She could see lights from the river barges and steamboats every so often, and the Arch to her left. Hushed conversations swirled around them, none close enough to hear, but loud enough to drown out the nerves threatening to take her under once more.

"So, here's how I see this evening playing out," Alex said, his voice serious and his hands clasped on the crisp linen tablecloth. "We're going to have a nice dinner and enjoy this great view. Then we'll turn into pumpkins tomorrow when you go back to elementary school and I hike around the park." That wicked grin glinted in the soft light and Paige chuckled.

"Is this your way of saying, 'Enjoy the moment, Paige'?" she asked.

"It is."

The waitress filled their glasses. Alex held his up. "What do you say?"

Paige waited until she left and then lifted her glass. "I say you forgot one thing we're going to do tonight."

"Really?"

She nodded. "You remembered dinner and the great view. You didn't say anything about a walk along the river."

"I thought that was implied."

"I don't like implications. I like things to be spelled out. Teacher and mom, remember?"

"Then here's to a night filled with atmosphere, good food and a walk. And since you like things spelled out, a good-night kiss." Alex clinked his glass against hers.

They placed their orders. Paige wasn't sure what to say. The old Paige would flirt, keep that kiss conversation going. Maybe play a little footsie under the table. She hadn't been on a date, not with anyone she was this attracted to, since she'd locked the old Paige in a box and shoved her under the bed. Alex didn't seem to mind the silence. He looked out the window at the steamboats on the river as if they fascinated him.

He was an outdoors kind of guy. Maybe they did. Why not find out?

"What is it that you do? You know, when you aren't hiking and suntanning and filling in spreadsheets?"

"I make a killer mac and cheese. The odd last-minute babysitting gig."

She grinned and sipped the wine. "I'm serious. This is a date. Dates are when people get to know one another. What is it that you do?"

Alex shifted in his chair. "I play basketball, although that used to be a lot more fun than it is now. Bad knee. Tuck keeps asking me to join the Low Bar Bowling League with him but I'm pretty sure joining that league means I have to grow a mullet, so I've avoided it so far."

"A mullet is not a good look. Good idea on the avoidance."

He grinned. "I thought so."

"What else?" Paige crossed her legs under the table and her toes curled when they lightly brushed against his khakis.

"I don't know. I work, I mow the lawn. Nothing incredibly special."

"Why not something special?" He made her curious, not just because he was holding back. She could see him measuring his words, and that was okay. First date, she reminded herself. And he likely hadn't been on one in longer than she had. Mostly he made her curious because beneath the laid-back ranger facade she knew there was more to him. A man didn't just go against family tradition or turn down an accounting degree to hike the Missouri wilderness.

"Hiking is kind of that thing for me. When I'm out there, even though I'm on the job, it isn't work. It's me and nature. I guess that's all I need."

"I've never been much for hiking. Or anything that leads to sweaty, smelly clothes at the end of the day."

"Employ a yard boy, do you?"

She fluttered her eyelashes at him and executed her best Deep South accent. "As any Southern woman with breeding would."

Alex's laugh was deep and rumbly and did funny things to the tiny hairs at the nape of her neck. Her skin seemed to prickle and she couldn't resist leaning across the table.

"Tell me about your favorite place to hike."

He was quiet for a long moment. "At the far end of St. Francois Park there is an overlook. You can climb to the top and it's almost like you could touch the sky. I know full-on mountain ranges are a lot taller, but the county spreads out below with some of the old quarry hills glinting in the sun, tall grasses blowing. In the summer you can see the corn and wheat fields in the distance. Maybe catch a cloud of dust from a tractor. It's so quiet that if a chipmunk moves in the trees you can hear it, and even if you go there alone, you're surrounded by life."

"That sounds lovely." Paige twirled her glass by the stem. She was surrounded by her students all day and had Kaylie at home in the evening hours. She thanked her lucky stars to have a friend like Alison in her corner. Still, there were times she felt totally and utterly alone. Like she might be the only single twenty-nine-year-old in St. Francois County. "That picture you sent me, of the barn, is it near there?"

He shook his head. "It's at the corner of the property so I don't get there as often as I'd like. We stay on the main trails for the most part because those are the most trafficked areas." He leaned in to the table. "And what is it you do? When you aren't teaching art to ruffians in the public school system, I mean."

Paige chuckled. Her mother hadn't called her students ruffians but the implication was clear in every conversation at every lunch and dinner: Paige was wasting her time teaching art. She should be creating it. Dot couldn't see that teaching her students was creating, and that painting for her daughter or friends was enough for Paige. The way Alex said it made the words okay. Like it was their joke and that he understood teaching art was the better use of her time. He got it.

"My mother is pretty transparent, isn't she? She means well, but she's just never understood that her dreams for me aren't my dreams for myself. I always thought she'd come around. So far she hasn't." Sometimes Paige wondered if her mother ever would come around. If her father would ever be even a shadow of the TV dads she'd wished for growing up. She was too old for wishes but as the first star twinkled through the city lights, she considered wishing one more time.

She changed her mind and wished instead for another night like this one. Talking with Alex. Flirting a little. Getting to know him. Changing her life, once more, in a way that would bring her what she wanted: a family.

"It kind of sucks when our parents don't live up to our expectations, doesn't it?"

More than sucked, even for a woman who was about to turn thirty. "This is a date, though. Let's not get all maudlin over my poor-little-rich-girl childhood."

Alex was quiet for a moment, like he wanted to say something else. There was an emotion on his face that she couldn't decipher and then it was gone.

"What is your dream? Other than teaching art and being one hell of a single mom?"

"I do juggle those hats well, don't I?" Paige finished the wine and Alex topped her glass off once more. "I want to paint a mural. At the school, I think. Something that takes up an entire wall, and I want the kids to help. Kind of put their own stamp on the school."

"Not fair, that's a work-related dream."

She lifted a shoulder. "What can I say? My work is my passion."

"Is any of your reluctance to send something to that art guy a reflex against your mother's dreams?"

"Not fair, we're not talking about my parents, remember?"

"I'm not asking why your mother is so desperate to see one of your paintings at the St. Louis Museum of Art. I'm asking why you aren't."

"I didn't say I don't want that." She did. A little corner of her heart wished she were good enough, not for her mother's sake. For her own. Because when she painted she got lost in the moment, in the act of creating. Seeing other people get lost in her work would be…amazing, she decided.

"You didn't say you do."

Paige fiddled with the linen napkin in her lap for a moment. She straightened her shoulders and looked into Alex's eyes. "Because I'm not good enough. And I don't want some favor to my mother to be the reason people wonder why an average painting of a daisy is in a gallery filled with Monets and Baroccis."

"I'm no critic, but it didn't seem average to me."

She offered a smile, hoping that and the dim lighting would hide the pain she felt from her eyes. "And my paintings aren't average to me, but I'm not foolish enough to think I'm on par with any of the masters. My mother, on the other hand, doesn't care if I have the actual talent as long as she can lay some sort of claim to a piece of displayed art in a major museum. For a long time I played along with her game. Then I decided it was time to stop playing and go after what I really wanted."

"And what is that?"

"A real life. With real friends. The kind of life that's filled with memories as vivid as the clips they show on those sitcom flashback episodes. That's my dream. You know, along with that mural at the school."

Alex lifted his glass again. "To dreaming, then."

Their dinners arrived and for a short while neither spoke as they enjoyed the meal. Finally Alex said, "Did you really compete for Miss Missouri in college?"

"Who—who told you that?"

"I had you investigated," he joked.

"Alison told Tuck and Tuck told you." Paige's face burned. She was going to kill her friend. Friends didn't have pillow talk about their friends with their boyfriends. But there was no going back and erasing that colossal mistake. "I did. And I played the water glasses as my talent."

Alex choked on his drink. "You're kidding, right?"

"It was that or paint something live and, well, that first day you saw what I'm like when I paint. I'd have killed my formal gown with splatters."

"How do you play water glasses?"

Paige lined up the glasses on the table—two filled with wine and two filled with water, all at different levels—and pushed her finger around the rim. A low hum sounded from the fullest glass, and when she switched to the water glass with barely a sip left, the low hum changed to a higher octave.

Alex clapped softly. "Where did you learn to do that?"

"Boring dinner party with Hank and Dot when I was nine. Mother grounded me for a week."

"So you stopped?"

Paige shook her head. "I played them louder. Ended up being a four-week sentence."

"I guess now I know where Kaylie gets her stubborn streak."

"Yep, comes by it naturally," Paige said proudly.

Alex signaled the waiter and paid the check but instead of getting into the truck, he took Paige's hand and started toward the walk along the river. Fairy lights hung low from tree branches and spotlights on the Arch were bright in the night sky. Although the evening was warm, only a few other pedestrians walked with them. Alex led them up the stairs to the Arch, where they circled and then started back along the path to the restaurant. This time the silence didn't bother Paige. She just enjoyed the sounds of the night and the nearness of Alex.

The last of the steamboats docked and Alex paused so they could watch the crew set the ropes and get the walkway ready for passengers. He pulled Paige to his side and they continued on to a quiet area filled with trees and a few park benches.

"I was thinking about Sunday and the weekly barbecue," Paige said.

"I'm uninvited already?"

She poked him in the ribs as they walked. "I was thinking Tuck and Alison should have some alone time. My parents don't know about all this yet, but they probably should. You know, they were distant and cold and they still want to run my life, but it isn't fair to them. Not knowing about your relationship with Kaylie. So what if we make it an us-and-them thing, without the friend buffer?"

He took her hand in the darkness. "And what about my relationship with you?"

"That, too." Her words were a whisper in the dark, beneath the tree branches with stars and fairy lights twinkling above them.

"I'd like that. If you're sure?"

Paige nodded, glad he couldn't see her face in the dark. Because she wasn't ready, not really. There would never be a good time to tell her parents Kaylie had a father and the father was a park ranger. Alex and his job were great in Paige's mind, but Hank and Dot were two completely different people. "Would you like to invite the Parkers? We might as well all start getting to know one another."

The thought of meeting his former wife's family made Paige's stomach lurch, but it wasn't like he didn't have a past. This was one date, but she wanted another.

Alex was quiet for a long time before he spoke. "I don't think that is a good idea," he finally said and something painful stabbed at Paige's heart. "I told them about Kaylie. It didn't go well. I'm not sure they're ready to actually meet her. Or you."

He kept hold of her hand, but Paige sensed a distance between them, brought on by whatever was happening with his in-laws. She didn't like that their pain or whatever it was was pushing against Alex. A hot ribbon of anger streaked through her when she thought of them not liking Kaylie solely based on the fact that Paige, and not their daughter, was her mother. That was quickly followed by icy coldness at the thought of Kaylie dying and some other woman trying to take her place in the far distant future. Paige swallowed.

"Then we should give them more time. I'll call my parents, but we'll wait for the full-on family introductions."

Whether they were still dating in a few months or not, she would always be Kaylie's mom. He would always be Kaylie's dad. Whatever was starting between them seemed solid and she wanted to test the boundaries, but not at the risk of causing Alex more pain. If he wasn't comfortable inviting the Parkers to lunch she would wait.

She was used to waiting.

CHAPTER THIRTEEN

"Do you have those pictures?" Sue's voice was quiet over the phone. It was Thursday morning and Alex was hiking along Mooner's Hollow again, taking advantage of another Indian summer day because surely there weren't many left. Cold winds would begin pouring in, dropping the temperatures. There would be an ice storm, maybe two, and then a few light snowfalls before spring thawed the ground and he was able to get back out onto the trails. Maybe he could convince Paige to bring Kaylie out, before it got too cold.

Maybe they could come out, just the two of them, for a picnic.

He'd been daydreaming about Paige. Again. Thinking about kissing her under the trees last night. Thanking whatever lucky star shined down on him that she didn't push when he said he didn't want John and Sue to come to the barbecue. Keeping her separate from his past, or the past away from her, had seemed like a simple thing in theory. One little test of the decision, though, and he got antsy.

"Alex?" His mother-in-law's voice brought him back to reality. "Do you have the pictures you mentioned the other day?"

Pictures, pictures. Attic. The remembrance book for John. That picture of Dee on the lake as the cover. In the attic were two boxes of scrapbooked pictures and several Dee never got around to putting into books.

"In the attic. Do you have any idea which pictures you'd like?"

"How could I know that when I haven't seen them?" This time her voice held acid and crackled over the line. This was the Sue he remembered. The Sue who took no prisoners, had plans and didn't take guff from anyone. Not that he was throwing guff; he thought she would have an idea which pictures she wanted. She'd helped with the books, after all.

Not that he would risk getting her more upset by pointing that out.

"I meant types," he tried as cover. "Casual, portraits. I can go up in the attic tonight and pick some out."

Sue sighed over the line, the sound long and mournful. "I hoped you wouldn't mind if I came over. If that wouldn't be too much bother."

Alex tilted his head left and then right, as if that might relieve some of the tension pouring over him. Sue wanted to come over and it likely had nothing to do with the pictures. If he knew his mother-in-law this visit would be about walking down memory lane. Making sure he was still… what? In mourning? God, was him spending a single Saturday away from the Parker farm such a big deal? He wiped his hand over his brow and then pulled the black ball cap from his back pocket. Looked into the distance.

It was Thursday. He had no plans. There was no chance Paige would show up at his home unannounced. They weren't at that point of their relationship. He could invite Sue and John over for a quick dinner, and while John watched *Thursday Night Football* Sue and Alex could look at a few pictures in the attic.

Only he didn't want to do that, not really. Not tonight. Not when he was working so hard to make this work with Paige. It felt like a betrayal of sorts. He was thirty-two years old and he wanted a life again.

"I can see I've overstepped," Sue said, her voice brittle. Angry. Maybe a little bit scared. "I thought you meant it when you said this new part of your life wouldn't take you away from us."

Damn it, now he'd upset her even more because the fear outweighed the anger as Sue spoke. It was the fear that got to him. *Separate boxes, remember?* Paige was in Bonne Terre. The Parkers just outside Farmington. He was the middle ground, in Park Hills. Simple enough to invite them over for dinner, and do the family thing. Then he would call Paige tomorrow and set something up with her.

He could balance it. Balance the past and the present. Neither had to disrupt the future he wanted to build.

PAIGE SETTLED AGAINST the sofa and read Alex's text.

Should I bring anything?

It was Saturday morning and, just like Monday through Friday, Kaylie was still sleeping. Paige, on the other hand, had forgot to turn off the alarm, and once she was awake there was no going back to sleep. She'd decided today should be a fun day—swimming at the indoor rec pool, and before she could change her mind she'd invited Alex to join them.

Just yourself. Swim trunks. I know rangers are always supposed to be prepared, but I don't think the lifeguards would appreciate you swimming in jeans.

It was a natural progression. Meeting with Kaylie with a group of people, coming to her lesson. Their first date and now a playdate with just the three of them. Normal. And the fact that he didn't want his in-laws at the barbecue on Sunday was understandable. Why put pressure on them when neither Alex nor Paige were positive where the personal part of their relationship was going?

She wasn't upset, not at all. His extended family, his prerogative. That scary little voice that kept bringing his reluctance up, kept reminding her of the mistakes she made in the past, could go to hell.

You just want to see if my bottom half is as tanned as my top half, don't you?

Paige chuckled. She did wonder, mostly because her summer tan was long gone but Alex's was still holding on.

If I wondered about that, I'd have said to leave the trunks at home.

Too late, she realized how that sounded.

I swear I did not mean it that way.

A moment later her cell pinged and the light burn on her cheeks deepened.

You're blushing, aren't you?

Paige texted back a nodding head.

See you in a couple of hours. With trunks.

ALEX WAS EARLY. He jumped into the warm pool water and swam a lap, just to take the edge off. He needed to be relaxed. Pleasant. The Alex he'd been after another text-flirting incident with Paige.

Instead, his insides felt balled up. He couldn't stop clenching and unclenching his fists. He shouldn't have taken the call. When Sue and John's home number had popped up on his caller ID Alex's first instinct had been to ignore it. Thursday-night dinner hadn't gone well. Sue brought food, as she always did. Food that was themed "Deanna and Alex." Dee's favorite veggie casserole, Alex's favorite dessert. John watched football while Alex showed Sue the boxes of pictures he brought down from the attic. Held her hand as she cried over their vacation albums. Scolded him because he didn't finish the projects Dee left behind.

Reminded him—over and over—that Dee had treasured her memories. Which had to mean Alex didn't. That he was trampling all over their memories because of Kaylie. Thank God she didn't know about Paige.

Friday morning she called in a panic because a storm blew their power and John had left for the day. Alex hurried to the farm reset breakers to find a hot breakfast on the stove and cold orange juice on the table, which would have been impossible to make. Added to that, John would never leave Sue home without power. He bit back the sharp tip of his annoyance at Sue's manipulations and reset the breaker. Was firm when he turned down her breakfast invitation.

She turned on the waterworks a moment later, telling him how distant John had become over the past weeks. Blaming it on Alex's absence from their lives.

John didn't seem absent to him. They'd talked on the phone a few times. Texted when the Rams won their first game of the season. He was fine at dinner on Thursday, but Sue didn't want to hear that and the more she carried on, the less Alex wanted to listen. He'd snapped at her, damn it, snapped when she just needed a little attention.

He swam harder, trying to push the hurt look in her eyes away with his own exhaustion, but it didn't work. He could still hear her voice. Could still feel the pain in his chest because he didn't want to hurt her, but he couldn't run to her rescue every five minutes.

Not any longer.

He completed five more laps of the pool before Kaylie's high-pitched squeal rent the air.

"Alex! Mama lost her swimsuit," she exclaimed, kicking her flip-flops toward an empty chair as she ran across the floor.

"Walk!" Paige and Alex both exclaimed and Kaylie skidded to a stop, dropping her towel in a puddle.

"Sorry, no running. I 'member." Her leggings

and tee were next to hit the damp floor and then she fiddled with the buckle on her swim bubble.

"I didn't lose the suit, sweetpea. I just forgot it was in the dryer. Sorry we're late." She picked up the towel and spread it over a nearby chair to dry before offering Alex a quick wave. "I see you've cleared the place for us."

He shrugged, and just like that the annoyance at Sue was gone, replaced by Paige and Kaylie. "I have my ways."

"I supposed you ordered up the sunny day, too, just to make sure everyone enjoyed what could be the last warm day of the year?" Paige clipped the bubble in place on Kaylie's back and the little girl cannonballed into the pool.

"What can I say? We rangers have connections in all the right places." Kaylie swam over to him and demanded he watch her sink under the surface and hold her breath.

Alex watched but his focus was on Paige, still sitting on the poolside bench. He sank to the bottom with Kaylie and quickly kicked to the surface. Blew the water from his nose and tried to refocus on Kaylie. But Paige still held his attention.

She sat on the bench seat, untying her shoes. Her tankini top skimmed over her flat tummy to rest just above the waistband of her jogging pants. Once her feet were bare she hooked her thumbs into the pants and pushed them over her hips, revealing a long expanse of creamy white legs, delicate knees and ankle bones his mouth begged to taste.

Alex's mouth went dry as he watched her and the fact that she was oblivious to him made it all the more enticing. She wasn't putting on a show, not with Kaylie in the pool. This was Paige being Paige. Natural.

Sweet.

Sexier than anything he'd seen in longer than he cared to remember.

"What did you think, Alex?" Kaylie splashed around him, having given up on him counting while she held her breath. She flicked water toward him but the water did nothing to cool his reaction to the woman across the room. Kaylie splashed again and Alex forced himself to refocus.

This day was about Kaylie, not getting wet and wild with her mother.

Well, not yet, anyway. Paige finished folding the clothes into her oversize tote and walked to the side of the pool. Her legs were firm, her toes painted a delicate pink, and for the first time she didn't have splatters of oils or watercolors across her feet. He kind of missed those speckles of color.

She dove into the pool and surfaced a few feet away. Pushed her wet hair away from her face and joined Kaylie in splashing around the shallow end of the pool and singing silly songs. When Kaylie paddled off to push plastic boats around the ladder area Alex turned to Paige.

"You look amazing."

She blushed. "I, uh… Thanks for coming today. Kaylie hasn't stopped talking about swimming with you since I woke her up this morning."

"Thanks for inviting me." He swam closer to her and his lightly kicking feet connected with hers. Through the water he felt a burst of heat. He cut his eyes toward the lifeguard stand but the teen in the chair seemed more intent on the book in his hands than on the people in the pool. Kaylie was perfectly safe at the ladder with her bubble on. "I have this overwhelming urge to kiss you," he said, pulling her into his arms and then kicking out of the deep end until he could set his feet on solid ground. He wrapped his arms around her waist but Paige pushed away.

"That isn't a good idea."

"It's a great idea."

She kicked away, putting a few inches of space between them. "Not with Kaylie at the other end of the pool."

"She's going to figure it out soon enough."

"Figure what out?"

"That we're dating. That we kiss like the princes and princesses in her movies."

PAIGE DIDN'T WANT to be the voice of reason. Didn't want to be the grown-up who was too old to make out at the pool.

But that was what moms did. They were the

voice of reason even when it took all their strength not to reach out and touch the muscled chest of the hot guy before them.

"Even so, I'd prefer to have the conversation with her at home and not in the locker room at the rec center," she said primly.

A devilish light came into Alex's eyes and he swam toward her. Paige backed away but he just kept coming. She turned, put her face in the water and struck out for Kaylie's corner of the pool, not caring if she was the prissy girl who wouldn't kiss the guy in the pool.

She'd nearly gone up in flames when he mentioned wanting to kiss her.

Paige had the feeling if he actually followed through the heat from his touch would empty the entire pool of water. She reached Kaylie just as Alex's hand closed around her ankle. She held on to the side, inviting Kaylie to join their game of chase. It seemed like the best option.

After all, he was chasing her.

She wasn't opposed to him catching her, as long as it wasn't in the pool with her daughter a few feet away. At least not just yet. Maybe when Kaylie knew everything.

Maybe when the relationship was on more solid ground and Paige could answer the questions she knew would come with certainty and not just wishful thinking.

The three of them played in the shallow end for

an hour, blowing bubbles in the water, practicing Kaylie's favorite strokes and racing the small plastic boats around the entry steps.

Paige caught Alex watching her several times and the look in his eyes wasn't one of fun. Her toes curled when his hand innocently brushed her shoulder. Her abs tightened as the back of his hand came in contact with her belly. She fanned herself. She was burning up and it had nothing to do with the water temperature and everything to do with the man floating on his back in the deep end of the pool.

Alex worked with Kaylie on her floats and then her arm movements and the little girl ate up the attention. Paige's heart clutched. She was a good mom, she knew that, but the more Alex was around the more obvious it was that Kaylie had missed something in her life.

No, not something. Someone.

"Kaylie, focus." Alex's voice brought her out of her thoughts and back to the pool. "Watch my hands, see how they turn when I point to the ceiling?" He demonstrated but Paige was more interested in her daughter than Alex's swimming abilities.

Her daughter's eyes were wide and attentive, but she was tired. Breathing heavily even with the bubble helping her stay afloat. She was exhausted, Paige realized. An hour in the pool was easy when you could touch the bottom but not so simple when you had to kick the entire time.

"Alex—" she began but Alex cut her off, intent on Kaylie reaching up and over in her back float with the proper form. Kaylie tried again but her little arms were too tired to hold the form and she dropped them into the water before her finger-tips could point toward the ceiling. Kaylie's face crumpled and Alex pressed his lips together in frustration.

He isn't used to this part of it, Paige reminded herself. He wasn't used to the limits even rambunc-tious and energetic children had, not used to teach-ing on a toddler level rather than an adult one. Still, she couldn't keep the frustration from her voice.

"Alex." Finally, she caught his attention. "She's had enough."

He looked at Kaylie, really looked, and Paige saw his face pale when he took in the little girl's exhaustion and the fierce glint of determination in her eyes. Paige gathered Kaylie to her, holding her up, but she kept wriggling.

"I want to try." She repeated the words as Paige held her still. "I can do it. Just like Alex."

He sank into the water, his arms making ripples in the waves as he reached to push a wet strand of hair off Kaylie's face. "No, sweetpea," he said, "you've tried hard enough. Let's just have a float, no kicking." He turned his troubled gaze to Paige and mouthed an "I'm sorry" as she floated on her back, pulling Kaylie by her little hands. Paige shook her head.

"It's okay," she said, reassuring him.

The three of them floated for a few minutes, meandering around the shallow end. Kaylie soon became interested in the little boats and returned to the steps to sit in the water and play. Alex took Paige's hand.

"I wasn't paying attention, not to what was going on. How did I not see how frustrated and tired she was?"

Paige squeezed his hand in hers. "She doesn't let on when she's tired. But in the end, nothing terrible happened. We took a break and we'll try again another day. It isn't a big deal."

"I won't be one of those parents." He said the words fiercely and steely determination glinted in his gaze. "I won't be the dad who relives his own athletic achievements through his child. You have to check me on that." He shook his head. "No, that isn't fair, either. I'll check myself. Check my expectations at the door and focus on encouraging her. Like you."

"That isn't what she needs, though. I could probably stand a little of your intensity. You could use a little of my laid-back approach." Paige looked to the shallow end and, seeing Kaylie was still occupied with her boats, kicked her feet to float on her back. She reached a noodle and flipped over, still floating but using the noodle to hold her weight.

"We don't have to mirror one another's strengths. We have to be what she needs, and the kid has a talent for swimming."

Paige realized the words weren't just a comfort for Alex, who kept a watchful eye on Kaylie and her toys. He thought not only that he'd overstepped, but that he might have put Kaylie in danger. He hadn't. He wouldn't. Paige didn't need a crystal ball to tell her that; she only had to watch him with the little girl. Wearing Paige's apron, playing silly breakfast games. Showing her over and over, patiently for the most part, how to use her hands to swim better. Alex would never put Kaylie in danger, not on purpose.

He took another noodle and together they watched Kaylie in the shallow end, their legs tangling beneath the water from time to time. "I was thinking," he said after a few minutes, "that you're right about the barbecue. I'm not sure my in-laws are completely ready for this, but I think the sooner we all start interacting the better. If you still think it's a good idea?"

A shot of victory poured into Paige's heart. Another step forward; just one step, but it seemed like a leap forward. She nodded. "I think it's a great idea."

Alex spent the rest of day with them, treating them to hamburgers for lunch and helping Paige grill chicken for dinner. He didn't try to kiss her again. Didn't tease or taunt her the way he'd done in the pool, but that didn't ease the tension Paige felt every time his hand brushed hers or she caught him watching her.

Because he would kiss her. She would kiss him back. It was the best tension she had felt in a long, long time.

"Can Alex sleep over sometime? Like Auntie Alison does at Thanksgiving before we shop?" Kaylie asked when Paige pulled the covers over her at bedtime. "We could camp in the backyard. He has a tent," she said hopefully.

"Maybe." If she couldn't slow things down, Paige had a feeling he'd be sleeping over before Kaylie knew the truth about him. She might have promised to have an open and honest relationship with her daughter, but Paige wasn't ready to let her know that Alex had come over to do more than just camp out in the backyard. "Sleep, sweetpea, we have a big day tomorrow."

Kaylie's eyes drifted closed as she said her prayers, and when Paige turned out the light she turned onto her side, snuggling her favorite yellow bear to her.

Alex sat on the sofa in the family room when she returned downstairs. He'd paused an old sitcom episode and patted the cushion beside him. Paige pulled two bottles of beer from the fridge, offered him one and then joined him.

"Today was a fun day," she said.

"One of the best Saturdays I've spent in a long time." He took a long pull from the beer but didn't restart the show. "I'm sorry for overstepping at the pool."

Paige held up her hand. "We talked about this. Kaylie was fine—"

"Not about her," he interrupted, "about kissing you. I wanted to, but you were right. We have to be careful about what she sees for a while longer. She might not understand."

"It isn't like I don't want to kiss you," Paige began. "It was more that I don't know how to explain it all. Not you being her father. Not what it means when you kiss me. This is total uncharted territory for me because since she was born I've been on exactly two dates and both were friendly kinds of things."

"If it makes you feel any better, I haven't been on a date in eight years. Not since before I was married." His voice was quiet in the room and Paige caught another flash of emotion she couldn't define on his handsome face.

She turned her body so she could rest her elbow against the sofa back. Then tilted her head against her fist. "None?" She couldn't imagine a man as good-looking as Alex had a hard time attracting women. Even if he wasn't interested, wouldn't they have tracked him?

"There was one, but it wasn't a date so much as an…an incident."

Paige's eyes went wide. "You had a one-night stand."

Alex shifted uncomfortably. "After one of the rec leagues. She wanted to, and I didn't not want to. But it wasn't a date, and I never saw her after that."

"Are you apologizing to me for something you did before you ever met me?"

"Not apologizing. Explaining, maybe. This is weird, talking about a one-night stand and not dating and my former wife with the woman I'm dating now."

Paige's heart glowed at the words. "We're dating?"

"Yeah." He raised his startled gaze to hers. "Aren't we?"

Smiling, Paige nodded. "I didn't think we were defining it."

"I definitely think we should." He leaned closer, until his words were a whisper against her cheek. Paige swayed forward.

"And what is your definition?" she asked as his lips descended on hers.

His mouth was hungry against hers, as if he might devour her. Which wasn't far from the truth. The more he was around, the more Paige felt Alex destroyed all reasons to keep her distance. Right now, on the sofa with his lips on hers, with their knees touching through denim and his hands pressing on either side of her thighs, she didn't care about their destination.

She only cared about following the trail of his lips as they nibbled along hers, tasting and then following her jaw until he reached the sensitive spot behind her ear.

Paige's head fell back, and Alex pressed forward, his hands spanning her waist and his thumbs playing with the strip of skin between her jeans and tee. He shifted again and canned laughter poured into the room. Paige stiffened as Alex drew back. He breathed hard, just as she did. The look in his eyes was dangerous, as if by muting the television he might strike down the laughing viewers. Paige giggled. Alex hit the button to do so, then dropped the remote onto the coffee table and sighed.

"I think I'm a little rusty at this."

"I think we're both doing just fine," she said. He put his arm around her shoulders and they were quiet for a moment. She couldn't stop her next words. "What kind of dates did you go on with Deanna?"

"Dinner, movies. A couple of random frat parties. The usual. We were married right after college, so I don't have a lot of non-school-dating experience."

Paige needed more. Not blow-by-blow accounts of his life, and she didn't want him to relive any of the horror that had to come with cancer treatments. But there had to be more between them if he'd been with exactly one woman since his wife's death. "What kinds of movies did you like?"

His hazel eyes shuttered and though he didn't move away, she felt a chill in the room.

"Oscar winners, mostly. I should get going," he said. "We have a busy day tomorrow. Your parents, my in-laws." He pressed a quick kiss to her forehead and slipped out the back door.

Paige watched the door for a long time, hoping he would come back so she could apologize. Alex had practically beat himself up with his apologies for pushing Kaylie too hard in the pool. It was her turn. A man didn't kiss the way he did if he wasn't interested, but obviously his feelings for his former wife were…still near the surface. She swallowed hard.

He'd spent the entire day with them, dropping whatever plans he'd had for a Saturday to go swimming and have hamburgers. Not wanting to talk about the details of his life with his former wife didn't mean anything.

It was silly, worrying about his memories as if they were a human being she could touch.

CHAPTER FOURTEEN

PAIGE WAS TOO busy Sunday morning to worry too much about her attraction to Alex and what it meant that he couldn't—or wouldn't—talk to her about his late wife. At the last minute, Alex had decided to invite his in-laws to the barbecue and they would arrive at noon.

A weird, unsettled feeling had kept her up most of the night after he left so abruptly. Worry that he would change his mind or find that Paige was lacking compared to his wife made her so jittery she couldn't paint.

During their weekly phone call she thought briefly about telling her mother the whole truth about Alex, but Dot was on a tangent about a new curator at a minor gallery in St. Louis. This was not the time to mention Alex's paternity, their developing romance or his steady relationship with Kaylie. Now she was glad she hadn't talked about the date with Alex. One big change at a time, and finding out Kaylie had a father was a big enough change.

Kaylie was in a mood and Alex would be here

any second. The dress she'd worn the night of their first date caught her eye and for a second Paige considered wearing it. She liked the way the silk felt against her skin, how the color seemed to make her skin glow.

A dress.

To a family barbecue.

She was losing it.

Paige pushed the dress to the back of her closet before grabbing her favorite jeans and a pair of ballet flats, along with a side-tie blouse with pretty flowers along the hem.

It was a family dinner. Not a big deal. Things like this happened every day. She would be thirty in less than two weeks, damn it. What was the big deal?

Paige caught her reflection in the mirror. Her eyes a little too wide, her smile a little too dreamy. Her skin slightly pale because she hadn't slept soundly in more than twenty-four hours.

Alex was the big deal. They talked on the phone every night, he'd been on Skype with Kaylie on Friday and text-flirted with her through the week. She'd learned he loved sushi and Mexican food, professional baseball but not basketball and that he was slightly obsessed with *Downton Abbey*. Which seemed odd until she remembered how good he looked in her apron and wearing Kaylie's hot-pink umbrella. Obviously Alex was a renaissance man.

They had similar taste in music and movies and

he'd teased her unmercifully when he learned she was the fan club president of a boy band in junior high. Paige had teased him about working out to a mix of Lady Gaga, Kid Rock and Van Halen, even though she found his taste in music endearing.

Then there were those hot moments in the pool yesterday. That kiss on the sofa last night and his abrupt departure when she pushed him about the past.

She poked her head into Kaylie's room to find the little girl lying on her stomach on the floor with a mountain of Lalaloopsy dolls beside her. Nightgown flung across the bed, the clothes Paige had laid out still on the dresser, and she was wearing only her undies. *She's only four, Paige. She's distracted by her dolls, not willfully disobeying you.*

Paige mentally repeated the phrase again as she reached for the little girl's jeans and tee. Kaylie raised her hands over her head but fiddled with putting her arms through the armholes. She lost focus entirely when Paige handed her the jeans.

"Kaylie, we have to get dressed. Alex will be here soon, and then everyone will be here for lunch." Kaylie held the jeans by the cuffs as if she'd never seen a pair before and, exasperated, Paige grabbed the dolls from the little girl and tossed them across the room into the toy box. "No more dolls until you have your clothes on. Now get dressed and then come into the bathroom to brush your teeth."

Paige finished brushing her own teeth and ran a brush through her hair. "How's it coming, Kaylie?"

"They don't fit!" Kaylie wailed, and then Paige heard tiny feet banging against the hardwood. She hurried down the hall to find Kaylie sitting on the floor, the legs of the jeans pulled to her knees while the waist puddled at her feet. Paige wanted to bang her head against the wall but she didn't have time for a migraine, not today.

Paige sat on the bed, pulled the upside-down jeans from her daughter's chubby legs and held them the right way. "Step in, remember?"

Kaylie smacked her forehead with her hand. "Silly Kaylie," she said.

"Yeah, goofy sweetpea. Come on, we're going to be late to our own party."

The doorbell rang. Paige reminded Kaylie to brush her teeth and started downstairs. Alex stood at the door, wearing an athletic polo and jeans. Looking like he should be modeling for a sports gear magazine.

"Hey, we're running late," she managed with just the tiniest catch in her throat.

"You look beautiful," Alex said, tucking a loose strand of hair behind her ear. His hand lingered near her jaw before dropping back to his side. "About last night—"

Paige waved a hand and talked over him, not wanting to hear whatever explanation he had about his past. It didn't matter. Today was about Kaylie, about introducing both sets of grandparents. They could deal with the rest later.

"Thank you. I couldn't decide what to wear and then just grabbed the first things I could reach." She couldn't think of anything else to say and so just stood in the doorway as they both sized each other up.

"Can I come in?" Alex finally asked.

Paige's brain finally kicked into gear. "Jeez, sorry, yes, yes. Come in." She ushered him into the living room, where the painting of Kaylie's daisy was almost finished. He stood before the easel, tracing his hands over the paint, lingering on the delicate brushstrokes of the flower. She'd added shadow to the painting and one night this week she planned to stretch it onto a nice frame and wrap it up. "Do you want a bottle of water? Some tea?"

"I'm fine. This is really good, Paige."

She blushed beside him. "Thank you." She thought so, too, but it pleased her that he liked the piece. She couldn't wait to hang it in Kaylie's room. Alex's arm snaked over her shoulders and he squeezed her to his side. Paige rested her head against his shoulder for a moment, enjoying the sandalwood scent of him, the weight of his arm across her shoulders.

The fact was he was in her house again and now she didn't care that they were running behind. Because Alex was here.

Which was silly. They'd had a single date, shared a few kisses.

This wasn't love. It was chemistry and attraction but—

She barely knew the man. It wasn't love.

Still, she couldn't bring herself to step away from him. She thought about him all the time, and not just in the daddy way. He brightened her day just by showing up. He was falling in love with her daughter.

God, she loved him. God, what was going to happen?

His lips brushed over the crown of her head and the glow within her intensified, coupled with a sinking feeling in her stomach. She loved him and he couldn't tell her about his past.

"Would you consider contributing a painting to one of the parks?"

His words came out of nowhere and Paige blinked. She stepped away from him, automatically ready to tell him no. She didn't need another person in her life pushing her into...

Alex held up his hands. "The department is adding a couple of indoor nature areas, for school trips and things. I just thought one of your paintings might fit well in the entry area. You know, local places like the old barn or even a lakeshore. I could give you the email address of the corporal who's heading up the project, if you're interested."

"Oh." It wasn't what she'd thought. He wasn't

pushing her work on other people. It wasn't like with Dot, who used her money and contacts to try to get Paige's art in major galleries. It sounded fun. Her fingers had itched to paint that old barn since Alex had sent her the photo. "I'd like that. Thank you."

"Alex!" Kaylie hopped off the bottom stair step and into the living room. "You know what?" She didn't wait for him to guess, just plowed on ahead. "I forgot to tell you yesterday, at my lesson I swimmed across the pool and then turned around and came back. That's a whole lap. I'll swim it for you next time we go. And I'll raise my arms up high."

"Cool, Kay," he said, kneeling before the little girl and offering a high five. "Don't worry about making them stiff and straight, just keep your hands in the right position, okay? If it's okay with your mom, maybe I'll come to your lesson this week and you can show me." He shot Paige a glance and she nodded her assent.

It was okay. It would be okay. She could handle being in love with Alex, could handle her daughter falling in love with him, too. She could share her parenting role and everything would be okay.

It had to be okay.

"Guess what?" Alex waited a beat and Kaylie's eyes grew round like quarters. "One of the horses got skunked this week and we had to buy five hundred tomatoes to get him cleaned up."

"Ewww." Kaylie wrinkled her nose. "Skunks are stinky. Why didn't you use soap?"

"Well, because soap only works a little bit, but the acid in tomatoes cuts through the smell."

Paige felt that odd tug in her chest again as she watched father and daughter talk about the cleaning benefits of tomatoes versus soap. She had a feeling Kaylie would ask for a tomato bath that night and mentally went through the contents of the crisper drawer in the fridge.

Alex ruffled his hand over Kaylie's hair and she took his hand, pulling him into the family room where her tablet lay on the sofa. Paige glanced at her watch. They could take a few minutes to play while she finished prepping the kabobs.

This was your brilliant idea, remember?

Yeah, she remembered. But it had seemed like a much more innocuous plan—their families meeting, deepening the bond between Alex and Kaylie—in theory than in reality. The reality was everything from Paige's work to her dating Alex would be fair game to her mother. And once Hank and Dot learned she was dating a park ranger those little hits would turn into full-on missile strikes. The Parkers might hate her and Kaylie.

The bigger reality: that Alex might still be in love with his dead wife. No matter how attached to Kaylie he was, Paige might always be just the woman who came along with the daughter package he'd chosen to accept.

As if sensing her sudden nerves, Alex reached across the seat to hold her hand. "It'll be okay," he said.

"I know," she lied. After today, nothing might be okay. Everything might be okay. Things might still be in this weird limbo that made her twitchy.

"Really. I know what to expect from Hank and Dot after their last barbecue appearance. As for John and Sue, they're quiet people. They won't cause a scene."

Paige glanced at Kaylie and even though the little girl seemed focused on her coloring book she pitched her voice lower. "They weren't crazy about me being a single mom but they've mostly adjusted. I'm not sure how they'll react to the daddy news."

Alex joined her on the other side of the counter. "They'll react badly." He shrugged when Paige cut her eyes to him. "Based on their last stellar barbecue performance. They love Kaylie. They'll feel threatened by me, maybe by John and Sue, too. They'll blame you."

"You read another psychology book, didn't you?"

Alex grinned. "Seemed like the smart thing to do. It was a book on blending families."

"And?"

"And in theory we're doing everything right already. In reality, your parents and my extended family aren't expecting what they're about to get today and…" He trailed off and stared into space for a moment, as if thinking about something unpleasant. There was a hint of anger in his gaze, a heaviness in the slant of his shoulders.

Paige squeezed his hand in hers. "And?"

"And John and Sue are good people, but they've never really gotten over Deanna's death."

Translation: Paige would be the interloper in their eyes while Alex was the unwanted party for Hank and Dot.

"Are we crazy for trying to make this as easy as possible?"

He shook his head. "No, and no matter what happens this afternoon, I'm glad we're at least trying."

CHAPTER FIFTEEN

ALEX TURNED A kabob on the grill, wondering how to start a conversation. Not the conversation, that could wait, but standing at the grill on Paige's deck while Hank and Dot sat a few feet away and not talking was just too weird. Paige bustled inside and out, getting the table ready. Kaylie colored quietly at the umbrella table and he wondered again what to say to Paige's parents.

He rolled his shoulders as a particularly heavy stare rested on him once more. Not Hank—he'd been oblivious to everyone at the barbecue since they'd arrived. Dot, on the other hand, seemed overly curious about why Alex was there. Dot Kenner was obviously not convinced this was a casual friendship.

Alex was torn equally between telling Dot exactly how things were and just leaving it at the friendship stage. Because until they told Kaylie everything, he didn't feel right about telling anyone else; it seemed unfair. Especially unfair since his in-laws probably at least suspected there was more between him and Paige than a daughter.

What foolish part of his brain thought this was a good idea?

The smell of burning vegetables and chicken brought Alex back to the present and he quickly put the kabobs on the upper rack so they could stay warm until lunch was ready.

"I'm going to check on the rest of our lunch. Can I get either of you anything?"

Hank shook his head. Dot, hands folded in her lap, said, "Thank you, no."

Alex briefly considered slipping a shot of Jaeger into whatever they were drinking with lunch. Hank and Dot needed to relax.

Paige dumped more ice into a container as he stepped through the sliding door.

"The Parkers still aren't here." Paige chewed on her lower lip, a habit he'd picked up on that first day. Her small white teeth worried the corner of her pink mouth as if she might solve the world hunger crisis if she only had the time.

"They're never late. I told them noon, they'll be here." But it was almost that time and he wondered if maybe this event was too much, too soon for the couple. "I can call them, if it'll make you feel better."

Paige nodded and put two more glasses on the large serving tray.

Alex hit the speed-dial button on his cell phone and waited while the phone rang.

"Hey, did I tell you about the horses getting

skunked?" Paige needed a distraction so Alex plunged into the story he told Kaylie when he first arrived. Paige held up a hand to stop him.

"Kaylie can be distracted by stories about skunks and tomatoes, not me," she said, hugging him around the neck as the phone kept ringing. "But thank you for trying.

Alex clicked off the phone. "No answer, which means they're on the way." Paige's shoulders were stiff so Alex hugged her tighter, rubbing her shoulders gently, and hoping she would relax. He knew most of her tension was from her own parents already being outside, but meeting his in-laws couldn't be an easy thing. He slipped his arms around her waist and squeezed. Paige's hands held on to his forearms and she leaned against him for a brief moment.

"I know. Everything will be fine." But she didn't sound fine. She sounded upset.

"It will. No matter what your mother or my in-laws say, everything will be fine."

Maybe if he repeated that to himself enough times he'd actually believe it. No, that was the tension talking. How could everything not be fine? He had a wonderful daughter, was dating a beautiful woman and most nights now he fell asleep thinking about her rather than listening to the sound of a canned television laugh track.

Most nights he didn't dream about Deanna or those last few weeks of her life. Didn't worry that she would hate him for moving on. Alex pulled Paige more firmly against his body. Just the other night he'd had a rather erotic dream about Paige, in his big sleigh bed. He'd woken up feeling guilty about the dream and then convinced himself it was natural to feel guilty about having another woman in Dee's bed.

And Friday he'd donated that bed to a local charity and bought a new four-poster in Farmington.

He felt reasonably sure the next dream he had about Paige wouldn't have the guilty afterglow.

The grandmother clock chimed noon and right on cue the doorbell rang. Paige's shoulders went tense again. Alex turned her around to face him.

"It will be okay. And if it's not, we'll still be okay. Okay?"

She nodded. "I'm sorry I'm kind of falling apart."

"Please, I'm a park ranger, remember? I'm trained for high-stress situations." He shrugged one shoulder and pasted a goofy smile on his face. It worked. A genuine smile stretched across Paige's face and the tension in her shoulders drained away.

"I don't think your course load of horticulture and accounting has anything on Dot Kenner."

Together they answered the front door.

Ten minutes later, all the introductions had been made and everyone sat around Paige's deck table, passing the plate of kabobs and bowls of vegetables and salad. No one said more than "please pass the peas," and the silence was killing Alex.

Kaylie seemed oblivious as she chased a pea around her plate with her small fork, and he watched the sets of older couples with trepidation.

"So, Mr. Parker, how is planting going? Is the nice weather making it easy to get the winter wheat in?" Paige's voice sounded desperate to Alex's ears.

John swallowed a bite of chicken and tilted his head to the side. "Well, winter wheat planting finished a couple of weeks ago, and the nice weather has made it a little easier to get the soybeans in, too."

"Great." Paige squeezed his hand beneath the table, but before he could keep the conversation going Dot interrupted.

"So you're farm people then," Dot said from her side of the table. The way she said "farm" made it sound as if John and Sue might be from a leper colony.

"John's a centennial farmer." Alex joined the conversation, hoping everyone at the table would chill out. "His family has owned the same plot of land since the eighteen hundreds."

"Mmm. That must be...stimulating," Dot said as she pushed two peas onto her fork and daintily ate them. Damn, but Paige's mother was a piece of work.

"There is a lot that goes into farming, Mother,"

Paige said from beside Alex. "They have to know weather patterns like meteorologists, have a head for banking like financiers. They read the ground and know when to rotate fields or let one go fallow to build up the nitrates. It's a complex job."

"Well, I'm surprised you never brought one home before, being that they're so insightful and brilliant."

"Mother." Paige clenched her jaw and the single word carried a warning.

"Alex saved a kitten." Kaylie gave up on her fork and popped a couple of peas into her mouth using her fingers. "And he gave a horse a bath with tomatoes."

"I'm sure he's done many interesting things," Dot said and then turned her attention back to Paige. "I only meant—"

"We know what you meant." This time Sue joined the conversation, her voice solid and strong and not at all the voice Alex remembered from her phone call a few days before. Maybe it had just been a bad morning. Maybe seeing him drop everything to come out to the farm had been enough to right her shaky world once more. "You meant farmers aren't good enough for your precious daughter. Maybe a farmer wouldn't be, but Alex is no farmer. He's a brilliant conservationist and has wonderful ideas about bringing more people to the parks, and preserving the land for future generations."

"I'm sure his job is...challenging. I'm just not certain it's the kind of job that can support a family."

Kaylie kept talking, oblivious to the adults' conversation. "Alex is going to take us camping sometime."

Dot talked over her granddaughter. "And he is *D-A-T-I-N-G* a family, not just a single woman."

"And he comes to my swim parties and he—"

"Kaylie, hush, the adults are talking." Dot flung her hand toward Kaylie, whose little face crumpled. Alex saw red.

"Mrs. Kenner, that is enough."

Paige took a bewildered Kaylie inside and settled her with a book and her tablet before calmly closing the door to return to the deck.

"First, don't ever speak to my daughter that way again. Now, Mother, since you're hell-bent on having your say, say it." She returned to the table to sit beside him.

Alex wanted to applaud Paige for standing up for their daughter. For his in-laws, in a small way.

"I think you're making a mistake, dating this hiker when you could be working on your art or dating a doctor or a lawyer. How many men have I introduced you to in the past four years?"

"Zero. You've seemed content to tell me what a mistake I've made being a single mom. But who I date is my decision. Mine. And yes—" she took Alex's hand under the table "—I choose to date

this man. Who is kind and decent and likes ou—
my kid." She stumbled over the word *my* and Alex
knew why. They'd agreed not to tell her parents
about his paternity, not yet.

"If you'd like I can fax my resume to you tomorrow," Alex said, trying to lighten the mood. Two
pairs of angry eyes focused on him while the other
couple, John and Sue, seemed to look anywhere
but directly at him.

"We aren't concerned about your degrees,"
Hank said, speaking for the first time. His voice
was deep and carried across the backyard, much
like it would carry across a packed auditorium
when he taught at the college, Alex thought. "Our
concern is that anyone who comes into contact
with Kaylie could change the trajectory of her life.
Are you willing to take that risk?"

Change the trajectory? Alex stiffened his shoulders. What the hell was the man talking about? She
had no trajectory other than kindergarten and from
what Alex could see she was bang on target there.

"You don't have to worry about Alex messing up
any trajectories," John said from across the table.
"He's a smart, capable man. Paige and Kaylie are
lucky to have him in their lives."

Finally a reasonable voice at the table. Alex
wanted to reach across the table and hug his father-
in-law. He settled for squeezing Paige's hand. She
threaded her fingers with his and squeezed back,
as if John's words had bolstered her spirits, as well.

"Kaylie's trajectory is amazing. She's a smart kid," Alex said.

"And you know this how?"

"Can't you see it?" Hank's question baffled Alex. Who couldn't see the sweet, smart, funny girl for exactly what she was? "She reads those two- and three-word sentence books, she knows her way around technology. Her teachers and classmates love her."

"People liking her will have little impact on her future career choices—"

Alex cut him off. "People liking her will have a huge impact on her self-esteem and that will determine her career choices." The older man scowled at him but didn't say anything more.

Sue sniffled, the strength she'd displayed earlier seeping away. "I guess I can see why they've pulled you away from us. Ready-made family and—"

"Sue." John's voice held a warning but his wife ignored it.

Sue focused on her husband, as if the rest of the table had disappeared. "It's plain to see the connection he has to Kaylie. I understand it—she is a sweet little girl. Even a blind man who couldn't see the physical resemblance would know it." She turned to Alex. "I guess—I guess you really are moving on." Pain filled her voice along with a breathiness that made it seem as if Sue was ready to break. Before Alex could comfort her, Dot gasped.

"Physical… My God, Paige, he's the donor?" From her tone, it seemed Alex had joined the farmer/leper colony with John and Sue. "How could you invite that man into Kaylie's life without telling us about it first? This changes everything. Do you even know what he wants?"

"Yes, Mother, I know what he wants. He wants to sue me for sole custody and make sure you never see your granddaughter again." John and Sue, Hank and Dot all focused on Paige, who rolled her eyes and seemed to gain strength from their close inspection. "He wants to get to know his daughter, Mother. *We* want to get to know one another. No matter what happens between us, we're committed to raising Kaylie to the best of our abilities." She focused on John and Sue. "He's told me about Deanna and she sounds like a wonderful woman."

Alex felt a little stab to his heart with that, because he hadn't told Paige much about Deanna at all. Yet she was willing to try to comfort Dee's parents, who were obviously having trouble with his change from widower to father and boyfriend. He wasn't giving her enough credit, not nearly enough. Alex didn't want to bring Dee into their relationship, for his past to impact his future, but it seemed she was already there. And that seemed okay.

Tears pricked the corners of John's eyes and he

hastily wiped them away. Sue sniffled. Alex patted Sue with one hand but held tight to Paige with the other. It was as if holding on to her helped steady him in the storm of Sue's anguish.

"Who is Deanna?" Dot's voice ran imperiously across the table.

"His wife. She died a few years ago."

"You're dating a widower?" Apparently being a park ranger was only the tip of the iceberg of things wrong with Alex in Dot's eyes. "Paige, really."

"Mother, stop. It's my choice."

Dot put her fingers to her forehead. "You're dating Kaylie's biological father, who was married to someone else, and you see nothing wrong with this picture?"

"No, I don't."

"Alex is a fine man." Sue sniffled out the words from her side of the table.

Dot ignored that. "You had a future. A gallery showing in St. Louis, a chance to make something of yourself. And now you're pinning your future— Kaylie's future—on a park ranger who's already been married and is a sperm donor to boot?"

"He wasn't a donor. Alex and his wife were undergoing fertility treatments, and there was a mistake made at the clinic." Alex saw Paige squinch her eyes closed and grit her teeth. "We've been over the gallery showing, Mother, and it's always going to be a no. As for my future, how about I'm dating a strong, caring man who happens to enjoy spending time with my kid?"

"You have no idea the can of worms you are opening, Paige, and I, for one, know nothing good will ever come of it."

John stood, pulling a still-sniffling Sue up with him. "Thank you for lunch. It was nice meeting you, Paige, but I think we should go."

"You don't have to—"

"Thank you for allowing us to meet Alex's... your daughter." He cleared his throat. "Thank you." He and Sue began walking around to the front of the house.

"Now that they're gone, I hope we can have a real conversation about the ramifications of you dating this man," Dot began, but Alex cut her off.

"The ramifications are that I'm staying." Alex stood, towering over the table. "I like your daughter and granddaughter and I'm a part of their lives now. Our hope in inviting you here today was that we could all get to know one another on an adult level. I can see now that isn't going to happen."

"Well, I never—"

"Well, you should." Paige stood beside Alex. "We are dating, Mother and Dad. We plan to see a lot of one another. Alex is building a bond with Kaylie and we'll tell her the whole truth about who he is when she is ready."

Dot stood, hands fisted at her sides and all traces of the headache she'd pretended to have a few moments before now gone. "You're allowing him to walk all over you. Just like every loser you've brought home before."

Paige's skin paled but she stayed steady and Alex's anger level rose on her behalf.

"You can leave. Now," he said.

"I will finish this conversation. You had us both fooled, Paige Julia Kenner. You made all these proclamations about how great a mother you would be and we truly hoped having a child dependent on you would help you change. But you're still the spoiled brat who ran off to Texas on spring break and who nearly ruined the career of a second-year law student. You'll never change and if we have to, we'll be the proper parents that Kaylie deserves."

Paige gasped.

"Get out." Alex had had enough. He grabbed Dot's slim clutch from the outdoor sofa and pressed it into her hands. "You have no idea the kind of woman your daughter is. She's an amazing mother with an infinite ability to love and care." Alex looked from one parent to the other. "You can't scare her into shutting me out of her life or Kaylie's. And if you follow through on your threat of a lawsuit, you'll lose."

He took Paige's trembling hand in his again. Together they watched Hank and Dot stride across the yard, backs straight and shoulders tense.

"I'm sorry." Her words were barely a whisper

but they stabbed against Alex's heart. How could parents be that cruel?

"I'm sorry, too." He wasn't sure if he was sorry for causing the ruckus or for the hell she'd obviously experienced growing up. Maybe both.

His parents weren't perfect but hers were so much worse than he had ever imagined. And yet, here she was, standing beside him. Raising Kaylie on her own, holding down a job. With a full life, friendships, and she'd welcomed him into her life, too.

Alex tilted his head against hers. "What do you say we go play with our kid?"

CHAPTER SIXTEEN

"I SHOULDN'T HAVE spoken to my mother that way." Paige sat on the lounger beside Alex, looking at the starry sky. She'd put Kaylie to bed a few minutes before but asked him to stay. "I pushed her buttons with that whole 'he wants sole custody' thing. That's what pushed her over the ledge into hysterical country."

"I don't know about that." Alex put his arm around her shoulder and the warmth of his embrace was welcome in the chilly night. "I think she was gearing up for a fight from the moment she got out of the Caddy."

"The Cadillac is her transport of choice when she has a mission in mind." Paige shook her head. "Still, I shouldn't have goaded her. I should have kept my head, kept things calm. You didn't deserve the things she said about you. Neither did John and Sue, who seem like really nice people, by the way."

"They are really nice people. John's a bit more steady than Sue, at least over the past few years. As for goading your mother, she was spoiling for a fight. You stood your ground, there's nothing wrong with that."

Still, Paige knew better than to engage. She'd learned the hard way that when Dot was on a rant the best defense was to say nothing. Maybe she could have said nothing if her mother hadn't snapped at Kaylie or been downright insulting to Alex and his family.

In a couple of days Dot would call, Paige would cave and apologize and their relationship would return to the status quo.

No, that wasn't happening. Not this time. Not when Paige's intentions with the barbecue were to forge a new path for her family—Kaylie and Alex deserved better. They deserved a path of unconditional love and support. Caring. There would be disagreements, Paige wasn't fooling herself, but there would be no accusations or throwing a person's past in her face. Speaking of, maybe it wasn't such a good idea for Alex to only know about post-Kaylie Paige. New leaf, starting fresh. She didn't dwell on the mistakes she made in the past, but it wasn't fair to him to pretend nothing had ever happened.

"Those old boyfriends my mom brought up—"

Alex held up a hand. "I didn't expect you'd never dated anyone. It isn't important."

"Thank you for that. But I think it is." Paige took a deep breath. She hadn't thought about the events leading up to the spring break fiasco for a long time. "When I turned sixteen, I was attending a day school in St. Louis. My mother hinted there would be a big celebration, but at the last minute a law school cocktail party came up and they canceled. Literally, the last minute. The limo hired to pick me and my friends up didn't show. We sat on the curb for over an hour waiting. One of the girls finally called her mom. I was so embarrassed and, of course, when the parents started calling, the blame was put on my shoulders. My birthday was the inconvenience, not my parents' choosing a Halloween work party over standing plans from weeks before."

"Your birthday is October 31?" Alex asked.

"We haven't talked about birthdays, have we? Yes, I was born on Halloween at midnight, which is a cool birthday for a kid because, dress up. Anyway, they'd stood me up before, but never in front of my friends. I got mad and I swore I'd embarrass them as badly as they'd embarrassed me—which is where the mom in me now winces. They decided we would go on a family cruise for spring break and I was still spoiling for that fight. I had visions of the Caribbean or Hawaii or some Greek islands. They chose a spring tour of New England so we could see the trees and flowers blossom."

"Not that exciting for a teenager."

She shook her head. "So the night before we were to leave, I left. This guy at a local bar we always snuck into invited me to South Padre with him. He was supposed to be on his college's spring break. I didn't tell them where I was going so God knows how they found out, but they found me in a seedy motel in Texas with a twenty-five-year-old mechanic. The flirty guy had lied about his age, his school. And I know now how dangerous what I did was. At the time, though, I just wanted them to…"

"Come after you? Take you home?"

"I wanted them to see me. I was angry and once I figured out the guy was a liar I was terrified of the mistake I'd made. And why? Why did I do that, anyway? Because my parents were flakes? I was mad that I let them get to me. I've worked hard to stop being angry and stop taking the bait they throw at me and this afternoon I took it. I'm sorry. And I'm not that girl anymore."

"I know."

Paige blinked. "You do?"

He nodded in the darkness and pulled her body closer to his. "Everything about you, from your job to your friends to the way you treat Kaylie, screams that you're a competent, complete, caring woman. Every kid makes a mistake now and then. What happened when they got you home?"

The compliment made Paige glow. "They shipped me off to another boarding school, this time in Switzerland. I was the only one who didn't speak French or German so I was automatically an outsider. They didn't let me come home for summer break. But I guess the joke was on them because I met Alison there the next fall. Her parents were going through a nasty divorce. My mother has never let me live that trip to Texas down. It's always her first strike."

For the first time, though, it didn't hurt to tell the story. Uncomfortable, definitely. But her parents' dismissal of her didn't hurt this time. It was merely a part of her past.

"Thanks for listening."

"Thank you for telling me about it." They were quiet for a long time, watching stars twinkle to life in the night sky.

"What about you? Tell me why your parents weren't perfect. I dare you," she joked.

"They were more Dan and Roseanne Conner, from that sitcom. Sarcastic and a little scary."

"Scary? I think Hank and Dot have that emotion cornered."

Alex shook his head. "They heckled school plays."

She slapped at his shoulder. "They did not. No one heckles school plays."

"My parents were the first of their kind." Alex nodded. "They yelled at umpires and referees, usually on behalf of the other team."

"Nuh-uh."

He held up his hand in the Scout salute. "Swear.

And they made me swear, every Christmas, that Santa was real."

"Every Christmas?" Paige laughed along with him.

"Until I was eighteen. The end of childhood meant it was okay to believe in only the spirit of Christmas, not the big man in the red suit."

"That Santa thing must have been hard when you hit puberty."

"You have no idea."

"They don't sound so bad."

He smiled in the darkness. "They don't, do they? I had a good childhood. I guess you realize that more as you grow up." He pulled her into his arms and she went, willingly.

His lips were warm in the dark and he tasted of dark chocolate from the cake they'd eaten after dinner. Paige thought she might nibble those lips all night, but there were more questions to ask. More things she wanted to know, and after declaring their relationship status to both sets of parents this felt like the right time to ask.

"What else? Have any deep, dark secrets you want to share? I mean, swearing about Santa is one thing, but I hopped on a Harley and disappeared for spring break." Funny, that was the first time she'd been able to joke about that night.

Alex reached for a light blanket at the end of the bench and covered their legs. "I'm an open book. Ordinary childhood. My parents were different but not terrible, and then they died. I think I might have more anger toward them, but…" He trailed off.

"But?"

"But I started seeing Deanna soon after their deaths and her family pulled me into their circle without any drama. I think that helped me come to terms with their not being around any longer, even though there had been times I wished they weren't around."

Paige settled against the bench seat and pulled the blanket over her arms. "You still love her, don't you?"

He was quiet for a long moment but Paige didn't feel him pull away. Not physically or emotionally as they watched the night sky and he considered his answer. Finally he said, "I think I'll always love her. I don't want that to scare you."

"It doesn't." Relief washed over Paige as she said the words. She wasn't scared, not about his feelings for his former wife. She wasn't upset about the barbecue with their parents and she wasn't nervous about what might happen down the road. It all felt normal. Like life, and wasn't that what she wanted? A real life with real people and real emotions? "What was she like? Not the kind of work she did or her bad driving. What did you love about her?"

"You can't want to hear this."

But she did. Paige needed to know what made him love his wife. What kept her in his heart. Not out of jealousy or a need to quash his feelings, but to understand him. She loved Alex. Love meant accepting every part of the person, not just the easy things. "She was important to you. You're important to me. That makes your past important."

His Adam's apple bobbed up and down when he swallowed. "She played the piano, mostly when I annoyed her. I think I annoyed her a lot, at least in the beginning, because the first few nights we lived in our home she banged on the keys for hours."

"Annoyed her about what?"

"I wanted a man cave. You know, leather furniture, sports posters and trophies. She wanted pink and flowers and roosters in the kitchen. God, I hated those roosters. On the backsplash and the tile floor and the freaking pot holders. I still use the pot holders and I hate them."

"But you can't get rid of them?"

"They were her, you know? We watched foreign films—subtitles, the whole nine—and I never knew what the hell was going on, but she liked them so I watched because being with her was more important."

Paige's heart pinged as he talked about Deanna, how she loved the summer sunshine and being on the lake. The way she shoveled the walk sideways so that the piles of snow made a kind of fort leading to the mailbox. That she worked out to Lady

Gaga and Van Halen and that no matter what she cooked for breakfast, it always burned.

"That's why you're such a good egg chef."

He squeezed her hand. "Breakfast is the most important meal of the day."

"I've heard." They were quiet for a long time, but Paige didn't mind. The Monday-morning rush would begin by seven the next morning, but she was content to talk with Alex. Sit with him.

Be with him.

"Thank you for telling me about her."

He nodded and after a moment said, "So Halloween. What a birthday."

She chuckled. "It was more than awesome when I was a kid. Who doesn't want more candy and chocolate? Now it gets lost in the shuffle of costumes for Kaylie, but I don't mind. Speaking of, I need to make a trip to the costume store in St. Louis sometime this week. Kaylie's still stuck on Snoopy and none of the local stores have him in stock." Alex's heart thundered beneath her cheek and Paige sat up. "What's wrong?"

"Nothing. I just… I can maybe help with that. If it isn't overstepping the new-dad bounds?"

"What, you have a Snoopy costume in your truck? SuperDad to the rescue?" Paige joked but Alex didn't smile.

"On the counter at my house, actually."

Paige had trouble computing what he was saying. "You have a Snoopy costume?"

He nodded. "Kaylie mentioned it, and I saw them online. Then I decided to send them back because you didn't ask for my help, but—"

"You bought a Snoopy costume for Kaylie?" Why were tears pricking at the corners of her eyes? He had overstepped. She hadn't asked him to swoop in to the rescue with a Halloween costume, but Paige couldn't muster even a hint of anger toward him. Because he bought Kaylie a costume.

"And Sally and Lucy and Charlie Brown, too, in case we all decided to go together."

The tears spilled over. Of all the overstepping, thoughtful things anyone had ever done for her— for her daughter—this was at the top of the list.

"It's okay, I'll send them back." He swiped his thumb over the tears streaming down Paige's cheeks. "I didn't mean to upset you. Halloween is your birthday, your time with Kaylie. It's not a big deal."

Paige could only shake her head. She pushed his hands away from her face and swiped the sleeves of her jacket over her eyes. Put her hands on either side of his face so he had to look at her. "Don't you dare send them back. Come trick-or-treating with your daughter, in a Charlie Brown costume. Please."

"Really?"

Paige nodded. "Other than Alison and me, no one has ever thought about what Kaylie would want." Tears threatened again and Paige cleared her throat. "These are happy tears. Stupid, crazy, happy tears. Please, come with us."

"Okay." He put his arms around her, pulling Paige into his lap. He dropped a kiss on her cheek.

The happy tears were dwarfed by her response to the simple gesture. Paige wanted more than a chaste kiss from Alex. She wrapped her arms around his neck and pressed her lips against his, feeling his immediate response to her. Her heartbeat thundered between them as he tasted her, as she inhaled the sandalwood scent of him.

Alex tested her boundaries, teasing the tip of his tongue against the seam of her mouth. Paige opened to him, allowing him entry. His hands at her hips urged her forward a hair, until she was seated over his hardness. Paige dug her fingers through his short hair as his hands worked over her ribs close, so close to her breasts. His knuckles teased the undersides of her breasts, and heat pooled between her legs at the near contact.

Then he was gone, leaving her cold and shivering on the bench seat. Alex paced to the railing, running his hands over his head as he bent at the waist. "We can't. Not on your back porch. Not with Kaylie a few feet away in her bed. Not when she still thinks I'm the guy who comes to her swim lesson and gives horses a tomato bath."

He was right. Realization of what they'd nearly

done washed over Paige, chilling her to the bone. They couldn't make love on her deck.

She'd nearly made love with a man in her backyard.

"We need to figure out how to do this when a toddler is underfoot."

"I think the basic rules still apply." Paige couldn't stop her smart-aleck half from saying the words.

Alex's laugh was loud in the dark. Rich and inviting. He took her hand. "We need to make a few plans."

OVER THE LAST week of October, Paige and Alex fell into a familiar routine. He stopped by her house most nights and the three of them would eat dinner together. He'd tell Kaylie silly stories about the parks or show her pictures from his hikes, if the weather had been nice enough for him to get out of the office. On Wednesday they took Kaylie to swim practice together. They hadn't been on another date, but once Kaylie was down for the night Paige and Alex would watch TV, sitting close together on her love seat. Or Alex would build a fire in the pit on the deck and they would watch the sky.

They talked and kissed and Alex went home most nights to take a cold shower. At least that was what Paige supposed he did because it was what she did once he left. Not that it helped. She wanted him.

Badly.

Privately Paige referred to this routine as the New Normal. And she liked it.

She looked out the window but no blue truck had parked before her house and the street was quiet outside. The clock ticked on past five-thirty and she reminded herself people were late all the time. He would be here. He wouldn't disappoint Kaylie.

She peeked her head around the corner, watching Kaylie for a moment. She was dressed and ready, the Snoopy costume's head making her own neck bobble a little. Her hot-pink jack-o'-lantern bucket sat by her side as she drew a picture at the low coffee table.

Paige sat down with her. "What are you drawing, sweetpea?"

"You and me, at the pool." She held up the picture, which had a tall stick figure and a shorter one floating on a blue square. Both figures had long hair and big smiles.

"Nice job. Are you ready for trick-or-treating?" Paige tacked the picture to the fridge and returned to the coffee table to sit with Kaylie on the floor.

"Mmm-hmm. Do you think Mrs. Purcell will have caramel apples again this year?" Kaylie put a new dress on the doll next to her.

"We will have to wait and see. Sweetpea, do you like it when Alex comes around?" Paige helped her put the doll arms through the narrow sleeve openings, watching her face for any uncomfortable emotions. Kaylie seemed unfazed by the question.

"Alex is my swimming buddy."

"Right. Alex likes you a lot."

"Alex is funny. Like you, Mama."

"I'm funny?" They finished with the doll and Kaylie admired the new dress.

"You smile a lot when Alex is here. Smiles are for funny things."

Paige tucked a strand of hair behind her ear and hugged Kaylie to her side. She had been smiling more over the past couple of weeks. "I love you, Kay."

Kaylie snuggled against her neck. "I love you, too, Mama. Can I play 'Angry Birds'?"

"Sure, but just for a few minutes." The clock read five forty-five and she checked the front door. She should get ready.

It only took a few minutes to secure her long hair in a bun, don the blue-and-black dress and saddle shoes. She put more blusher than normal on her cheeks and pulled the black foam wig over her head, still wondering where Alex might be.

She settled into her favorite wicker chair on the porch with her sketchbook and pencils, doodling.

Why was she so antsy? Things were going well. She felt warm and cozy when he texted her a picture or a funny thing that happened during the day. Or just wanted to say hi. Those were her favorite texts, the ones that had absolutely no reason. They just were. Like Alex. He could text her a "happy Monday" note and her day was made.

Even her mother's usual haranguing didn't bother her. Or maybe it was that Dot seemed to have given up on the backhanded compliments since that last blowup. She'd called twice, reminding Paige of gallery deadlines, but didn't bring up Alex. Or his connection to Kaylie. She'd been… almost normal.

Maybe that was the cause of her discontent. Dot was never this laid-back about anything.

No, that wasn't it.

The phone rang, and Dot's number glowed on the readout. Paige sighed. "Think of the devil," she muttered but picked up the call. "Hello, Mother."

"Paige, sweetheart. I was just calling to remind you that if you want to send something in to the curator, the deadline for local artists is today. Halloween, of all days, can you imagine?"

Halloween. Maybe that was the source of her angst. She turned thirty today. Paige twisted her mouth to the side. No, thirty was a big number, but she wasn't worried about gray hairs or sagging boobs. What was wrong with her?

"Paige, are you there?"

"I'm here, Mother. We talked about this. I have a lot on my plate with school, and there is a new project we're planning for the spring—"

Dot cut her off. "Please. You know you could

snap off a canvas that would thrill them, if you'd just try. I talked to the curator today and he said as long as you emailed him the plan for your painting, he would get it in the next showing."

Paige gritted her teeth and held back the angry retort. Dot wasn't turning over a new leaf. All her quietness over the past two weeks had been a buildup to this call. Paige should have known.

"He leaves at seven. You only have a little time left," her mother continued. "Why don't you go ahead and email your ideas? You know, I think a landscape around the Chain of Rocks bridge in St. Louis would be a great addition."

Except the area didn't interest Paige. Not that Dot would care.

"Did you need anything else, Mother?" Like to wish Paige a happy birthday? "I'm planning to take Kaylie trick-or-treating in a few minutes. We need to get ready."

"No, I only wanted to remind you of the gallery deadline."

The words were like a punch to Paige's midsection. They shouldn't have been, not really. Over the years her parents had forgotten more of Paige's birthdays than they'd remembered. And she didn't want to argue with her mother, not again. Not with Kaylie just inside the house. Not on her birthday.

"Don't forget to email a picture of Kaylie's costume. She's a fairy princess again, right?"

Paige sighed. "No, Mother, she's Snoopy this year. She didn't want wings and a crown."

"But Snoopy is a boy's costume. A boy dog. Surely you told her that."

No, Paige hadn't. Who cared if Snoopy was a boy dog? Her kid wanted to be Snoopy so Paige would let her be Snoopy. She closed her eyes and counted to five. Getting upset with her mother would spoil their evening with Alex and Paige was loathe to do that.

He deserved better than more Kenner family complaining. "She insisted Snoopy was the costume," Paige said in a level voice.

Dot sighed. "Well, I still want a picture, I suppose. Don't forget about emailing the curator. He's waiting for you."

Right. "I'll think about it."

"That's all I ask, darling. Your father just walked in the door, would you like to speak with him?"

"No, that's okay. Tell him I said hello. Would you like to talk to Kaylie?"

She went in search of her daughter and found her playing "Angry Birds" on the iPad. Her completed drawing showed a little girl, a dog and a tall man. Paige smiled. No matter how messed up her own childhood, she had to admit she was raising a pretty cool kid.

Kaylie chattered about preschool for a few minutes with Dot, and Paige imagined the indulgent expression on her mother's face. When Paige was a child, the indulgent expression meant Dot was distracted and not really listening. With Kaylie it meant she was taking in every word. Absorbing them, tucking them away so she could ask questions later.

Paige frowned. Now she was jealous of her daughter? She really had to get a grip on her emotions. A few minutes later Kaylie handed the phone back and returned her attention to the game. Paige gave her a five-minute warning before turning her attention to the phone.

"You will send something to the gallery tonight?"

She closed her eyes. She could lie, say yes and deal with it later. Or she could grow up and deal with it now. Including not letting what happened next cloud their evening with Alex.

"No, Mother, although I appreciate you talking me up to the curator, and reminding me about the opportunity. I have too much on my plate right now with school and Kaylie and—"

"And that man, I suppose." Dot's tone cooled immensely, not that it had been overly warm from the moment Paige said hello. "Paige, you cannot continue to allow men to run your life or shape your career."

"I'm not, Mother. My career is my choice. Teaching makes me happy. Painting for Kaylie or the school makes me happy." *Alex makes me happy.* She didn't say those words aloud, thank goodness. "I wish you could be happy for me."

Dot sighed, the sound more menacing than sad. "I wish you could see how much talent you're wasting in a classroom when you could be painting landscapes around the world. You could be showing Kaylie that world—"

"She has school, Mother, and I'm not interested in painting the lost landscapes of France or Turkey." Although she wouldn't mind painting the barn on Alex's parkland. She twisted her mouth to the side and walked into the living room to turn the empty canvas on its side. Just enough space.

"Please. Nannies and tutors would be better for Kaylie than that backwater town you live in."

"Mother, stop. You lived in this 'backwater' town for fifteen years, remember?"

"And then we realized you needed more than reading, writing and arithmetic. Paige, you had an international education. You know the benefits of experiencing other cultures, learning new languages. It would be so good for her."

Yes, she knew all about being dropped in a foreign country, not knowing the language, not knowing a single soul.

"Mother, thank you." Paige put a hard note into her voice. "Thank you for believing in my talent, but you have to accept that we have different dreams for me. I like living in a small town, I like teaching school and, yes, I like Alex. I have a good life and it's exactly what I want. I'll talk to you soon." She hung up before Dot could say anything more. Set the phone back in its charger.

And realized she still held her sketch pad in her other hand.

She doodled her name with Alex's across the page. She'd drawn a unicorn and a few hundred hearts. Sketched his hand holding hers in a corner.

The sound of his truck snapped Paige back to the present. She closed the book and put it under one of the couch cushions.

She loved Alex Ryan.

Tonight might be the perfect time to tell him.

ALEX'S PHONE BLEEPED and he glanced at the read-out. Alison.

When will you have you-know-who out of the house?

Trick-or-treating starts at six, so anytime after. I'll keep them on candy watch until at least seven. You have the cake?

She texted him a googly-eye-rolling smiley face.

Of course I have it. You have mad cake-ordering skills. The house will be perfect by seven.

Thank you.

He pocketed the cell phone. He could have planned Paige's surprise birthday party without Alison's help, but he couldn't have readied the house while still having his first trick-or-treat night with his daughter. And Paige deserved to be remembered on her birthday.

The clock on Sue's stove clicked past five and Alex folded his hands together. He'd taken a half-day off work because Sue called that morning, asking him to help her move a few things from Deanna's childhood room into the attic. A good sign, he thought, but then the moving of things was sidetracked by every piece of memorabilia Dee had collected during her teenage years.

"Can't you stay? Just for one cup of coffee?" Sue's faded blue eyes begged him to stay.

"I can't, Sue," he said, feeling like a heel because he couldn't bear the thought of spending five more minutes inside this kitchen that now housed a few high school yearbooks, some cheerleading ribbons and various other paraphernalia. He didn't have the words that Sue needed to hear. She studiously avoided talk of Kaylie or Paige, keeping the conversation focused on life precancer, and Alex was sick of it. "I'll call you tomorrow. Why don't we plan to have dinner next week?"

She dabbed the corner of her eye with a tissue and nodded. "I guess I'll have to accept that you have other priorities now." Her voice cracked on the last words.

"I'll call you to set it up," Alex said before he could think twice about coffee and holding Sue's hand until she felt better. Before he could say his priorities were the same as they had always been: family, work, fun. It was just that his family included more people now.

"When you're here, it's like nothing has changed."

Okay, he had to suggest it. "I think you need to talk to someone. Someone other than me or John or your friends." He felt like the worst kind of son as he said the words. Sue had been fragile since Dee's death, but over the past few weeks her depression had become a breathing thing that changed her from the woman he knew.

Sue scraped her chair across the tile floor and stood. Stalked to the sink to rinse out her coffee mug. "I've lost my daughter."

"But we're still here. John. Me. Dee is gone and she isn't coming back," he said, echoing Tuck's words to him from a few days before. "We are still here."

She put her hands on the counter and rocked. "Go on, whatever your plans are you go ahead. I do not need mental help." She choked out the words.

"Sue—"

She cut him off. "No, go, Alex. You obviously have something more important than your family to deal with tonight. Just go." She whispered the last words, her shoulders shaking.

Alex started to reach across the space between them but let his hands drop. Because he couldn't soothe Sue's pain, not this time.

Paige and Kaylie had given him a glimpse of life and he was damned if he'd put that light out. Not even for Dee's mother.

CHAPTER SEVENTEEN

AT SIX O'CLOCK on the nose Alex's truck pulled to a stop before Paige's house. Her heart skipped a beat when he jumped from the cab with the cellophane-wrapped Charlie Brown costume in his hands. She shook herself, mentally wiping the goofy grin she knew was on her face off before she opened the door.

"Sorry, I got held up. Two minutes and we'll be in sugar-heaven." He rushed by her and into the powder room but was back in a heartbeat. "You look amazing. I don't think Lucy van Pelt had legs like yours." He kissed her, a quick, hot press of lips. "And I'm positive she never kissed Charlie like this."

"I don't know. That psychiatrist couch had to be good for something."

He waggled his eyebrows. "Do you have one of those around here?"

Paige pushed him toward the powder room. "Two minutes. I don't think I can hold Kaylie back any longer."

As if on cue, Kaylie hurried into the hallway with her bucket on her arm. "Is it time yet?"

Alex whirled around, grinning at the little girl. "Sorry, Snoopy, we'll head out in two minutes."

She giggled. "I'm not Snoopy, I'm Kaylie."

He pushed the costume head back, examining Kaylie's face in the small opening. "So you are."

Paige distracted Kaylie with setting up the candy bowl and sign reading "Please take one" for the neighborhood kids while Alex changed, and then they started down the street. She shot a glance in his direction. Even in the skullcap that made him look as bald as Charlie Brown, Alex drew her attention. Made her tummy flutter and her knees go weak. The man was a menace in the best possible way, she decided, and then made one more decision: just for tonight, as her birthday present to herself, she wasn't going to worry about loving him. She wouldn't think about his past or hers. She would enjoy this moment with all her heart.

Paige snapped pictures as Kaylie skipped up driveways and sidewalks, telling the adults she could do this on her own. Love clogged her throat as she watched her little girl, who had been too afraid to go near any of the houses even though she knew everyone in the neighborhood just last year, sing the Halloween chant and come running back with more and more candy.

Mrs. Purcell, dressed in a black witch's robe with a pointy hat on her head, handed out cara-

mel apples. She offered Paige a finger wave and a
wink when she saw Alex making the rounds with
them. Paige tried not to feel too optimistic that her
elderly neighbor seemingly approved of her choice
in men, but nosy and curmudgeonly or not, Mrs.
Purcell was a good judge of character.

By six-thirty Kaylie was slowing down, and
Paige had emptied her bucket once already. They'd
made it around half the neighborhood.

"I think she's had it. And we've definitely gotten enough candy for three families," Paige said.

Kaylie disagreed—loudly. "I haven't gotten to
Brie's house yet. I wanna keep going."

"I definitely think that is enough, young lady,"
Paige said, cringing when she sounded more like
Dot than herself. She shook the plastic bag filled
with candy and then Kaylie's bucket. "We have
enough candy here to last 'til Christmas."

Kaylie batted her hazel eyes at Paige. "Please?"

Alex joined in, complete with batting eyelashes.
"Yeah, *pleeeze*?" He drew out the word.

Paige laughed. "You two are incorrigible. Fine,
we continue on. But I'm not carrying you."

Kaylie was already off, scampering across the
next neighbor's yard in search of goodies. She got
a pencil with Snoopy on it and crowed. Just after
seven, they turned the corner to Paige's house and
she blinked. At least ten cars sat along the normally quiet street as the sun sank lower in the west.

"What is going on?"

"They must be coming in from all over the county," Alex said quickly. "Good thing we got started on time." He took Kaylie's hand and started walking again. Paige couldn't put her finger on it but something was off about this. There were cars, but where were the people?

She hurried to catch up with Alex and Kaylie, who were talking about the merits of Lemonheads versus SweeTarts—SweeTarts were winning but mostly because Kaylie kept using the "because I said so" defense. Paige smiled. Maybe it was time to come up with another reason besides that for when Kaylie didn't want to follow the rules.

"I'll replenish the candy bowl for any latecomers. Why don't you two go on around back? We'll build a fire and finish off the night in style," Alex suggested.

Paige didn't want this night to end. Not when it had been such a crappy afternoon. Not when she had decided not to let said crappy afternoon kill her birthday.

Kaylie pulled Alex's hand and when he bent down, whispered something in his ear. He shot a quick glance at Paige, a smile she couldn't quite decipher on his full lips. Nodding, he said, "Yeah, it's time," and Kaylie squealed as she jumped up and down. Before Paige could ask what was going on, Kaylie grabbed her hand and began pulling her around the house to the backyard.

"Fire pit! Fire pit! I get to stay up for the fire

pit!" she chanted all the way through the side yard. Together they rounded the corner and Paige stopped dead in her tracks.

Fairy lights blinked throughout her trees and along the rails of her deck, casting a comforting glow in the dusky evening. A few Chinese lanterns glowed from low-hanging branches and Tiki torches lit the paving stones leading from the trampoline in the yard to the large wooden deck.

"Happy birthday, Mama," Kaylie screeched, pulling Paige forward as Alison, Tuck and a host of her friends yelled, "Surprise!" from the deck. They tossed streamers into the trees as they yelled and they broke into the Happy Birthday song as Alex came through the sliding glass door. There were two Dorothys, a Scarecrow and a few witches and superhero costumes, as well. Alison and Tuck were dressed as Rhett and Scarlett from *Gone With the Wind*.

Paige put her hand to her heart to keep it from pounding through her ribs. Tears prickled at the corners of her eyes and she swiped at them to keep the tears from falling.

Scratch that crappy afternoon. Scratch everything. This was the best thirtieth birthday she could have asked for.

Alex pulled a long-handled lighter from his back pocket and began lighting candles on the cake as the group started in on a second verse. Paige noticed Mrs. Purcell and a few other neighborhood ladies on the porch singing loudly and off-key, and then Alex motioned her to join them.

Kaylie bounded up the steps ahead of Paige but didn't swipe at the icing like she normally would have. She turned, beaming, and said proudly, "I didn't spoil the surprise, Mama."

"No, baby, you made the surprise perfect," Paige managed as the singing died down.

"Make a wish! Make a wish!" Kaylie ordered from her perch beside the small table set up with more of the colorful streamers and a hot-pink plastic cloth that read, "Thirty But Still Flirty."

Alex smiled across the shimmering cake, decorated with splashes of her favorite purples, blues and greens, and it was as if the moment stretched out until just the two of them were there. Alex watching her, Paige watching him and the cake between them.

Paige squeezed her eyes closed. Squinted through one eyelid at the man across the table from her and then made her wish. Everyone clapped and Alison appeared with a knife to cut the cake while their friend Hannah took drink orders and the neighborhood ladies took up position in the most comfortable of Paige's wicker deck chairs.

After cutting the cake, Alison hugged Paige. "Happy birthday, bestie. I hope it's been amazing."

"If you'd asked me earlier, I'd have said no, but now I think this is the best birthday ever." Paige looked around at the friends filling her deck and yard. At the man playing a hand-slapping game with her daughter. At the fairy lights and streamers swinging in the light breeze and all her friends dressed up in kid-friendly costumes. "I can't believe you're all skipping the bar parties for my birthday."

"Oh, I think some of us will hit the bars later," Alison said. "We can't let the senior citizens think we're getting old, you know."

Paige took a bite of chocolate cake and sighed. "You bought me a Breanna's Chocolate?" she mentioned a bakery in the next town.

Alison shook her head. "Alex did. This whole thing was his idea. Good guy, remember?" She tapped her head against Paige's shoulder.

It was getting harder to remember any of her reservations about the man or the relationship, Paige admitted.

"Yeah, good guy. Speaking of, how are things with your good guy?"

Alison chuckled. "Good. Distracting. Easy, believe it or not."

Paige could believe it. Tuck seemed steady, just like Alex.

Alison picked up a slice of cake and took a bite. "So, tell me Kaylie and I aren't the only loves of your life anymore." She tilted her head toward Alex, who was cornered by Mrs. Purcell. "He's been over a lot lately."

Paige couldn't help the smile that stretched across her face. "He has."

"A-a-and?"

She watched him chat with her neighbor and then detach himself to stand with Tuck in the yard. "And…I think he might be the best relationship I've ever had, Al."

Two hours later the last of the birthday guests left for the parties at the local bars or their own couches. Paige looked over the backyard and decided cleanup could wait. There was no way she was climbing trees in the dark to pull down hundreds of streamers or to unwind the strings of fairy lights. Kaylie lay on the sofa in the family room; someone had thrown a light blanket over her legs with her Snoopy head cuddled into her chest. The rest of the costume was puddled on the floor.

Alex brought a stack of plastic cups into the kitchen to throw in the large garbage can. "I'll take her upstairs, if you want to go relax on the deck," he said.

Paige usually put Kaylie down for the night, even when Alex was visiting, but maybe tonight wasn't just about presents for herself. "She'll want a drink of water and a story, no matter how exhausted she is."

He nodded and picked the little girl up to snuggle her against his chest. "I'll handle it. Meet you outside in five." He disappeared into the hallway and she heard his soft footfalls on the steps. Paige filled two fresh cups with wine and then boxed the last few pieces of cake and stuck them in the fridge before settling into her favorite chair on the deck. She turned off the deck lights so the only illumination was from the full moon and the fairy lights.

Alex slid the door open and closed and joined her in the other chair. "Happy birthday, Paige."

She rolled her head against the cushioned chair. "You already said that."

"I know, but you only have three hours of birthday left. I figure you could stand to hear it a few more times." He reached across the space and took her hand. "Happy birthday."

"Thank you. It has been a happy birthday."

"How does thirty feel?" he asked in the dark and she thought she heard a smile in his voice.

"Thirty feels very much like twenty-nine, to be honest." They were quiet for a minute and she asked, "When did you come up with all this?"

He raised his eyebrows.

"Alison said it was all you."

"I ordered the cake and asked who to invite. She came up with the decorations and turned the 'maybes' into 'yeses,'" he said.

"Whatever the division of duties, you gave me one of the best birthdays. Ever."

"Better than eighteen?"

"By at least a hundred points."

"Twenty-one?"

Paige waved her hand. "Twenty-one, schmenty-one. It pales in comparison."

"Since twenty-one is usually the barometer for all birthdays, I'll accept that I am a party-planner extraordinaire."

"We all bow to your prowess," she said and leaned across the low table between them. Laid her lips on his and sighed. The kiss started slow, a gentle caress of his full lips against hers. Paige wanted more. And, damn it, it was her birthday. Why shouldn't she take more? She pulled away long enough to leave her own chair and join Alex in his. "Kaylie's asleep?"

His hands spanned her waist, burning her through the coarse fabric of her Lucy costume. Paige pushed the skullcap from his head, letting it drop to the floor. He nodded. "Until another rush of sugar kicks in."

"Thank you for remembering my birthday."

"Thank you for taking me trick-or-treating." He removed her wig and freed her hair from the bun atop her head. Paige shook out her hair and Alex buried his hands in it. She pressed her mouth to his once more, tasting the sweetness of the wine and the cake. "I don't care if she ate the Mount Everest of sugar, there is no way she'll wake up tonight. This much excitement always equals exhaustion for our kid."

"You never said that before. 'Our kid.'"

"She is. The best of you, and the best of me." His

tongue tasted her and Paige sighed at the intimate contact. Alex tilted his head, deepening the kiss, and Paige followed along, content to taste him. Content to play with the stubble along his jaw. His hands inched along her ribs and Paige arched her back, wanting more than the easy touch, wanting to feel his hands against her skin.

But with the thick Lucy costume covering her neck to knees there was no chance of that happening. His hand closed over her polyester-covered chest, rubbing through the layers of fabric, and Paige decided there was something to be said for making out fully clothed.

The combination of lacy bra and fabric played against her nipples with Alex's hands giving just the right amount of pressure. She moved her torso closer to his, wanting more of his heat. More of the sweet pressure on her breasts. More of the liquid warmth pooling between her legs.

And then his hand moved from her breast to play with her knee and inch slowly over the smooth skin of her thigh. His hands were smoother than she had imagined, or maybe that was just his moves. Obviously the man knew how to make a woman want him. His fingers played over the backs of her knees while his other hand kept up the pressure on her breast until Paige was a writhing, moaning mess. She buried her hands in his hair, but it wasn't enough so she walked her fingers down his chest and over his abs to the hem of his bright yellow tee.

Pulled it up and played her fingers over his washboard abs. Alex sucked in a breath and bit down on her lower lip gently. Then soothed the burn with his tongue. Paige sighed against him, liking the feel of his quivering muscles beneath her hands. Liking more how his hands were playing against her upper thigh and breast.

She could feel his hardness against her hip and she wanted it. God, she wanted it. Inside her, pushing her over the brink.

"People make love with kids in the house all the time."

"Are you sure?" His voice was rough, as if he might already be at the edge. The knowledge shivered up Paige's spine.

"I'm sure."

He led her up the stairs and into her pink-and-brown bedroom, locking the door behind him as it closed. He left a small light burning on her dresser and was across the room in a flash, and the heat of him burned through the heavy polyester of her Lucy costume. So slowly she could hear the zipper as it opened over her back, he drew his hand over her spine. Little jolts of electricity followed the light touch and Paige swallowed hard, reaching for the hem of the Charlie Brown shirt and lifting it over his powerful chest.

Everything became frenzied. Alex's lips descended on hers as his hands pushed the costume to the floor. Paige pushed the black shorts off Alex's hips and he tugged the tee over his head.

She couldn't get enough of the feel of him. Her hands met his warm flesh and she felt his abs ripple beneath her questing fingers. She walked them up, up to play in the light dusting of hair over his flat nipples. Alex pushed his index finger under the thin strap of her lace bra and she shivered. His eyes darkened from hazel to almost brown in the dim light and Paige bit her lower lip.

"Beautiful, Paige, you're beautiful." Alex's finger trailed over the side of her breast, down her ribs to play with the elastic below her belly button. Paige gasped and closed her eyes, concentrating on the feel of his hands on her. Tracing the indentation of her spine. Squeezing her buttocks. Playing her ribs like she was the most expensive piano on the planet. But always, always coming back to her breasts. Barely touching the undersides. Lightly flicking his thumb against her nipple until she wanted to scream at him to flatten his palm and grind it against the sensitive flesh.

But he seemed to be in no hurry.

Finally, not content to be fondled, Paige reached her arms around his neck until they were skin to skin.

It was glorious.

He was hard where she was soft. Warm where her body had cooled. His lips met hers, caress for ardent caress. His scent tantalized her nose—

woodsy and fresh—and her belly tingled where his hardness pressed so firmly against her. She could feel him through the thin layers of her lace and his cotton. Wanted to feel him without any barriers between them at all.

Alex led her to the bed and lay her down, kissing his way from the sensitive flesh of her collarbone through the valley of her breasts and over the shivering skin of her tummy. His hands played under the soft edges of her bra, teased at the sensitive flesh under her lace panties and then he went lower, pressing a soft kiss to her belly button. Tracing his tongue over her hip bone and finding erogenous zones where she'd never imagined. Like the outside of her thigh, the inside of her ankle. And when he found an area that made her writhe on the bed, he focused his attention until she was breathless and desperate.

"Alex, please." The heat that had been pooling in her center from the moment he'd parked the truck threatened to go molten. To burn her from the inside out, but still he seemed content to kiss and caress. When Paige didn't think she could take any more, Alex hooked his index finger under the elastic of her lace undies and pulled, exposed her fevered skin to the coolness of the room. She moaned but he caught the sound in his mouth and chuckled.

"Little ears. Quiet, remember?" She could only nod as he reached behind to unclasp her bra and pull it from her shoulders. "Paige, you are so... everything," he said finally. "And I can't believe this, but I didn't come prepared."

Paige grinned, glad that he was as taken by the moment as she, that this wasn't planned. But she *was* prepared, because since their evening in St. Louis she had thought about when they might make love. She motioned to the nightstand and said, "Top drawer."

Alex made quick work of the condom and then his hardness pressed against her wetness and Paige opened for him. Cradling his hips between her legs, wrapping her arms around his chest as he pressed into her.

He slid in, inch by delicious inch, and Paige forgot to breathe. Forgot to do anything except feel the weight of him against her. Inside her. It was the best feeling she had ever experienced and she couldn't define it.

"Mmm," she mumbled when he slid in to the hilt. He didn't move for a moment, as if he waited for something. When he started to move in a slow rhythm, Paige matched him, letting him take her over the edge into blinding heat.

CHAPTER EIGHTEEN

ALEX'S ARM WAS ASLEEP. Pins and needles shot through his veins. He wasn't about to move, not with Paige sleeping so soundly against him. He brushed a lock of hair behind her ear and she settled in, breasts pressed flat against his ribs. One leg insinuated between his. Hip to hip.

Skin to skin.

Nothing between them.

No guilt. Wasn't that odd? To some degree there had been guilt, on his part, between most of their interactions. Tonight there was only Paige and the future. Nobody's feelings but his own.

It was liberating, lying in bed with her and being able to simply enjoy the moment. To look out the window and watch the stars. It was enough to be with Paige.

Enough to have the certainty in his chest that this relationship was headed somewhere permanent even if the start was a bit rocky. He ran his fingers over her silky hair, thinking that this moment was a long time coming.

He loved her. It wasn't the same as loving Dee,

but it was just as real. Just as scary and just as wonderfully surprising, with a unique set of obstacles still to overcome. There was telling Kaylie. There was dealing with her parents and his.

There was telling Paige how he felt when he didn't know how she felt. She liked him, was attracted to him, but did she want more?

She stirred against him and pressed her lips to his nipple. "Is it morning?"

"I don't think so. The clock is blinking midnight. I think it's broken."

"I must have unplugged it yesterday."

"Shh, go to sleep."

Her breathing evened and he thought she must have drifted off. "Stay." The word was a whisper in the dark and sent a jolt of heat to his chest.

"For a while."

"For the night. Stay." Her fingers drew circles around his flat nipple and Alex drew in a breath.

"Do you think that's a good idea? What about Kaylie?"

"Your running shoes are next to Kaylie's by the sliding glass door. You left them on Sunday." She raised up on her elbows. "The book you picked off the shelf is still on the coffee table from Wednesday evening and almost every drawing Kaylie has made since the night you babysat her has included an image of you. I don't think she would mind waking up to find you're already here."

He had to be the voice of reason, didn't he? One

of them needed to remember why they wanted to tell Kaylie he was her father before they took things to the next level. Except he was already naked in her bed. "What about that conversation you said you didn't want to have? The one where she's a teenager and realizes my sleeping over wasn't about camping in the backyard?" he said before he could talk himself out of it. Because he wanted to stay.

"We've thrown some other cautions to the wind." Paige steepled her hands on his chest and rested her chin on her fingertips. "Maybe I was thinking too much."

"Maybe we should think about this, really think about what it means for Kaylie to see me here in the mornings, before she actually does." Damn, he didn't like this voice-of-reason crap. Didn't like it at all.

Alex flipped Paige over and settled her against the pillows before sliding from the bed. He slid his legs into the Charlie Brown shorts and pulled the shirt over his head since his street clothes were downstairs in the little powder room.

"Since when are you the experienced parent?" she teased from the bed. Paige pulled the sheet over her. "I know you're right. This responsible-adult thing blows."

He chuckled and sat beside her on the bed, just as he'd done when she'd come home from the lock-in at school. Kissed her forehead because if he allowed his lips to touch hers he would be lost. Again.

"WHEN ARE YOU going to tell Paige you love her?" Tuck's voice seemed overly loud in the quiet office. Not that he'd spoken loudly. No, it was more that the topic of conversation wasn't exactly welcome to Alex.

He brought a stack of mail into the office today. Spending so much time with Paige, he was behind on clearing out the junk from his bill statements and other mail. Thankfully, he used automatic bill pay or he might have fallen behind on something. That's how distracted he was lately: he couldn't be bothered to throw out a few envelopes or file his receipts and statements.

"Well?" Tuck sat back in his chair, waiting.

Good question. One he didn't know how to answer because he had no idea how to tell Paige how he felt.

Should he tell her?

Last night they talked about Dee and his old life and she accepted his words. Didn't seem affected when he said he still loved Dee.

How could he love Dee and love Paige at the same time? It didn't seem possible, yet the only definition he knew for his feelings for Paige was love. He thought about her, wanted to be with her. Her touch sent pulses of electricity over his skin. When she smiled, he smiled, and when she was angry he wanted to fix the problem. Or at least hold her hand while she fixed it.

When he thought about Dee his chest didn't clutch and he no longer wanted to destroy anything in his path because of the overwhelming grief. It was harder to pull up her image from his memory banks, but he could hear her laugh. Smell her perfume sometimes. Those memories made him smile, in a different way than being with Paige did, but both felt like love.

"Alex. You alive over there?" Tuck waved his hands in the air as if signaling for an airplane landing.

"I don't know." It was the best he could do. *How did you tell a woman you loved her, but that you still loved someone else, too?* She would think he was crazy. As accepting of his past as she had been, this would be too much.

"Don't know if you're alive or don't know when you'll tell her?" Tuck leaned back in his office chair and put his booted feet on the desk.

"Why do you think I'm in love with her? Don't answer that. I don't need your advice." Alex shot Tuck an annoyed look. He didn't need advice from a guy whose longest relationship, pre-Alison, was five days. Not even if the guy was his best friend.

"Yeah, you do. Because Paige is the best thing to happen to you since that first date with Dee and if you can't see then you're more than blind. You're dumb, to boot."

"Tuck, stop."

"She is a beautiful woman to start with—"

"I don't need you to recount the ways Paige is amazing." He knew all those ways by heart. What he didn't know was how he could love her without stopping loving Dee.

Tuck ignored the interruption. "She's a good friend and a good mom. Has a steady job that she loves and refuses to cow to her overbearing mother. Still with me?" Alex could only nod his head. Tuck was right, Paige was all of those things and more.

She was funny and attentive. Had seemingly unlimited patience with Kaylie. Was an incredibly talented artist. Her nose crinkled when she laughed and she bit her bottom lip when she was contemplating something. Or when she was nervous. She tasted like the most decadent of desserts and her body fit his like it was made for him. Alex pulled at the collar of his shirt but the room was stifling.

"I can't vouch for the way she tastes but I will say you two have a definite connection. It's obvious to anyone in a five-mile radius." Tuck interrupted Alex's thoughts.

Wait. How did he know what Alex had been thinking? "Did I just say all that out loud?"

Tuck nodded. "You did, and not quietly, either."

Thank God they were alone in the office. Alex pressed the back of his neck against the cool leather of his desk chair. What was he going to do?

"Dee isn't here, you know."

He beetled his brows. Tuck wasn't helping. "I'm aware."

"She isn't coming back."

"I know that, too."

The phone rang and Tuck picked it up only to hang up immediately. "I don't think this has to be an either/or thing. I think you can be in love with Paige and still keep your memories of the past."

Alex couldn't look at his friend. He wasn't a blubbering, emotional wreck, but he knew if he took his eyes off the ceiling tiles he would embarrass them both. "Thank you," he said finally, wondering when shallow, self-absorbed Tuck had become such an insightful friend.

And hoping beyond hope that he was right.

"I THINK WE could use a shower," Alex panted as they topped the steps leading up to the Arch on Tuesday evening. The boiler at Paige's school had blown up that morning and until Thursday there were no classes. Tuck was covering for Alex at the parks, Dot, whose animosity toward them both seemed to have cooled, asked to take Kaylie to the zoo for the day and he and Paige were having their second official date.

Their first since they made love on Halloween night four long days before.

Alex had suggested one of the steamboats and dinner aboard the ship, but Paige preferred a picnic dinner beneath the Arch. And then challenged him to a race along the Gateway Arch Trail.

Paige shook her head and then put her hands on her knees as she breathed deeply. "I'm more of a bath girl. Should I have mentioned that before? Bubble baths. Long—" she kissed him, sweaty nose to sweaty nose "—and hot—" her teeth nipped his lower lip "—and absolutely not G-rated."

God, she was perfect. The right amount of sass and sweet. The responsible mom and the flirty girlfriend all at the same time. He loved her. Why couldn't he say it? Alex took her hand, hurrying them to the hotel where they were staying for the night.

She drew a bath while he poured chilled wine into glasses. Paige's eyes widened. "Ooh, I see you have your own idea of what a bath should be."

"You have no idea," he said.

In the tub, Alex pulled her back against him, playing his hands over her flat stomach. Teasing her, letting his fingers graze over her core and then bringing them back to play with the undersides of her breasts.

But Paige didn't let him have all the fun. She reached behind her, which pushed her firm breasts higher into the air, to take his member in her hand. Squeeze and caress and play her thumb over his sensitive tip.

If he didn't slow her down this would be over

before either of them was ready. Alex set her away
from him, immediately feeling as if there was a
vacuum between them. But he needed the space,
just for a little longer. He picked up the rough
sponge and ran it over her smooth back, squeezing the hot water over her skin and making her
shiver. Rubbing the coarseness over her sensitive
breasts and making her moan. Her body shook
against him when he pulled her to him and slid two
fingers into her heat. She ground her hips against
his hand and reached behind his head to press his
lips to hers.

"Alex, more," she gasped.

He gave her more, pressing his thumb to the tiny
bundle of nerves in rhythm with the motion of his
fingers until she writhed in the water, eyes closed,
hands gripping the smooth sides of the tub as the
jets pounded against them below the surface. Alex
felt her tense beneath him but didn't let up until her
back bowed and he felt the flutter of her internal
walls against his fingers.

He lifted her from the steaming water, toweled
her dry and carried her back to the bed. She was
boneless, holding on to him as if she would never
let go. Alex lay her against the pillows and took
his time, licking droplets of water from her skin.
Sucking her nipples into his mouth and pressing
his thumb against the sensitive bundle of flesh. Her
reactions to him were fascinating. The indrawn
breaths. The way she bit down on her lower lip.

How she hiked her legs around him, wanting everything and all at once. Alex left the bed long enough to pull another foil packet from his wallet, then slid it over himself and rejoined her on the bed.

Paige ran her hands through his hair and over his shoulders, pulling him against her. Wrapping her legs around his waist. "I want you," she said as he pressed against her center.

Her walls gave willingly, inviting him in. Exciting his flesh. Alex's natural rhythm took over as his lips met hers. She twined her fingers with his, panting against him. Tension rose in her body. Her hands tightened against his shoulders, her feet flexed against his buttocks.

"Alex, please," she said as her back bowed and he took her over the edge once more.

Breathing heavily, Alex balanced his arms on the bed, keeping most of his weight off her until he could move again. Then he rolled onto his back and brought her with him, snuggled into the curve of his body once more. She shivered and Alex pulled the duvet over them.

Paige wrapped her leg around his and twined his fingers with hers. She breathed deeply, as if she might sleep, but he felt her heart thundering against his side.

"I love you," she said as her eyes drifted closed and her heart stopped pounding.

Alex ran his fingers over her damp hair, twisting it lightly around his fingers until her breathing quieted and she sighed. Her body went limp and he knew she was asleep. He kissed her lightly on the forehead and whispered to the room, "I love you, too."

CHAPTER NINETEEN

THEY SPENT THE first two weeks of November much the same as they'd spent the last two weeks in October: Alex would come to Paige's house after work. They would cook or go out to eat. He would spend time with Kaylie and after she was down for the night, Alex and Paige would sit on the back deck or cuddle up on the sofa to watch television. They touched and they kissed. Held hands.

Talked about telling Kaylie who he really was.

And with each passing day Alex felt more settled. They would tell Kaylie about his paternity soon. It would be their first holiday season as a family.

At quarter to five, Alex found Paige and Kaylie sitting on the floor picking leaves from color-coded piles on the tile floor. He waited at the sliding glass door and watched for a moment, taking in the scene. Paige with dirt and pieces of leaf caught on her hands, Kaylie holding up leaves to determine their worth and chattering about decorating her classroom in one breath and her swim test this evening in the next.

God, he loved them.

He wanted them. Wanted Kaylie to know he was her father. Wanted to build a full life with Paige.

Tonight. He would tell them both. Tonight. He opened the door and said hello to his family.

AT THE POOL Alex sat on the familiar bench seat, watching Kaylie push through the water. In just the few weeks he'd been coming to her practices he saw a marked improvement in her stroke technique. He shouted encouragement to the little girl and was rewarded with a grin and a wave.

"I still say fun is the most important part of lessons at this point."

"I think you're right."

Paige's jaw dropped. "What's this? Ex-swimmer Alex Ryan says stroke technique isn't the most important thing for a four-year-old to master?"

He grinned at her teasing. "I still say it's better to learn correctly than to erase old habits. As long as she's having fun, I'm good."

The coach caught their attention as she readied Kaylie and one other child for their test. She gave them their instructions—swim to the rope and then tread water for five seconds. The instructors moved into position and Kaylie waved at them from her position at the wall. The coach called out and Kaylie kicked off. Her kick was low and she held her head out of the water more than it was in, but her arms were almost perfect and she made it to the rope without stopping. The instructor gave her a high five and helped her to the ladder as she gave the next group the instructions.

"Mama, Alex, I did it!" she squealed as she shook water off her legs. "I got to the rope. I'm going to Level Three." And she started running.

Alex and Paige both stood, telling Kaylie to walk, but the little girl was too excited. She rounded the corner of the pool and stepped in a puddle of water. Alex's stomach pitched when her legs flew up from behind and her body flew forward toward the pool. He lunged to catch her but was too far away.

The sound of Kaylie's head hitting the hard side of the pool wall was sickening. Both instructors lunged for her. Kaylie's face was white and a trickle of blood trailed from her hairline over her chubby cheek and into the water.

"No, no." Paige sobbed as she reached for the little girl from the side. A lifeguard ordered Alex to keep Paige back while the swim coach cradled Kaylie's body from the water and the other instructor grabbed the backboard from the wall. It was the hardest thing he'd ever done, holding Paige back from her daughter. Not diving into the water himself.

They had Kaylie strapped to the board in a second. And within another, the other lifeguard told them the ambulance was on the way. Paige held Kaylie's hand but she wasn't moving.

God, let her move. Let her cry. Anything. The words were a jumble in Alex's mind, not making sense. Tripping over Kaylie's voice from when she'd excitedly told them she leveled up. Why wasn't she moving?

Alex reached for Paige's free hand and it was cold, as cold as his own heart. In the distance he heard sirens but all he could see was Kaylie's pale face.

He couldn't let it happen again.

He couldn't lose another person that he loved.

PAIGE PACED OUTSIDE the room housing the big X-ray machine, allowing anger at the doctors to take over from the cold and fear she'd felt from the second Kaylie pitched forward into the pool. They said it didn't matter that she was a baby, Paige could only watch from outside the room.

While her baby lay quietly in the room.

She didn't care about protocol and she didn't care about the risk to herself from the X-ray machine. She wanted to be with her daughter.

Alex hurried through the door from the waiting room and relief swept over her. She took his hand and together they watched as the technician took images of Kaylie's head. A moment later they wheeled her out, and although she was still groggy from the fall, Paige thought she was a bit more alert than she had been when they'd arrived in the ambulance.

The orderly settled Kaylie in the emergency room once more and Paige pulled a chair over to sit beside her.

"My head hurts," she said in a weak voice.

"You slipped and fell, sweetpea. You'll be okay."

"Did you see me swim? I got to the rope all by myself."

"We saw it." Alex stepped forward and took Kaylie's other hand when she reached for the bloodstained bandage on her head. "You did so great."

The emergency-room doctor hurried in, followed by Kaylie's pediatrician. "Ms. Kenner, Mr. Ryan. Kaylie is going to be fine." The doctor put Kaylie's X-rays on a lighted board and indicated a dark spot on the screen. "She has a nasty bump and there is a small subdural hematoma here, but we don't see any bleeding on the brain."

Paige sagged back against her chair and Alex put his hands on her shoulders. "Thank you," she whispered. "Thank you. Can we take her home?"

Dr. Laffay, Kaylie's pediatrician, shook her head. "Kaylie needs to stay with us for tonight. We'll watch her closely, just to make sure there is no damage we haven't spotted yet."

"Can I stay with her for the night?" Relief swept over Paige at the doctors' words, but she didn't want to leave her baby, not tonight.

"You won't get much sleep. The nurses will be

in periodically to wake her, make sure things are moving along smoothly," Dr. Laffay warned.

"I don't care, I want to stay."

"We'll have a cot brought in for you, then."

Ten bustling minutes later Kaylie was settled in a new room in the children's ward outside the ER. A nurse checked her vitals and made sure she was comfortable before telling Paige to buzz if they needed anything.

She needed Alex, Paige thought, but although he was beside her she could tell he wasn't really there. He'd held her hand all the way to the hospital. Taken over at the admission desk, giving the pertinent insurance information to the intake worker. Held Kaylie's hand when she was scared and hurting before the doctors gave her any medication. Through it all he was physically there, but he wasn't present, not the way he usually was.

Everyone responds differently in a crisis.

Except he was a park ranger. Used to stressful situations, taking charge. From the second Kaylie had started to fall it was as if Ranger Alex was gone, replaced by a stranger.

"You don't have to stay."

"I can stay." His words were hollow and now that there was no work to be done, his face was pale, even in the dim light of the hospital room.

"I know you can. You don't have to." As much as she wanted him to stay, she needed to focus on Kaylie. Not him.

He paced the room. Picked up Kaylie's chart and thumbed through it as if he could decipher the scribblings on the page. "I'll stay. For you." He glanced at Kaylie, tucked under a white blanket with an IV in her little hand. "For her."

Paige went to him. "You don't have to. If it makes you uncomfortable."

"I was going to tell you tonight."

"Tell me what?"

"Tell you I thought it was time to tell Kaylie I'm her biological father."

Paige's breathing quickened and she squeezed his hand in hers. "I think it's time she knew, too."

Dr. Laffay entered, interrupting Paige. "Your cot will be delivered shortly, Paige." She turned to Alex. "Visiting hours were over a long time ago, though. You'll have to leave."

"He isn't visiting. He's—" Paige paused for a split second and then plunged ahead. If anyone would understand this crazy situation, it would be Kaylie's doctor. "He is Kaylie's father."

"You're adopting her. That's wonderful." The doctor called for another cot. "We'll make an exception. It's important for Kaylie to be with people she knows for the next few days. She's going to be in quite a bit of pain as the hematoma heals."

The cots arrived and Paige and Alex settled into the darkened hospital room with the beeping machines and the occasional sigh from Kaylie.

"You told her I'm Kaylie's father." Alex reached

across the darkness to take Paige's hand. He felt warm, familiar, and she was glad for the contact.

"You are her father. I would have corrected the adoption part of it, but I'm exhausted. I know we wanted to tell Kaylie first, but I don't think she'll mind, since you get to have your first sleepover because of it."

He chuckled in the darkness but his voice was heavy when he spoke. "When I saw her fall I felt like I was falling, too."

"Alex." Paige squeezed his hand in sympathy.

"I had this terrifying thought that I would lose someone else I loved. I do love her, Paige."

"I know." His words warmed her in a way the blankets and his touch couldn't. "She loves you, too." She settled her head against his shoulder. "I love you," she said for the second time.

He was quiet for a long time. "I know," he finally said into the darkness. "I love you, too."

Paige fell asleep holding Alex's hand and listening to the quiet beep of the machines in the room. He loved her.

They were the four best words she had ever heard.

ALEX PACED THE hallway outside Kaylie's hospital room with Paige by his side the next morning. The doctors were examining her. He wanted to be in there. Wanted to know she was okay. Now, not in five or ten minutes when they finished the examination.

Fathers all over the world had to be feeling the exact same way, he thought.

Finally, the door opened and the nurse gestured for them to come inside. Kaylie was still groggy from the pain medication but she offered them a thin smile when they came back into the room.

"She'll sleep for a while yet, and we'd like to do a CAT scan this morning, just to make sure there is no bleeding on her brain. But if everything goes well, she should be in her own bed tonight.

"Really?" Paige's voice was a squeak.

"Really." Dr. Laffay looked uncomfortably from Paige to Alex and then the ceiling. She opened the door and a small man with a gray comb-over came in. Alex recognized him as Nelson, from the fertility clinic. Dr. Laffay continued, "We made an exception last night, because of the circumstances, but *if* Kaylie needs to stay another night, only you will be allowed to stay, Ms. Kenner."

Paige looked blankly at Alex and then the doctor. "But he is her father."

"Adopting father. Until the paperwork is completed—"

"Biological," Alex said. "We should have corrected you last night, but with everything going on we didn't. I am Kaylie's biological father."

"No, you aren't." Mr. Nelson spoke from the other side of the room.

"Yes, he is." Paige's voice sounded reedy to Alex's ears, like she was trying to remain calm and failing. She focused on the pediatrician and not the man from the clinic. "You know about the insemination, but there was a mix-up at the fertility clinic. Alex is Kaylie's father. We just found out a few weeks ago. Mr. Nelson can explain."

"It was only Alex's name and identifying number that were mislabeled," Nelsen said from his side of the room. "I stamped the letters notifying you of the swab results myself before handing them over to the mail clerk two weeks ago. When you didn't respond, we began calling."

"I put the envelope with my important papers, because you were so positive Alex was the father. I didn't read it." Paige whispered the words, then pulled her cell phone from her purse to scroll through the recent calls.

She showed Alex an unidentified number with repeated calls, but no voicemails. He swallowed hard and did the same. The same number called him several times over the past week, but there were no voice messages.

"This isn't the number I programmed into my phone, but it's yours?" Nelson looked at the readout and nodded.

"The number you programmed would have been the receptionist, not my direct line. I felt it would be best to speak directly to you—"

Alex cut him off. "What does this mean?"

"The tests were conclusive. You are not the girl's father." He softened his tone and turned to Paige. "When no one answered your phone this morning, I called the emergency contact in your file. Your friend directed me here."

"But you said—" Paige reached for Alex's hand but he stepped away. He couldn't touch her. Not now. Not when the steady life he wanted to build was being snatched away from him.

He wasn't Kaylie's father. He had nothing to offer them.

Nelson swiped a handkerchief over his beet-red face. "It was only your name. We are certain of this now that the tests have come back." He focused on Alex. "Your name was placed on one wrong vial, and during our records switch over the paperwork indicated that vial was used for insemination. The actual sample belonged to the donor she chose. Not you."

He couldn't breathe. Alex fisted his hands and concentrated on taking one deep breath and then another until he didn't feel like his chest would explode. "You're sure about that?" Alex said sarcastically.

"It was human error."

Dr. Laffay picked up Kaylie's chart and turned her sympathetic gaze to him. "Human error sounds about right. You filled out Kaylie's records? And the extra paperwork about donating blood if there was a need."

The muscles in Alex's jaw tightened. "I did. We didn't know how serious the situation was."

"It's protocol, especially with traumatic injuries. You entered your blood type as A positive."

"That's right." What was she getting at? What did his blood type have to do with anything?

"Kaylie's blood type is B negative. Paige carries A positive, as well. It is highly unlikely, just from a blood standpoint, that you're Kaylie's biological father."

Alex felt the world shift. Not her father? How could he not be her father? There was the physical resemblance. The call from the lawyer.

He'd been playing dad for over a month, for God's sake. Paige crossed her arms over her belly. What was happening to his life? He was fine eight weeks ago. Cold and alone but fine. Now he could feel the cold creeping over him once more and felt powerless to stop it.

He wasn't Kaylie's father. This entire messed-up month, his guilt over moving on, the stress put on the Parkers. The ordeal Paige had to slog through with her own parents. All because a bumbling intake worker slapped his name on the wrong vial.

"I don't understand. You said you were sure. You offered a settlement." Paige and the doctors kept talking but Alex refused to listen. He didn't need halfhearted explanations or consoling. He looked at the little girl in the hospital bed. Physically she looked like him and his heart ached.

"The hospital could run a separate DNA test to corroborate the clinic findings, but I don't think it's necessary," Dr. Laffay said. "Of course, you're welcome to stay in the room during visiting hours."

"How long will that take? Another test," Paige asked. Alex stared out the window. The voices all sounded so far away, like the television sounded when he was waking up in the morning after forgetting to shut it off.

"The results could be ready within the week."

Alex could feel his heart, every slow, labored beat, as the world came back into focus. "When your lawyer called, I was told my sample was used in the insemination."

"We were trying to rectify the situation as quickly as possible. Our investigator noticed the difference in your records and those of Ms. Kenner. We pulled the donor samples and had all of them tested. They all match the actual donor, not you. We are very sorry." He cleared his throat. "You will, of course, both be compensated for the trouble."

"Compensated?" Alex swallowed back the anger. "A month ago your lawyer turned my life upside down and now you believe you've rectified the situation because it was just a typo on a form?"

This wasn't happening, not again. He would not accept that Kaylie, beautiful, smart Kaylie, wasn't his daughter. They had the same hair, the same eyes. He loved her, for God's sake. How could she not be his?

He gripped the windowsill as if that might anchor him to the room. To Kaylie.

To Paige.

"Please go," Paige told the doctors. "We would like to have some time with our daughter."

The doctor and Mr. Nelson shuffled out. Paige came to him, put her hands on his shoulders. He didn't want her sympathy. Didn't want words that would tell him it didn't matter. This mattered. If he wasn't Kaylie's father, who was he? Paige chose to be a single mom, and seemed to accept him into her life easily, but that was when he had the right to be there. The drama with her parents, his in-laws... Without a biological reason to keep fighting those external forces... If he wasn't Kaylie's father, why would Paige want all that upheaval?

"Where does this leave us?" he finally asked.

"It leaves us as Kaylie's parents." There was a tremor in her voice, a question, like she wasn't sure, and Alex moved away from her touch. He couldn't do this, couldn't watch this break down before him.

"You're her parent. I'm nothing."

"You are a part of her life. She loves you. She doesn't care about DNA or mislabeled vials in a lab somewhere."

"She will. Someday."

Paige scoffed at him. "Biology is only a small

part of what makes a family. If you saw anything over the past six weeks, it should have been that. Biological or not, she loves you. She wants you." She reached out but Alex backed away. "She deserves to have a father."

Alex couldn't look at her, couldn't look at Kaylie, so he focused on the beeping of the machine instead. Beeping machines were still familiar after all these years. "She deserves to have a *real* father. It will be better for both of you if I walk away now, before things get more complicated."

Anger shot from Paige's gaze as she turned on him. "So you would choose to fight for *our daughter* because you think she has the right DNA, but now she doesn't meet your standards because her genetic material isn't what you expected?"

"I don't give a damn about chromosomes."

"Then fight for her. Fight for us."

He spun on his heel and walked out of the hospital room before he could change his mind.

Paige and Kaylie were a unit. He was the unwelcome addition neither had ever asked for.

CHAPTER TWENTY

A FEW DAYS later Paige dumped sacks filled with the makings for sushi and wontons onto her kitchen counter. She pulled a chopping board and knife from a drawer and began slicing and dicing. Kaylie lay on the sofa, a Biscuit book in her hands. The hospital released her the same day they'd learned Alex wasn't her father. For the first time Hank and Dot had no recriminations for Paige. They called daily to check on Kaylie, and to make sure Paige had everything she needed.

Her daughter was healing; that was all she could ask for.

"Can I get up?" Kaylie asked from the sofa.

Paige crossed the room, felt her forehead for fever and checked her pupil dilation like the doctors showed her. Kaylie seemed normal, although she still complained of headaches now and then. "Do you want to color?"

Kaylie sat up, nodding. "The Belle book, please."

Paige got colors and the book, setting them up on the coffee table. The book Alex had been reading caught her eye. She picked it up. Thought for a second about putting it back on the shelf and instead tossed it into the recycling bin.

"Is Alex still working?"

Paige didn't know how to explain he wasn't coming back so she had taken the easy road so far, telling Kaylie Alex had to work and couldn't come over.

"I think so, sweetpea."

Kaylie was quiet for a long moment, rolling a yellow crayon over Belle's dress on the coloring page. "I miss Alex. Is he mad that I ran and bonked myself?"

"No, kiddo, he isn't mad." Paige hugged her close and kissed the crown of her head. How could she explain that simple DNA changed how Alex felt about Kaylie?

Who was she kidding?

DNA changed how Alex thought about Paige, too. She settled in with Kaylie, coloring the opposite page and wishing she could go upstairs and pull the covers over her head. Forget about the fertility clinic, the accident. Forget about Alex.

No, she didn't want that. The accident she could do without. What had she said to Nelson during their first visit? She didn't want his money because, no matter what had happened on the day she was inseminated, it had brought her Kaylie.

The same applied to Alex.

Whatever had happened on the day they discovered the mislabeled vials, it led to her meeting Alex. How could she regret that?

It was ridiculous that she was still crying over him, really. It had been four days.

"Did I tell you Auntie Al is coming over for dinner tonight? Why don't you finish this picture for her while I finish dinner, okay?"

Kaylie nodded and went back to coloring.

Paige was done feeling sorry for herself. Her daughter was okay. Celebration was in order. Celebration and thank you. Tonight she had invited Alison over for dinner, to thank her for stepping in so often over the past few weeks.

She chopped carrots and cabbage and set tiny cubes of beef and chicken aside to cook later. Alison loved Paige's sushi and wontons, and it was about time she showed her friend how much Paige appreciated her.

Paige swiped at the corner of her eye with her shoulder.

No more tears over what might have been. She had put her life back together several times before, and she could do the same one more time.

Alison arrived a short time later. Paige turned on the local radio station and then filled wonton wrappers and cooked the rice while Alison oohed and aahed over the coloring page.

"What did I do to rate your wontons and sushi?" she asked, coming over to the counter.

"I want to say thank you, for helping out so

much during the Alex thing," Paige said. Alison reached for a wonton wrapper and together they rolled the ingredients. Paige concentrated on making each roll as symmetrical as possible while Alison slapped a little rice and some fish into each before plopping it back on the plate.

"So I guess you don't want to talk about it," she finally said.

Paige decided playing dumb was her best defense. "Talk about what?"

"The reason Alex has been in a short temper all week. Why you look like you've seen a ghost or you're dealing with an eating disorder."

"Not really." Paige rolled another bit of sushi.

Alison slapped her hand against the counter. "Too damn bad," she said, collecting the plates of ingredients and setting them aside. "I'm not spending the rest of this evening ignoring the fact that you look like you've been hit by a truck. This isn't just about Kaylie's accident, is it?"

"I thought it was an eating disorder." Paige tried to make the joke but it fell flat. "I'm not good company. Why don't you call Tuck and go have a late dinner on me?"

"Why don't you tell me what happened?"

Paige sighed. "That hole in the middle of the net that was supposed to catch us? It turned out not to be me."

"Him?" Alison said softly.

Paige shook her head. "The fertility clinic.

Alex isn't Kaylie's father. I have the paternity test to prove it." She slid a sheet of paper across the counter and tried to explain what she still didn't understand. "He says Kaylie deserves a real father and by 'real' he means 'biological.'"

Alison snapped her jaw closed, rallying for Alex after reading the damning sheet of paper. "Maybe he just needs time."

Paige sniffed and decided to hell with it. She was already depressed. A little wine wouldn't change anything. She finished the glass and poured another. "We were his replacements. The family he would have created with Deanna if he could, and now that he knows Kaylie has the wrong DNA, we're out of the picture."

Alison's next question caught her off guard. "Do you love him?"

"You know me, always in love with Mr. Wrong." Paige kept her voice light but she couldn't stop a tear from falling down her cheek. "He said he loved me, just before everything fell to pieces. I know he loves Kaylie. I think maybe he just said he loved me because I said the words first. Because he thought if he loved Kaylie he had to love me, too."

"I don't believe that. He's a good man, Paige. A solid guy whose life went horribly wrong and then took another weird turn a few weeks ago." She shook the paper in her hands. "Despite what this says and what he did when he walked out of the hospital, I still believe Alex Ryan is a good man."

"Don't tell me he needs to process, this is about more than processing a few emotions. Do you know he never takes us south of Bonne Terre? Our dates are in St. Louis, and he meets us for dinners or lunches here in town. I don't know what his house looks like. These are big, screaming warnings that he hasn't let go." Paige took a deep breath and plunged ahead, voicing the fear that had torn her up since he walked out of the hospital room. "There is a part of him that's still there, living it. I'm the new girl, the girl he flirts with and laughs with. The girl who reminds him of the guy he was precancer."

"I don't believe that. Not from what I saw when he was around you. Not from everything Tuck told me about him."

"I don't think he even realizes it. He put Kaylie and I in a tiny compartment of his life that would never touch the rest of his boxes, the boxes filled with his memories of Deanna and the life he wishes he still had."

ALEX SHOVED HIS truck into Drive and pulled away from the park office. He was tired. So damned tired.

Frustrated.

Every morning Tuck asked him what his problem was. Every morning Alex told him to back off. He didn't want to talk to Tuck about his world falling apart again so he did his work as quickly as he could and headed for one of the trails, not caring if it rained or was icy cold.

Tonight he pulled into downtown and took a left at the second light. Despite the late hour the gates were still open so he pulled through and found the quiet spot under the red maple tree where they put Dee's coffin to rest. Stared at it for a long time and then let the anger turn to sadness. Because she was gone. Really and truly gone, and there was nothing he could do to change that. No mantra he could chant that would change the way she'd died or the things they'd never gotten to do together.

Like raise a daughter like Kaylie.

He gripped the steering wheel and then banged his head lightly against his hands.

She wasn't his daughter. Why did he keep forgetting that?

"I'm sorry." His words were a whisper in the quiet cab. "I couldn't stop it." Emotion clogged his throat but he kept talking as if she might hear him. He apologized for the things they didn't have time for, apologized for the way he'd jumped into a new life with Paige, apologized because the cancer took her before she could have a little girl like Kaylie. Wondered what Paige and Kaylie were doing that evening.

"I feel obligated to tell you you're an ass," Tuck said through the open truck window as he surveyed the empty cemetery.

Alex refused to take the bait. "That's not news."

It was better for everyone, all around, if he stopped trying to be what he wasn't. He was a widower. He wasn't Kaylie's father. His past had messed up Paige's life and he refused to wreck it further.

It shouldn't be this hard to move on from her. He shouldn't hear her laugh when he was in line at the grocery store. Shouldn't see her face in his dreams. It had been a month, six weeks. Falling out of love with a woman he barely knew should be as simple as falling in had been.

So why wasn't it?

He snagged his bottle of water from the cup holder and drank, but Tuck was still there when he finished the bottle.

"Don't you have a date to go on?"

"Sure. I'm picking her up in an hour." He pointed to his car, parked behind the truck. "But I thought maybe I could talk some sense into you before I danced her through the night."

"I don't want you here."

"Doesn't look like you have a choice. What happened at the hospital?"

"Kaylie fell, slight fracture to her skull, but she's okay."

"I didn't ask why she was in the hospital. Alison told me that. I asked what happened at the hospital."

Alex gripped his hands on the wheel. "X-rays, pain meds—"

"God, you really are an ass. Why is it that pre-hospital you said you loved Paige and posthospital you won't mention her name? Haven't seen her and are stomping around like Godzilla destroying Tokyo?"

Saying it out loud wouldn't change anything. Wouldn't make losing dad status any worse, Alex decided. "I'm not Kaylie's father. The mix-up at the clinic was clerical only, only they jumped the gun and told Paige and I immediately."

Tuck whistled low and long. "Damn. I'm sorry, man."

Alex wanted to shrug, as if it wasn't anything big, but couldn't. "Yeah."

"Being pissed at the clinic doesn't mean being pissed at the world. What does Paige have to say about all this?"

"That we're still Kaylie's parents."

Tuck raised an eyebrow at Alex and waited.

"*We* aren't her parents. Paige is. I'm just…the guy whose name they put on the wrong vial."

"You think you can't be Kaylie's father because you don't have the same DNA?" Tuck said incredulously.

"That's kind of what DNA means. Family. Paternity. Relative. I'm not her father."

"Neither is the guy who donated the semen to make her. And he's got the same DNA."

Alex clenched the steering wheel. Tuck didn't understand. Couldn't understand what it meant to think he was Kaylie's father only to find out he wasn't.

To love Paige but realize he had nothing to offer her.

"I don't think Kaylie cares that your DNA string isn't a match to hers. I think she cares that you're teaching her to swim and give horses tomato baths."

A set of lights flashed behind them and the night watchman stopped, reminding Alex the cemetery would close in a few minutes. Alex waved the older man off and watched as Tuck got into his truck to drive away. After a long time he drove slowly through the gates, thinking about the fertility clinic. Kaylie. Everything circled back to Paige.

Why would she want him, a widower with family issues to deal with, if he didn't have a real connection to Kaylie?

It's just to find out. If there is a problem, we'll know and deal with it. Dee's words from that first conversation about the clinic echoed in his mind. *This is just step one on our journey to becoming parents. It doesn't matter how we do it, it only matters that we do do it.*

A peaceful feeling settled over his shoulders. What if Dee was right? What if it didn't matter how a family was made—through biology or pharmacy or choice?

For the first time since he'd met Paige he saw a light that wasn't dependent on her or on Kaylie. Because it was part of him.

CHAPTER TWENTY-ONE

PAIGE MOPED THROUGH the week, indulging herself in a few good, hard cries and a couple of pints of Ben & Jerry's salted caramel ice cream. Spent extra time watching movies and reading books with Kaylie, and after her daughter was asleep, turned on old black-and-white tearjerkers on late-night television.

Each day Kaylie seemed more like her old self.

Each day it seemed strange not to tell Alex about something Kaylie said or did.

It really shouldn't be this hard to get back into her routine, but it was impossible to finish the barn painting and lighting the fire pit brought back too many memories of Alex. Playing "Angry Birds" with Kaylie made her remember the night of the school lock-in and how Alex had filled in like a pro.

Here she was on a Friday night with zero energy for grading projects and no interest in anything other than staring at the wall. Which was ridiculous and so ending now.

Her heart might be bruised to its very core but

that didn't give Paige permission to stop being a mom.

"What do you say we make spaghetti for dinner?" she asked Kaylie after staring into the pantry for a solid five minutes. Nothing looked appetizing but spaghetti would at least be more nutritious than drive-through burgers or pizza. Again.

She twisted around on the sofa. "The long noodles?"

She nodded. "I won't break them up at all."

"Yay, just like *Lady and the Tramp*," Kaylie squealed and ran to her shelf to find the movie. "Can we watch while we eat?"

Maybe turning over a completely new leaf could wait for tomorrow. Spaghetti and her favorite Disney flick with Kaylie sounded like heaven. "Sure. But tomorrow, screen-time rules are back in force."

Kaylie tilted her head to the side, trying to decipher what Paige had said.

"It means tomorrow we go back to fifteen minutes of tablet and one hour of TV or movies per night."

"Oh. Okay. Alex calls that 'scream time,'" Kaylie said and handed the DVD box to Paige. Her heart pinched at the mention of Alex's name and she thanked the heavens Kaylie didn't follow that up with a "Where is Alex, anyway?" question. Again.

She got the movie going and popped spaghetti into the boiling water before warming the garlic bread and sauce. On the screen, Tramp convinced Lady to follow him away from Jim Dear and Darling's house. Just as Alex had convinced her they could make a future together.

Stop it, Paige. Stop thinking about him and start enjoying the evening with your daughter.

She drained the pasta and, while it cooled, set up two trays in the family room. Filled the plates and settled in just as Tramp and Lady shared their plate of spaghetti in the dirty alley. Kaylie giggled as she sucked a long noodle into her mouth, imitating the dogs on the screen. When Paige tried, and splattered sauce all over her shirt, Kaylie laughed even harder.

Paige wet a dish towel at the sink and tried to brush the worst of the sauce away. The doorbell rang, interrupting her.

"I can get it," Kaylie said and her tiny feet pounded out a rhythm against the hardwood floor as she raced to the door. "Hi," she said, excited as Paige rounded the corner.

And stopped short.

Alex stood in the entryway. He unzipped his jacket. "May I come in?"

Paige's heart beat a tattoo against her ribs. Oh, but he looked good. He had a bit of scruff on his cheeks, as if he'd been too busy to shave, and wore his usual jeans and polo. She wanted to run down the hall and throw her arms around his neck the way Kaylie had just thrown her arms around his legs.

"Mama said you weren't here tonight," she said.

"I'm just running a little late, sweetpea," he replied. Paige's nickname seemed to roll off his tongue as if he'd been saying it forever. But his focus was on her, not on Kaylie, as if what he said wasn't in reply to Kaylie at all.

Paige shook herself. Now was not the time to go all weepy because he used a nickname and happened to be looking in her direction when he did so. She motioned him inside and offered him a plate of spaghetti. He declined.

"I was hoping we could talk," he said quietly.

"Okay. But not in front of her."

He shook his head. "No, not in front of her." He motioned to the back porch. Paige made sure Kaylie was settled back with her movie and food and followed him outside.

The night was dark, with clouds blocking out most of the stars and seeming to put the moon on a dimmer switch. Paige wrapped her arms around her body and wished she'd grabbed a coat from the closet. Alex took off his jacket and offered it to her but Paige declined. She needed a clear head. Getting lost in the scent of Alex was so not going to happen.

"I'm sorry, Paige."

"I know. You're too good a man not to be sorry when someone is hurting." She couldn't get angry.

She would acccpt because she had to move on, for Kaylie's sake. She wouldn't let her pre-Kaylie past influence her life any longer, and she wouldn't let her post-Alex life change her, either. She deserved to be happy and she would figure out how to do that starting right now.

"I'm not sorry because you're hurting. I'm sorry because I hurt you." He reached out, trailing his fingers along her jaw. At the light pressure she looked at him.

"Alex—" She had to stop him before he said something he didn't mean.

Before she started believing in him again.

"I talk to her, sometimes. Go to her grave and tell her what crazy schemes Tuck's cooked up, tell her how much her parents miss her. I stopped doing that after the lawyer called." He took a breath but didn't break the connection of their gazes. "It was about a week before I met either of you, and I went to the cemetery. I couldn't get out of my truck. There was this pressure in my chest, like it was holding me against the seat. I drove away because I had no idea how to tell her that her dream of having a child led me to having one without her. And then I avoided it because you made it okay not to be Alex the Widower. You and Kaylie didn't have a connection to my past and I had no idea how to tell her about how you made me feel. Like I was Alex again. Just Alex."

Paige's heart broke a little more at his words

because she could feel the truth and the pain in them. "You're still Alex."

"But I'm not Kaylie's father. Not really. I told her about you, about that night at the pool. I told her about Kaylie and you. I didn't see a ghostly apparition and I didn't hear her voice, but once I said all that I felt peace. Like maybe she heard me. Like maybe she understood what I needed."

"Good." Paige tried to keep her breathing even. Because his finding peace didn't automatically mean she would find the same thing. "I want you to be happy, Alex."

"You make me happy."

Her heart jolted in her chest but still Paige couldn't allow herself to believe.

"I can't be the female accessory in your new life. And I won't let Kaylie be that, either." She crossed her arms over her chest. "We can't be the replacement family."

"You were never accessories, either of you. And you weren't replacements. I just had a hard time figuring out how to define you, and then after the accident there didn't seem to be anything to define."

"And now?"

He watched the stars for a long moment. "And now I think I'm ready to start making up my own definitions. I'm not Kaylie's father, but I hope you might still let me be her dad."

All the emotions she'd been holding on to so tightly spilled over. "You want us?"

"I love you," he said. "I love you and I want you. Both of you. I don't care what the paternity test says. I choose the future." He was quiet for a long moment. "I want the future, Paige. I want to be Kaylie's dad. I choose to love you and build the family we both want."

"Tell me again."

He smiled and pressed his forehead against hers. "I love you, Paige Kenner."

"Ask me something."

"Do you want to take a drive with me?"

She nodded. A few minutes later, with Kaylie buckled into the backseat, they were driving. "Where are we going?"

"You'll find out in a few minutes. Why don't you sing while we drive?" Alex suggested and turned on the radio. Kaylie sang, off-tempo and off-key, as they meandered around Bonne Terre.

Tall oak and maple trees dotted the streets and streetlights gave the area a glow. Alex turned left off Main Street and a few blocks later turned back onto her quiet street.

"Hey, we didn't go anyplace. We're just home," Kaylie said in annoyance.

Alex looked at Paige, a look in his eyes that made her heart leap. "Yeah, we are."

EPILOGUE

FOUR WEEKS LATER, Alex finished his chicken and speared a stalk of broccoli from Kaylie's plate.

"Hey!" she said, beetling her little brows at him.

"You said broccoli trees grow in your mouth."

"Cheese helps them go down."

Alex replaced the stalk on her plate and Kaylie happily demolished it. After clearing the dishes and setting the cook pans to soak, the three settled into the family room. Paige fiddled with the television remote and finally put it down.

"Before you watch your show, Kaylie, there's something Alex and I would like to talk to you about." Paige cleared her throat. "You know how it's always been you and me? Mommy and daughter?" Kaylie nodded and drew her knees to her chest. "Well, it's also been Alex for the past few weeks, and he has something he'd like to tell you."

The hawks in Alex's stomach flapped to life.

"I wondered if…" No, not the right way to go about this. He was her dad. "I want to tell you that you're my favorite four-year-old in the whole world."

Kaylie grinned. "That's cause I'm funny and I

swim good. And I don't run at the pool anymore."
She touched her head. The bandage was gone but
a small scar remained.

"Yes, those things are important. You're a great
helper and a good party planner, too. But the reason you're my all-time favorite four-year-old is because I love you." Kaylie threw her arms around
his neck and squeezed. He caught Paige's gaze
and she nodded.

"We both love you, Kay. I'm your mom and I
love you."

Alex cleared his throat. "And I'm going to be
your dad and I love you."

Kaylie tilted her head back and studied Alex for
a long moment. "I thought I only had a mommy."

"We all thought that, sweetpea," Paige said, rubbing her hand over Kaylie's arm. "For a long time I
thought it would just be you and me, but now we've
found Alex, and he wants to be part of our family."

Alex chimed in. "If it's okay with you, I'd really
like to be your dad."

"So now can you sleep over?"

Alex grinned when he saw the blush steal over
Paige's face. He'd been sleeping over, off and on,
since the night they took the drive. "Yeah, but no
matter where I sleep, I'll be here for dinner and
swimming and we'll watch movies and have the
best time."

Kaylie studied him for a long moment, tracing

her fingers along his nose and under his eyes. "Do I get to call you Daddy?"

Alex swallowed against the tightening of his throat. "Only if you want."

"I want," she said and bounced back to her seat between him and Paige. "Can I watch my show now?"

Alex studied their daughter for a long moment, thinking how lucky he was to have found not only Kaylie but her mom. Kaylie took Alex's hand and then Paige's and they settled into the sofa to watch her favorite program. Kaylie leaned her head against his arm and curled her legs under her like Paige did.

From friend to dad in the span of five minutes and now they were watching a cartoon like any number of families around the world. His heart expanded a little bit more at her easy acceptance of him into her life.

Paige waited until Kaylie's show was over and her daughter's eyes were drifting closed before suggesting a bedtime story, wanting the night to last as long as possible. Kaylie insisted Alex tell her a story and Paige sing a lullaby. She was asleep before Paige got to the second verse.

As they had before things briefly fell apart, Alex and Paige went to the deck to sit and watch the sky.

"My turn," he said after a while.

"For what?"

"Q and A, of course."

Paige crossed her legs primly. "I'm an open book. Ask what you will."

He sat beside her. "Do you love me?"

She nodded and wrapped her hands around his neck, pulling his face down to hers. The kiss was sweet, a caress of lips and a joint inhalation when they came apart.

"More than I thought possible. Alex?"

"Yeah?"

"Do you want to go steady?"

"Nope," he said and she froze. "Because you know Hank and Dot are going to have issues with the leprous farmers from St. Francois County. After the past few weeks I can vouch for the fact that my mother-in-law can be a master manipulator. I don't want to go steady. I want to be your family. Yours and Kaylie's, through all the bumps that are bound to come from blending us all together."

Paige couldn't breathe. She tried to inhale but the air seemed to get stuck somewhere between her nose and her lungs. Her heart pounded and her eyes got watery.

"If you missed it, that was a proposal without the question attached, in case you want me to officially ask that important question on a night that is just about us and not us-with-Kaylie."

"I didn't miss it," she said, and her voice wavered. "And I think a night that includes all of us is perfect. So why don't I ask the question?"

"Because that's my job?"

"We've made our family without paying so much attention to the rules so far."

"True." He looked at her and she could see the love shining in his eyes, brighter than the stars in the sky.

"Alex, will you marry me?"

He cleared his throat. "I'll marry you. And I'll love you—and Kaylie—for the rest of my life."

Paige reached around his neck and pulled his mouth to hers, sealing his promise with a kiss.

* * * * *

LARGER-PRINT BOOKS!

GET 2 FREE LARGER-PRINT NOVELS PLUS
2 FREE GIFTS!

☒ HARLEQUIN®

Romance

From the Heart, For the Heart

YES! Please send me 2 FREE LARGER-PRINT Harlequin® Romance novels and my 2 FREE gifts (gifts are worth about $10). After receiving them, if I don't wish to receive any more books, I can return the shipping statement marked "cancel." If I don't cancel, I will receive 4 brand-new novels every month and be billed just $4.84 per book in the U.S. or $5.24 per book in Canada. That's a savings of at least 19% off the cover price! It's quite a bargain! Shipping and handling is just 50¢ per book in the U.S. and 75¢ per book in Canada.* I understand that accepting the 2 free books and gifts places me under no obligation to buy anything. I can always return a shipment and cancel at any time. Even if I never buy another book, the two free books and gifts are mine to keep forever.

119/319 HDN F43Y

Name	(PLEASE PRINT)

Address		Apt. #

City	State/Prov.	Zip/Postal Code

Signature (if under 18, a parent or guardian must sign)

Mail to the **Harlequin® Reader Service:**
IN U.S.A.: P.O. Box 1867, Buffalo, NY 14240-1867
IN CANADA: P.O. Box 609, Fort Erie, Ontario L2A 5X3
Want to try two free books from another line?
Call 1-800-873-8635 or visit www.ReaderService.com.

* Terms and prices subject to change without notice. Prices do not include applicable taxes. Sales tax applicable in N.Y. Canadian residents will be charged applicable taxes. Offer not valid in Quebec. This offer is limited to one order per household. Not valid for current subscribers to Harlequin Romance Larger-Print books. All orders subject to credit approval. Credit or debit balances in a customer's account(s) may be offset by any other outstanding balance owed by or to the customer. Please allow 4 to 6 weeks for delivery. Offer available while quantities last.

Your Privacy—The Harlequin® Reader Service is committed to protecting your privacy. Our Privacy Policy is available online at www.ReaderService.com or upon request from the Harlequin Reader Service.

We make a portion of our mailing list available to reputable third parties that offer products we believe may interest you. If you prefer that we not exchange your name with third parties, or if you wish to clarify or modify your communication preferences, please visit us at www.ReaderService.com/consumerschoice or write to us at Harlequin Reader Service Preference Service, P.O. Box 9062, Buffalo, NY 14269. Include your complete name and address.

LARGER-PRINT BOOKS!

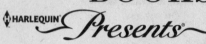 HARLEQUIN *Presents*

PASSION GUARANTEED SEDUCTION

GET 2 FREE LARGER-PRINT
NOVELS PLUS 2 FREE GIFTS!

YES! Please send me 2 FREE LARGER-PRINT Harlequin Presents® novels and my 2 FREE gifts (gifts are worth about $10). After receiving them, if I don't wish to receive any more books, I can return the shipping statement marked "cancel." If I don't cancel, I will receive 6 brand-new novels every month and be billed just $5.05 per book in the U.S. or $5.49 per book in Canada. That's a saving of at least 16% off the cover price! It's quite a bargain! Shipping and handling is just 50¢ per book in the U.S. and 75¢ per book in Canada.* I understand that accepting the 2 free books and gifts places me under no obligation to buy anything. I can always return a shipment and cancel at any time. Even if I never buy another book, the two free books and gifts are mine to keep forever.

176/376 HDN F43N

Name	(PLEASE PRINT)
Address	Apt. #
City	State/Prov.	Zip/Postal Code

Signature (if under 18, a parent or guardian must sign)

Mail to the **Harlequin® Reader Service:**
IN U.S.A.: P.O. Box 1867, Buffalo, NY 14240-1867
IN CANADA: P.O. Box 609, Fort Erie, Ontario L2A 5X3

**Are you a subscriber to Harlequin Presents books
and want to receive the larger-print edition?
Call 1-800-873-8635 today or visit us at www.ReaderService.com.**

* Terms and prices subject to change without notice. Prices do not include applicable taxes. Sales tax applicable in N.Y. Canadian residents will be charged applicable taxes. Offer not valid in Quebec. This offer is limited to one order per household. Not valid for current subscribers to Harlequin Presents Larger-Print books. All orders subject to credit approval. Credit or debit balances in a customer's account(s) may be offset by any other outstanding balance owed by or to the customer. Please allow 4 to 6 weeks for delivery. Offer available while quantities last.

Your Privacy—The Harlequin® Reader Service is committed to protecting your privacy. Our Privacy Policy is available online at www.ReaderService.com or upon request from the Harlequin Reader Service.

We make a portion of our mailing list available to reputable third parties that offer products we believe may interest you. If you prefer that we not exchange your name with third parties, or if you wish to clarify or modify your communication preferences, please visit us at www.ReaderService.com/consumerschoice or write to us at Harlequin Reader Service Preference Service, P.O. Box 9062, Buffalo, NY 14269. Include your complete name and address.

HPLP13R